6/10 3 9082 11390 9603

P9-CSS-511

ALSO BY STEPHEN McCAULEY

Alternatives to Sex

True Enough

The Man of the House

The Easy Way Out

The Object of My Affection

Insignificant Others

STEPHEN McCAULEY

SIMON & SCHUSTER
NEW YORK   LONDON   TORONTO   SYDNEY

WATERFORD TOWNSHIP PUBLIC LIBRARY
5168 Civic Center Drive
Waterford, MI 48329

3 9082 11390 9603

Simon & Schuster
1230 Avenue of the Americas
New York, NY 10020

This book is a work of fiction. Names, characters, places, and incidents either are products of the author's imagination or are used fictitiously. Any resemblance to actual events or locales or persons, living or dead, is entirely coincidental.

Copyright © 2010 by Stephen McCauley

All rights reserved, including the right to reproduce this book or portions thereof in any form whatsoever. For information address Simon & Schuster Subsidiary Rights Department, 1230 Avenue of the Americas, New York, NY 10020

First Simon & Schuster hardcover edition June 2010

SIMON & SCHUSTER and colophon are registered trademarks of Simon & Schuster, Inc.

For information about special discounts for bulk purchases, please contact Simon & Schuster Special Sales at 1-866-506-1949 or business@simonandschuster.com.

The Simon & Schuster Speakers Bureau can bring authors to your live event. For more information or to book an event, contact the Simon & Schuster Speakers Bureau at 1-866-248-3049 or visit our website at www.simonspeakers.com.

Designed by Jaime Putorti

Manufactured in the United States of America

10   9   8   7   6   5   4   3   2   1

Library of Congress Cataloging-in-Publication Data
McCauley, Stephen.
 Insignificant others : a novel / Stephen McCauley.
  p. cm.
 1. Gay men—Fiction. I. Title.
 PS3563.C33757I67 2010
 813'.54—dc22   2009051615
ISBN 978-0-7432-2475-8
ISBN 978-1-4391-8983-2 (ebook)

In memory of some very significant others—
Ed, Jones, Molly, and little Woodles.

Insignificant Others

Dinner and Monogamy

When I learned that Conrad, my partner of eight years, was seeing someone on the side, I wasn't completely surprised. A couple of years earlier, I'd noticed that the word "monogamy" had fallen out of our vocabulary, and I assumed he had as many reasons for no longer using it as I did. Even though it's usually not acknowledged, at a certain point in most relationships discretion supplants fidelity as a guiding virtue.

The slow, silent fade of monogamy in our lives reminded me of something that had happened with a particularly flavorful baked chicken dish we used to make. The chicken was spiced with cumin and ground caraway seeds, preserved lemons, and a handful of musky herbs I'd picked up at a Lebanese grocery store. It filled the entire apartment with a smell that was both exotic and homey, and it came out of the oven glistening, looking nourishing and vaguely pornographic. Conrad and I both liked it a lot—after the third or fourth year of cohabitation, it was among the few things we agreed upon wholeheartedly—and he or I ended up cooking it a couple of times a month. I took a great deal of comfort and delight in sitting across the table from him and talking in bland terms, like a long-married and slightly bored couple, about the honest pleasures of the meal. Then one day, I was rummaging around in the kitchen cabinets and came across the ground caraway seeds and realized that without discussing it or consciously crossing it off a list, we hadn't served it in over a year. I suppose both of us just got tired of the wonderful flavor. It happens.

While we'd stopped using the word "monogamy," significantly, we hadn't stopped using words of affection and fondness. We hadn't stopped saying "I love you" at the end of long-distance phone calls or when one of us was half asleep and wanted to signal the other to turn out the lights. Surely, those were the more important points.

Conrad frequently traveled for work, and when business was good, he sometimes spent ten or more days a month out of town. How could I have been surprised that he had an Insignificant Other as a source of entertainment? There are only so many ways to amuse yourself in a hotel room, and Conrad had never been a big one for CNN.

It was my own fault I learned about the I.O. Conrad had been striving for discretion. I was dashing around our bedroom stuffing my clothes into a backpack on a winter night, running late for an exercise class at one of the gyms I belong to, when I heard the buzzing of his cell phone. I was so shocked to realize it was on the bureau and not with him as it always seemed to be, and so, distracted by my own uncharacteristic tardiness, I picked it up. There was a text message on the screen from an Ohio area code that read: *Can't fucking WAIT for you to get here.* Conrad was leaving for Columbus in two days.

Conrad Mitchell and his friend Doreen McAllister ran Mitchell and McAllister, a consulting business. They traveled to cities all over the country where there was lots of new money and an attendant lack of taste they practically lived in Florida and Texas and advised people building multimillion-dollar houses on the artwork they should hang on their expensive walls. I could understand a client being excited about acquiring a Warhol, but the caps, even more than the "fucking," were a dead giveaway that the message was about something else.

Because he traveled so much, and because he was a highly organized and precise person, Conrad kept a small suitcase packed with toiletries, handkerchiefs, and clean underwear in the closet. It was an expensive black leather item capable of consuming vast quantities of clothes and supplies without ever appearing bloated. It was aging well, too—in any case, better than I was. From where I stood at the bureau in our small bedroom, I could see the suitcase leaning against the paper-bag-colored wall. (Conrad had chosen a hypermasculine decor and color scheme for the bedroom, an example of protesting too much, I'd always thought.) Suddenly, the black valise had a malevolent appearance, like a slim priest who was hiding explosives under his cassock.

Conrad was at the dining room table organizing a portfolio by slipping photographs of paintings and expensive sculptures into plastic covers, his lank and pretty blond hair hanging across his face. I left the apartment without mentioning the text message, hoping he wouldn't be able to tell I'd seen it. I wasn't eager to admit I'd looked at his phone, and more to the point, I didn't want to open up a discussion that would make me late for class. After decades of perpetually running behind schedule by eight or ten minutes, I'd reset my inner clock a few years earlier and was now fanatically punctual. Being prompt is one of those lesser qualities—like sending thank-you notes, wearing deodorant, and tipping the mailman at Christmas—that you can will into being with a little discipline. They don't rank up there with Talent, Intelligence, and Goodness, but past the age of fifty, they become essential if you want to get invited to dinner parties or have your sagging jowls overlooked.

No matter what, I was never late for exercise class. For about four years, I'd been struggling with a minor compulsion related to working out. At times it was a heavy burden, but it did have its advantages. Sneaking off to the gym six or more times a week to lift weights, take spinning classes, and listen to my personal trainer's relationship problems took up a lot of time I could have spent studying a language or reading George Eliot, but on the plus side, even at my fifty-something stage of life, I never had to worry about all the time it otherwise would have taken me to get *back* in shape.

The gym I belonged to near the Beacon Hill condo Conrad and I shared—versus the one I belonged to near my office in Cambridge—was a grimy basement, and the spinning classes were held in a corner room without light or ventilation. I appreciated the darkness and the privacy it conferred. The only people who crow about spending as much time as I do exercising are the ones who never get off the couch. Those of us who can't stop ourselves tend to exercise furtively and try to pass off our lean bodies as the product of genetics. As I pedaled in the dark, getting nowhere, trying to tune out the shrill voice of the instructor and the thumping music that I liked to pretend I was speeding away from, I reasoned that I had little to worry about. Conrad's eager friend lived in Columbus. I'd been to Columbus a number of times and had nothing against the city, but knowing Conrad's limpid snobbery, I knew someone from there was not a threat the way a paramour from New York or Los Angeles would have been.

Ego and the American Century

There was also the bigger picture. I'd reached the point in midlife at which everyone I knew seemed resigned to a low level of gnawing discontent and dissatisfaction, with their jobs, their relationships, their retirement savings, and their eyesight. For most, the ability to tolerate professional disappointment, drugstore eyeglasses, and domestic ennui was linked to moral fortitude and—provided it didn't devolve into physical violence or (nonprescription) drug abuse— was a matter of pride. Friends who'd once come to me for advice about how to change their lives—I was a psychologist by degree who'd segued into human resources at a software company—now bragged about their muted, comfortable despair, as if this somehow mitigated their overpriced cars, expensive tooth-whitening procedures, the frequent upgrading of countertops and bathroom fix-tures, and the purchase of digital cameras and software programs they never learned how to use. As a badge of honor, you couldn't do much better than stoically put up with joint problems or a toler-ably bad marriage.

In my opinion, their attitude was intimately connected to the end of the American Century. Six years into the presidency of one of the most reviled and ineffective men on the planet, there was a sense that our country had lost whatever position of moral author-ity it had once had and was headed for a fall. As a result, Americans, even the fringiest lunatics of the right wing, seemed to be undergo-ing a subtle but painful realignment of self-esteem. The dollar was worth less and less, our leader was an empty suit, our foreign policy was contemptible, and almost everywhere you went in the world, you found people speaking more elegant and precise English. The Iraq disaster had banished whatever empathy people felt about the 2001 tragedy and confirmed our status as global bullies.

The retreat into tolerable unhappiness was a self-imposed form of penance and ego adjustment. And if the behemoth of American ego could accept something other than its familiar spot on the top rung of the ladder, I supposed I could accept my partner's apparent lapse.

Faster, Faster, Faster

In the dark, humid exercise room, surrounded by several dozen sweating maniacs—my tribe—I decided I was dealing with the text message discovery pretty well. I was putting it in perspective, giving it only as much importance as it deserved. As compensation for the drawbacks of having been abandoned by my forties, a little emo-tional maturity and restraint was not a bad thing. Then I noticed that the instructor's piercing "Faster, faster, faster" was directed at me. Apparently, I'd stopped pedaling and was staring off into the emptiness of the mirror in front of me, as if I'd arrived at my destination and was trying to figure out where the hell I was. I didn't know when I'd stopped, but judging by Toni's frantic gaze and shrill admonitions, it hadn't been within the last minute.

"Rossi, Rossi, Rossi," she shrieked. "Crank it up!" The fact that she knew my last name was a shameful reminder of how often I took the class.

After class, I apologized to Toni for my slowdown. All of the spinning instructors at this gym were blondes with androgynous names—Toni, Marki, Danni, Frank—and bodies that were so defined and polished, they looked as if they'd been carved out of wood. I aspired to their lean musculature and ropey arms, even though I found them unattractive and missing some element of human softness. Gazing admiringly at her own thighs, she told me that I seemed distracted. I told her I had a lot on my mind. She began to pack up her iPod and rattled off the recipe for a drink she was especially fond of: a vitamin booster, four kinds of fruit juice, and three brands of alcohol. "It really helps me relax," she said.

When I returned home, Conrad was still at the table; had he really been at his organization project since I left? "You've been spending a lot of time in Columbus recently," I said. "Business there must be especially good." He finished snapping a page into the portfolio, and then looked up and swept back his blond hair. "Business and other things," he said. And then, almost spontaneously, he smiled.

Conrad spent a great deal of time projecting a sophisticated but sunny disposition. He had a repertoire of a dozen or more smiles he performed on a rotating basis. This was his "Isn't It Obvious I'm Busy, Darling?" smile, a close relative of his "I Love You, But Fuck Off!" grin. He was from a part of California where the weather was always warm and people were always smiling, so a good deal of the sunshine in his personality was learned behavior for which he couldn't be held responsible.

As we were getting ready for bed, I pushed him down over the desk (Danish, teak, mid-century, but not too) and had my way with him. Admittedly not a romantic encounter but a reminder that even if he did have superior taste in art and furniture, I was still the boss. It made me feel better about the stability of our relationship, my own vigor, and—because it had been a witness—Conrad's slim black suitcase.

Two days later, when Conrad was out of town, I told Benjamin what had happened. It was his concern about the matter that began to fuel my own.

The Best Position

"I don't see how you can be so calm about it," he said. "I'd be jealous and pissed off. It's a betrayal, Richard."

"I'm trying to fire up some righteous indignation," I said, "but so far, I've been having trouble with the righteous part. In case you haven't noticed, I'm not in the best position to judge him."

"I suppose not," Benjamin said. "But at least he doesn't know about us. That's a big difference."

It was late afternoon on a Tuesday, and Benjamin and I were at the Club. He was lying on the queen-sized bed, checking e-mail on his laptop, and I was pacing back and forth, checking messages on my phone. We were both fully dressed and had on our winter coats, but neither of us was ready to leave. The Club was our name for a studio apartment on the eighteenth floor of a faceless concrete building near MIT in Cambridge. He and I had been subletting it for a couple of years, even though our use of it was intermittent and increasingly infrequent. It was an ideal spot in that it was close to my office, had underground parking, and was near the entrance to the Mass Pike, the highway that took Benjamin back to the carefully organized pleasures and deceptions of his real life. Opposite the bed was a sliding glass door that opened on to a balcony, a nice feature, although neither one of us had ever stepped onto it. Ben was always too rushed, and among my assorted phobias is a fear of balconies, especially those made of concrete and steel.

"I'm surprised at Conrad," Benjamin said, his voice aimed at his computer screen. "To be honest, I'm disappointed. I didn't think he was the type to do something like this. I thought he was into his job and all caught up with that friend of his. What's her name?"

"Doreen. He is."

"Doreen, right. Sorry, I forgot. And he loves you, Richard. I'm sure of it."

"That doesn't mean he wouldn't welcome a distraction now and then, which is undoubtedly what this person is."

Benjamin considered this and then sighed, as if frustrated by the unwelcome complications of human emotions. "It's pretty inconsiderate of him to toss in that 'other things' line about being busy." He restated my report of Conrad's words verbatim. In many ways, Benjamin was absentminded, but he had a flawless memory for my accounts of conversations Conrad and I had had. "As if you needed to hear that. Conrad's always struck me as such a considerate person."

Benjamin had a high opinion of Conrad—without ever having met him—just as I had a high opinion of Benjamin's wife, Giselle, and their two kids. The lot of them had become familiar and dear to me, like characters in a play who are frequently mentioned but never appear onstage. I could tell that Benjamin thought I wasn't quite good enough for Conrad, in the same way that I believed he wasn't quite good enough for the long-suffering and glamorous-sounding Giselle. What that left, of course, was the belief that we deserved each other, at least to the limited extent and in the off-and-on manner that we had each other.

"I'm not leaping to any assumptions," I said, "and I wish you wouldn't either. This is hardly a crisis." I glanced up from my phone.

"You'd better do something about your hair before you leave, boy. It looks like you've been rolling around in bed for the past hour."

For a man in his late forties, Benjamin had a great head of hair, full and curly, gray only at the sides and only when the cheap rinse he used was washing out. He laid the blame for all of his vanity— the curly locks, the longish hair, the pubic trimming—on his wife. Married men always did. All in all, he showed fewer signs of aging than I thought he should by right, considering the messy tangles and contradictions he lived with. True, he suffered from ulcers, occasional panic attacks, and a nervous tic in his right eye that sometimes got so bad I had to cup my hand over it until it quieted down. But what decent person in his situation wouldn't show a variety of neurotic symptoms? Despite the multiple deceptions, Benjamin was an exceptionally decent person.

"You should at least tell him what you read on his phone," he said.

I was beginning to feel annoyed. Like most of my friends and business colleagues, Ben usually sought advice from me, and I was far more comfortable with that arrangement. I'd been trained in psychology and social work, and even though I was now employed by a software company, I was far happier assuming the mildly condescending pose of sympathetic, slightly detached listener, who was paid to evaluate and occasionally solve the problems of others, instead of owning up to my own.

My Husband

In the three years I'd known Benjamin, I'd come to think of him as *my husband*. He was, after all, *a* husband, and in some way that was heartfelt but also, I realize, entirely ridiculous, I saw it as my responsibility to protect his marriage from a barrage of outside threats and bad influences. It was the only way I could justify sleeping with him, and it wasn't an easy job. Among the bad influences was me, and chief among the threats was Benjamin's "sexual confusion," the term I'd agreed to use to describe his erratic but rapacious homosexual cravings. Frankly, the only thing I found confusing about his sexuality was fitting the production of a son and a daughter into my experience of it. There was the whole cushy, boring infrastructure of Benjamin's suburban life to preserve—the pointlessly large house, the cars, the dog, his wife's horse, the after-school activities, and the Christmas decorations. In my most deluded moments, I thought of myself as a distant, benevolent relative to whom his family had never been introduced. The Club and its distractions were things I chose, most days, to conveniently skip over.

By now, Ben and I had "forgotten how we met." The translation of this phrase was that one day three years earlier—when Ben's confusion was at a high point and I was feeling restless and abandoned with Conrad out of town—I answered an ad he'd placed on Craigslist. Pretending we'd just stumbled across each other made the meeting and the ensuing relationship seem all that much more accidental and therefore blameless, one of those things in life that just happen and can't be controlled. His ad had mentioned something about a married man looking for an uncomplicated, sweaty hour of distraction, with a cautionary clause about no drama or entanglements. I suppose there were a few lurid details, but those I really have forgotten.

Throughout my life, I've had luck with married men in this context. And in this context, there is an unlimited supply of them. Having been well trained by their wives, they're almost always clean and polite. The vast majority are sexually submissive and hugely appreciative of getting on the side what they can't get at home. You have to put up with their roiling guilt, but because I was brought up around a lot of Catholics—my parents, for example—I'm comfortable with that. The guilt often leads to a desire to be verbally humiliated and physically dominated, something that I, like most gentle and diffident men, am always happy to do. They're frequently not in the best shape, but much better that than the sculpted, oddly generic bodies of work-out addicts like me. On the whole, they're obedient, they get regular checkups, and they never call after business hours.

Benjamin had won me over with his very first comment: "Are you disappointed in my looks?" I found it so touching, especially coming from such a handsome man, that I never quite recovered. Even before I'd finished doing other things to him, I found myself wanting to help him. It didn't occur to me until it was too late that what I wanted to help him with were two contradictory things: to get satisfaction for his deepest sexual urges and, at the same time, to stay true (in some convoluted fashion) to his wife.

At the time I met Ben, I was still being faithful to Conrad, although it is true I'd expanded the definition of faithful to include an occasional impersonal encounter with an inappropriate person. What I was seeking in these indiscretions was not contact with someone I was attracted to but reassurance that I was still attractive to someone else. In that sense, they never seemed to be true betrayals. They only boosted my confidence, thus improving my relations with Conrad. Or so my rationalization went. I was certain Conrad engaged in the same kinds of activities from time to time, not because I had any specific evidence, but because he never showed a flicker of doubt about his physical appeal, even after turning forty, and because he spent an unconscionable amount of money on underwear. After meeting Ben, I made more adjustments to my definition of fidelity, and then simply eliminated the term, along with monogamy and a few others, from my vocabulary.

The At Least List

At some point in the past decade, I'd begun to deal with the various challenges and disappointments of aging, economic uncertainty, and reality in general by mentally compiling a litany of compensatory clauses I thought of as the At Least List. I resorted to the list when I made the mistake of taking certain actions, like opening my financial statements or looking in a mirror in a well-lit room.

Typical items:

- My funds are going down, but *at least I've still got money to lose*.
- I might be going gray, but *at least I've got hair*.
- I'm not entirely deserving of the promotion I want at work, but *at least my competition isn't entirely deserving of it either*.
- My face might look like a topographical map of the Andes, but *at least I don't have skin cancer*.

The final item on the list, the one I was headed toward but hadn't yet reached, was that all-purpose statement of defeat and despair: *At least I'm alive*. Hopefully, I had more than a decade to get to that.

My relationship with Benjamin offered an endless supply of logistically messy but otherwise reassuring items:

- *At least I'm never going to press for a relationship that would bring an end to his marriage.*
- *At least I offer him a sexual outlet that helps him stay faithful to Giselle.*
- *At least I'm 100 percent committed to my own domestic arrangement.*
- *At least I never call after business hours.*

The list helped me believe I was organizing my disappointments and betrayals, a lesser accomplishment than overcoming them but better than nothing.

As for my feelings about Conrad and my guilt about betraying *my* primary relationship:

At least Conrad was nearly a decade (seven years) younger than me, and immensely better looking. At least he was appealing and personable, and people had a way of gravitating toward him when we socialized as a couple, at least until he sideswiped them with a condescending subordinate clause. He was a natural blond. At least if you don't count highlighting as unnatural. These mitigating factors made my off-and-on arrangement with Benjamin feel less like a full-fledged transgression and more like a way to balance things out between me and my sexy and appealing partner. At least.

I'm not without my own good qualities, charms, and hidden assets, but given that the term "middle-aged" is unrealistically optimistic, given that I've always had a craggy face that's been deteriorating even more quickly these days, given the aforementioned awkwardly fit body, and given a tendency toward reserve in social situations that's been mistaken for sullenness or early onset dementia, I'm more of an acquired taste.

Tuscany

Benjamin and I were subletting the Club from a Massachusetts Institute of Technology scientist who'd moved back to Shanghai, the new center of the civilized world since the U.S. had become economically second-rate and irrelevant. Among the apartment's advantages was its view of a building MIT had paid the world's most famous architect a fortune to design. I'd heard the interior office space was so eccentrically laid out that there were no vertical walls

suitable for bookshelves in the offices and that one lecture hall in-
duced such severe vertigo in students it was unusable as anything
but a funhouse tourist attraction. And yet, from the windows of the
Club, the building was a triumph—a shimmering confusion of
curves and angles, sheathed in metal of various textures and tones.
At twilight on winter afternoons such as this one, it glowed below
us like a mad, marvelous Tuscan village as imagined by a Cubist
sculptor. I'd become enormously fond of the building in the time
Benjamin and I had been using the apartment. It was a perfect view
for two people who were in a relationship that was intimate and yet
unworkable, ill-advised, and surreal. Benjamin was a partner in a
small architecture firm that specialized in designing highly practical
buildings for mid-sized companies, most of which were located
along the highway sprawl of cities like Atlanta, Milwaukee, and
Portland. He became slightly melancholy whenever he looked down
at the jumbled building below; it reminded him of the inequities of
his profession, the creative limitations imposed by his standing in
the world, and perhaps the limitations of his own imagination. He
called it the Scrap Heap.

Anything

I was standing in front of the sliding door to the balcony, looking at
the snow that was starting to swirl in the lights below. I had a message on my phone from a colleague at work telling me that there
was something she needed to discuss with me. I texted back saying
I was in a meeting, true in a way.

"I think it's snowing in Tuscany again," I said. It had been a
balmy fall, but January had turned cold and snowy so suddenly that
now, more than three weeks after Christmas, the ground and rooftops were piled high.

Without lifting his eyes from his computer, Benjamin said, "If it's snowing on the Pike, it'll take me twice as long to get home." He snapped his computer shut, turned on his side, and faced me. "It might be that Conrad *wants* you to be upset. Have you thought of that?"

"You're misreading the situation," I said. "And you're making me nervous. Let's change the subject." I lay down beside him on the bed and put his computer on the floor. "How are the kids?" I asked, pulling him in toward me.

"Tyler's been impossible," Benjamin said. "Sometimes I catch him staring at me with this look in his eyes that's—I'm not sure what. Like he hates me or finds me disgusting."

"He's thirteen," I said. "It would be unhealthy if he didn't hate you. And just for the record, I occasionally find you disgusting, too." Since I'd just insulted him, I figured it was acceptable to kiss him. "In the nicest possible way, I mean."

"Sometimes I wonder if he suspects anything."

"Anything" always meant one specific thing. Benjamin lived in fear of his family and co-workers suspecting "something." It was my role to reassure him that he was merely paranoid. To the untrained observer, there was nothing stereotypically gay about him, but Benjamin had a look of hungry willingness to surrender in his pretty green eyes that was unmistakable to me.

"I wouldn't worry about it too much. Two weeks from now, you'll be in Tyler's good graces. Take him to see a violent movie. You haven't done that in a while. There's a new one opening on Friday. Excessively gory, void of human emotions, and filled with subconscious homoerotic content. It would be a nice father-son outing."

"In his current frame of mind, he probably won't agree to go, and I'll end up feeling rejected and miserable. You know how much I hate rejection. If it wasn't for Kerry, I don't know how I'd stick it out."

Kerry was Benjamin's eight-year-old daughter and the love of his life, a sweet child with a speech impediment and a minor deformity in one foot that caused her to limp. Most of Benjamin's arguments with Giselle involved her desire to fix their daughter's problems with tutors and surgery and his desire simply to bathe her in the kind of unconditional acceptance he'd never had from his own rigid parents.

Our relationship went in fits and starts. When a couple months of regular meetings brought us too close together, he'd retreat in panic, handing me his set of keys to the Club with unconvincing finality. Sometimes, when I felt he was getting attached in a way that was distracting him from his home life, I'd be the one to suggest a break. His panics and concerns were such convenient focal points that I rarely needed to worry about or acknowledge my own. In theory, the breaks were a good thing, but the fact that our friendship endured despite them, and in some ways became more solid, challenged our mutual agreement that we were just in it for the sex.

Still, I had no illusions. Like most relationships based on secrecy and a presumption that it would, ultimately, go nowhere, mine with Benjamin was like a series of one- and two-hour vacations on a calm, lovely island. When you're on holiday in Martinique, the fantasy of living there is unavoidably appealing; you have to keep reminding yourself you'd go nuts if you actually relocated.

In the past six months, we'd seen each other only two or three times, a fact that I found both disappointing and reassuring.

The Bad Guy

"What did you end up getting Giselle for Christmas?" I asked.

"I got her a gym membership. It didn't go over."

"Oh, Ben, come on. How could you? That's like telling her she should lose weight."

"She's thinner than you are. Have you been eating, Richard? You're probably more upset about Conrad than you admit. You probably haven't been sleeping, either."

"Whenever you've gained weight, you accuse me of being too thin," I said.

I'd carefully maintained my emaciation for nearly forty years to compensate for the trauma of having been an obese ten-year-old. Benjamin vacillated between rigorous running and compulsive eating. When he was convinced he couldn't put up with the stress of his contradictions and turned in his keys, he packed on pounds, as if he thought food would cure him of his homosexuality.

"Giselle told me she wanted a gym membership. She's been saying it for months. 'I want to join a gym, I need to start going to the gym. My resolution for the new year.'"

When Benjamin imitated Giselle, he used a slightly affected accent that I assumed was inspired by his class rage. Among the too-much-information I had about Giselle was the fact that she'd been educated in Switzerland and spoke three languages fluently. She'd been a skilled equestrian before law school and the children, and on the advice of her psychiatrist, she'd started riding again a few years earlier, around the time Benjamin and I met. It insulted and pleased me when Ben made comments about our relationship that compared it to a hobby and put it in the same category as his wife's pastime with animals.

"I give her one and now I'm the bad guy. It makes no sense."

Like most heterosexual men, confused or otherwise, Benjamin was happiest thinking of himself as a victim of his wife's unpredictable behavior and hormonal whims. Whatever the problems in their relationship, I was convinced that he adored Giselle. He sometimes spoke about her in tones of hushed reverence; had he complained about her in more than the mild way one always complains about a spouse or the weather, I probably would have lost respect for him—or perhaps lost respect for myself for carrying on with him.

"What she really wanted was for you to reassure her she *didn't* need a gym membership. I told you to buy her a purse, didn't I?"

"I don't know anything about purses," he said. Earlier, in preparation for going out, he'd put on his scarf, and now, seeing he was sweating, I loosened it from around his neck. It was one of those long woolen things, striped with the colors of the prep school to which his parents had sent him in order to compensate for the fact that they were French-Canadian. (I assume the name Benjamin had been another stab at assimilation.)

"There's nothing *to* know about purses. You go to Hermès or Gucci and spend a lot of money. Period. Keep it in mind for her birthday. Which, in case you've forgotten, is next month." My ability to remember the important birthdays in his life rivaled his memory for my conversations with Conrad. "You should always do what I tell you."

"I do, Richard."

"Yes, but I mean outside of the bedroom."

Going Down

A short while later, as we were going down in the elevator, I noticed that he had a far-off look in his eyes, always a bad sign. I fixed his collar and combed his hair back into place with my fingers. "You look distracted," I said. "You're not gearing up for another disappearing act, are you?"

"I'm worried about this whole Conrad situation," he said.

"Why?"

"Because you're not."

"It's my job to worry about your life. You don't have to concern yourself with mine."

"What if he leaves you?"

"I think you're jumping way, way ahead."

"But what if? You'd be single. It would throw off the balance of our friendship. You'd start looking for someone who's available and I'd be out of the picture."

Since I was usually the one being written out of the picture, I was touched that he'd expressed it that way. I reached for his face with both hands, even though I'd just put on a pair of leather gloves. I loved that he was an inch or so shorter than me. It neutralized whatever manhood credits he'd earned for having had a bachelor party thrown in his honor. "I'm flattered you care," I said, "but you're overreacting."

The elevator stopped on the third floor, and a young woman got on. She was wearing a calf-length down parka that made her look like an ambulatory igloo. She put an end to our conversation. When we reached the lobby, I said goodbye and shook Ben's hand, which, considering what we'd just done upstairs, seemed perverse.

"Keep me posted," he said, as if we served on a condo board together and were awaiting a bid from electricians.

"Lunch next week?" I asked, hoping, for Benjamin's sense of propriety, that it sounded credibly businesslike.

"I'll get back to you," he said.

Why Not?

It took about twenty minutes to walk from the Club to the flat on Beacon Hill where Conrad and I lived. The snow had started to come down heavily, but it was still a pleasant walk across the Longfellow Bridge, the great stone parabola that spanned the Charles River and connected Boston to Cambridge. Like much of the infrastructure in the country, it was crumbling from lack of proper maintenance. There was always heavy traffic on the bridge, and subway cars rumbled across it hundreds of times a day. I fully expected it one day to collapse into the river below. Until then, it provided beautiful views of Beacon Hill, all red brick and yellow lights twinkling in the snowy winter twilight. The steep old neighborhood where I lived looked, from this angle, like an archaeological site, with the skyline of the new city rising up behind it. A woman in an orange coat passed me walking in the opposite direction and made a complaint about the weather, the only acceptable greeting between strangers in New England.

I tried phoning Cynthia Viano, the co-worker who'd called me earlier. Her message had implied that there was trouble brewing at the office, and since I have an essentially pessimistic nature, I wanted to learn what it was immediately, so I wouldn't spend the night constructing worst-case scenarios. Unfortunately, she'd already left the office. Anne, our secretary, informed me of this in a disapproving tone that suggested I was in no position to judge anyone else for leaving early.

"The roads are pretty slippery," I said. "Have a safe drive home."

"That's out of my hands, Richard," she said.

This was a subtle reference to her relationship with Jesus, which, like most such comments, was really a subtle reference to my lack of a relationship with Jesus.

"Just make sure you buckle up," I said.

I liked to try and have the last word with Anne; it made me feel as if I were asserting my authority in a small way; meaningless perhaps, but it somehow compensated for her intimate connection to a higher power.

Walking across the bridge, I became increasingly unsettled about Benjamin's thoughts on Conrad. While I was willing to betray my partner, I wasn't ready to lose him. I don't mind being alone, but I prefer to be alone in the presence of other people. I'm not crazy about sharing the covers, but I like waking up next to someone else. I don't mind cooking, and I don't mind doing the dishes, but I prefer not to have to do both at the same meal. More than all that, it was just too late in life to start over.

When I reached Boston, I decided to do a little shopping. Conrad and Doreen were only gone for a few days, assuming he didn't elope with his Insignificant Other. Among other things, I hadn't made dinner for Conrad in far too long.

I went into Savenor's—a porn shop for gourmands—and bought a pricey, pampered chicken and some cumin and caraway. Why not? It would be a show of affection and a reminder of our past rituals. I hated to think that Benjamin, the world's least reliable authority on relationships, had more insight than I did, but if you don't keep an open mind about such possibilities, you don't learn.

Picking at Scabs

I tried calling Conrad, but there was no answer on his phone. That wasn't uncommon, but it was impossible for me not to imagine what might be preventing him from answering. The lurid scenarios running through my mind disturbed me and then, even more disturbingly, started to arouse me. I was too weary to head to the basement gym to distract myself, so I went to my computer and checked out my favorite political Web site. I was delighted to learn that the president had made yet another embarrassing grammatical gaffe earlier in the day. This was guaranteed to inspire dozens of spiteful columns and remix videos to keep me in thrall for hours.

In what now felt as remote as a former lifetime, I had been a literature major in college, with a focus on the Victorian novel. I'd planned to go to grad school and plunge into a study of Anthony Trollope, that thorough and nonjudgmental chronicler of human nature. But practicality had intervened at the last minute, and instead I'd gone to social work school where I could get a degree that would allow me to get paid to chronicle human nature on my own, albeit in a far more judgmental way. For decades, I felt I'd abandoned some crucial piece of myself in my career choice, and had spent the bulk of my free time working my way through Trollope, Thackeray, Dickens, and a few other similarly inexhaustible writers. But my enthusiasm for literature had waned sometime around my second gym membership, and half the boxes in the basement storage space of our building were filled with nine-hundred-page novels. (Conrad didn't approve of the way the cracked orange bindings looked on our shelves.)

These days, I didn't read much other than factually questionable political blogs that supported my own views and unsubstantiated opinions. Reading them was as pointless as picking at a scab, but equally irresistible. It was getting increasingly painful to read about what was going on at home and abroad, but nothing soothed me more than spending a few hours poring over rehashes, deconstructions, and psychological analyses of the president's malapropisms, mistakes, and smug facial expressions. It felt like a patriotic duty.

I fell asleep on top of the covers with my computer on my lap running a recording of an incoherent presidential sentence about education, over and over, a lullaby for the disaffected.

A Beautiful Disaster

The software company I worked for was housed in a compact, four-story former candy factory in East Cambridge, not too far from the river. At one time, a lot of candy had been made in and around Boston, but now that, like everything else, was made in countries that don't use the Roman alphabet. Still, on hot summer days, a faint odor of sugar and cocoa would seep out of the factory's bones, and people would suddenly begin craving childhood treats without knowing why. As I approached the building in the cold the next day, it looked almost like a structure in a black-and-white fantasy of small town America, back in promising days of yore, and gave no hints of the architectural marvels inside.

Two young men in hooded sweatshirts and tight jeans that accentuated their ridiculously skinny legs and a pale girl in sneakers and a long skirt were huddled against the building smoking and laughing. The ages and casual outfits marked this group as members of the creative team, the employees who came up with the company's apparently innovative products. Most of my work in HR revolved around the creative team, folks who were, on the whole, younger, more socially awkward, and harder to talk to than the marketing people. Jenny and Marcus, I decided, and drew a blank on the name of the third person. Fortunately for me, most of the socially clumsy creative team didn't expect to be referred to by name, and half of them gave no indication of knowing what to call me.

"Nice smoking weather," I said.

"Especially for pot," Marcus said.

I laughed along with them and opened the door, not sure if they were joking. The work ethic of this generation was still as mysterious to me, five years after joining the company, as their eerie fluency in all things computer-related.

The inside of the renovated factory was an example of form triumphing over function, but a magnificent example. The entire building had been gutted and then filled with offices that looked like little glass and steel boxes stacked on top of each other, all connected by narrow walkways and circular staircases. Connectrix manufactured and marketed software to assist in various forms of technology-based communication. The concept of the interior design had something to do with communicating—letting people see exactly what their co-workers were doing and thereby creating an atmosphere of open engagement. In reality, it had created a lot of paranoia and embarrassment, but the aesthetics of the building packed such a wallop, no one dared complain.

I'd once given Benjamin a tour of the building, and his wistful reaction had been: "A beautiful disaster. I wish I had enough stature to design mistakes like this."

Prayers

Compared with some, I was lucky. My office was high up and looked down into the atrium and the other offices, affording me enough privacy for the occasional nap. I never took the elevator but bounded up the circular steel staircase that hung in the middle of the building, as if suspended in space. In addition to the exercise issue, I had mild claustrophobia issues (the elevator was small) and a ridiculous belief that it was morally flabby to take an elevator to anything lower than a fifth floor. That morning, I reached the top level and received the usual look of disapproval from Anne, the secretary I shared with Cynthia Viano.

"How did you find the drive home last night?" I asked. "Slippery?"

"It was a challenge, Richard, but no one said it was going to be easy, right?"

Like so much of what Anne said, this sounded primarily like a comment on my weak character.

"Those stairs, for example," I said. "Getting less easy every day."

"With my back problems, I wouldn't even attempt them."

"I suppose not."

When I hired Anne, I assumed she was just one of those sardonic suburban wives and mothers who disapprove of everything. She took a great deal of pride in appearing unfazed by any news, disappointment, report of bad behavior, or human error. No matter what I told her, she responded with a dismissive "It is what it is" or a sarcastic "What can you expect?" Like everyone else at the company, she spent at least an hour a day on her cell phone making personal calls, most of which seemed to consist of her saying "It is what it is" or "What can you expect?" with varying inflections and levels of moral superiority. Most of her family and social circle appeared to be plagued by accidents, health crises, and marital discord.

I'd hired her three years earlier because I'd been impressed by her feistiness and her résumé, and because I thought she'd add a little diversity to a company made up of largely single, urban employees. It wasn't until she'd been working for several weeks that I noticed she ended most personal calls with the phrase: "I'm praying for you." I thought nothing of it at first—being a fairly ardent non-believer, such statements always sound amusing and ironic to me—but then little prayer cards began showing up on her desk and on counters in the employee kitchen, and I heard from a number of people that she had solicited them for donations to a religious organization that was "protecting marriage." With this new information, all of her asides began to sound sanctimonious rather than sardonic.

While I was personally appalled by her fund-raising activities, I hadn't figured out a way to address them. People were always soliciting money for some cause, charity walk, or international disaster relief effort. Undoubtedly, Anne disapproved of my life, but she was no more or less polite to me than she was to anyone else. The degree to which one is obliged, for the sake of tolerance, to be tolerant of the intolerant has never been clear to me. I found myself avoiding commenting on aspects of her work performance for fear I was merely biased because of her religious and political views.

Anne was thirty-five. I knew her height and weight, too. One of the pleasures of my position was having access to personal information about everyone—age, medical history, school transcripts—even if I rarely remembered the details. She was unsentimental about her two sons, both of whom had developmental problems, and was openly hostile toward her husband, an unemployable man she referred to as "the Slob." At first, I assumed the disparaging way she talked about Daryl was part of a cranky persona she'd crafted for the sake of self-defense, but after working with her for three years, I'd come to believe she genuinely hated her spouse. This fact made her whole "defense of marriage" campaign seem infinitely less threatening and serious. I was all for changing the laws, but based on what I knew of most marriages, I considered it and the PTA, the NFL, and all theme restaurants, institutions heterosexuals were welcome to.

"Anything happening I should know about?" I asked.

She gave me a once-over, an unnerving habit she had, as if she were searching for outward signs of moral turpitude. "Not much. The lawyer on the discrimination lawsuit called to cancel his appointment with you."

"Did he say why?"

Anne made a show of appearing appalled that I assumed she'd know. She was simultaneously proud and secretive about all her inside information. "Certainly not to me. He's calling tomorrow instead."

"Send me a reminder, all right?"

"And your sister called yesterday. She called when you were out." She articulated the word "out" with a bit too much care, almost as if she knew what I'd been doing and with whom. "She didn't want voice mail. She wants you to call her today. She phoned at five. You and she have different accents."

"I haven't lived in Buffalo for a long time," I said.

"Gee, it wasn't a criticism, Richard. I just meant most people don't go out of their way to change their pronunciation and all that, like they're trying to erase their past. Doesn't your sister have your cell phone number?"

"She has two kids and a husband she's devoted to," I said,

drawing attention to the fact that even if I didn't have a life Anne approved of, I was related to someone who did. "She's probably lost it. Best not to burden her by giving it out again."

I had no interest in giving my sister my cell phone number so she could call me at inopportune moments to remind me of the fact that she and I were different people.

I studied Anne's face for a moment, and she stared back at me defiantly. She had big eyes that were made to look bigger by the square glasses she wore. I associated her style of eyeglasses, along with the dirndl skirts she favored and the sweatshirts decorated with colorful appliqué flowers with her Bible studies. I liked that she was rarely intimidated by me, even though my life would have been easier if she occasionally cowered. "I had a message from Cynthia yesterday," I said. "She didn't specify, but it sounded as if there's some kind of trouble brewing around here."

"What makes you think I'd know about it?"

"There's not much you don't know about, often before it happens."

Because Anne pretended to care about nothing, people told her almost everything as soon as she nonchalantly probed. Unless you intrude into other people's lives to some degree, it's hard to assume moral superiority.

"You're flattering me," she said.

"I am. Is it working?"

She shrugged. "Apparently there are rumors floating around about Brandon Miller."

"Nothing new there. I've been hearing rumors about Brandon since the day he was hired." The whole practice of gossip was invented for dealing with people like Brandon Miller—young, handsome, alternately intelligent and doltish, and maddeningly, brilliantly unspecific about the gender of his friends and romantic interests.

"I know," she said, "but this isn't the usual character assassination. There's a buzz that he might be leaving us."

After working with Anne for three years, I'd acquired a few of her dismissive affectations to communicate a fundamental lack of interest. I used them only when, as now, I felt unsettled by a piece of information. I slipped out of my coat. "I don't believe that any more than I believe the stories about his piercings."

She held up her hands. "You asked. Maybe Cynthia knows more about it than I do."

I thanked her for the information, but since most of what Cynthia knew came directly from Anne, the comment was essentially meaningless.

The Brandon Factor

I wandered into my office and hung up my coat on the rack I'd placed to the side of my desk. In an attempt to create a semblance of privacy, almost everyone had odd arrangements of books and clothes and soshi screens and plants scattered around their fishbowl offices. The glass-box design was supposed to give the building a look of sleek elegance, but all the makeshift barriers made the interior look like a tenement in Brasilia. The architect, who frequently visited the building to see to a new leak or spreading crack, was always after me to write rules and company policies banning this. It destroyed the integrity of his design and muddied the metaphoric construct that was the linchpin of the entire Connectrix project. I refused, fearing a rebellion, not to mention a loss of my own faux solitude.

While much of the personal gossip in the company was a combination of exaggeration, jealousy, and outright fabrication, rumors that didn't involve sex, inherited wealth, or plastic surgery almost always turned out to be true. This information about Brandon was unwelcome news.

Brandon was the son and only child of friends of one of the founders of Connectrix. He'd been hired right out of college for a low-level HR position as a favor to his parents. It had been one of those mercy-fuck hirings that had been surprisingly common during the rapid expansion of the company a few years earlier. Many of the companies that bought Connectrix's multifaceted communication systems were multinational. Teleconferencing tools, e-mail systems, and certain kinds of Web designs were our bread-and-butter, although to be honest, I was never able to grasp the details of what we actually produced. The creative team—the goofy people I dealt with—were known for coming up with ingenious applications that made some tiny aspect of human interaction quicker and simpler. This, despite the fact that they had some of the worst interpersonal skills imaginable. After 9/11, when no one was eager to get on airplanes, Connectrix had seen its business increase exponentially. Money was flowing and everyone was working overtime to fill up the glass offices of the building.

While it was easy to hire people, one of the chief problems we had was figuring out how to keep the under-twenty-five crowd, the folks with the most up-to-the-minute skills and the most innovative ideas, to stay with us for more than a few months. They were a notoriously fickle bunch who'd been brought up by parents of my generation to believe that they were deserving of everything they wanted. Since birth, they'd been paid attention to and had their opinions taken seriously, so they treated the whole notion of a business hierarchy with a casual attitude that made it hard to discipline, demote, or co-opt them. Initial attempts at keeping them at the company long enough to develop ideas and advanced knowledge of systems had involved salary increases. These rarely worked.

It had been my idea to enlist Brandon Miller to work on this problem with me. He had been, up to that point, an affable, undistinguished employee most notable for being able to get along with everyone at all levels of the company.

He helped me understand, in a more thorough way than I'd understood before, that his peers tended to leave Connectrix mostly for serendipitous reasons. It wasn't necessarily that they'd been offered a better salary somewhere else, but that the new company was located closer to a favorite café. They had a longing to study anime in Tokyo for six weeks, and quitting was easier than trying to arrange an extended leave of absence. They just didn't feel we were making enough effort at recycling paper. The lighting in the bathrooms was depressing. Offering salary increases to try to keep them on only made them feel more confined and, oddly enough, less valued as people.

Brandon and I reconfigured the corporate culture in ways that made the company feel more like a fun campus than a workplace. There were free bicycles employees could keep for up to forty-eight hours. Every other week there was another gimmicky opportunity to win an iPod or a MacBook, even though everyone already owned several. Brandon helped get employee discounts at some of the more funky restaurants and used clothing stores in the neighborhood. There was a garden on the roof that produced organic herbs, lettuce, and tomatoes from late June until early fall.

As a result of the work we did together, employee attrition had decreased by 40 percent. Lewis Hall, one of the founders, had been delighted by the results and by the fact that I'd actually found something meaningful to do with the son of his distinguished friends. Brandon received a promotion, and I got a salary increase.

Losing Brandon would be a blow to morale and send the wrong message to the rank and file. And, if true, the news of his departure was coming at exactly the wrong moment. Lewis Hall had indicated that there was to be a restructuring of the HR department in early spring, along with some kind of major reshuffling of the entire company. The implication was that either Cynthia Viano or I would be promoted to a new position. I didn't want anything to happen between now and then that compromised my standing.

Cynthia dealt with the marketing people, the better groomed and more socially adept employees, but also—as is often the case with the well groomed—the ones with messy alcohol and drug problems, and addictions to sex and gambling. We'd always kept the competition between us unspoken and just below the surface. However, in recent weeks, I had seen a few more indications of it in the way she always tried to keep a few steps ahead of me in matters of news about problematic employees, even those who were not her responsibility.

Although Brandon's office was about fifty feet from my own, I knew better than to try face-to-face communication, something that was increasingly regarded as invasive. Instead, I sent him an e-mail telling him I'd like to have lunch the following week. I'd barely managed to hit the send button when I got an enthusiastic response from him suggesting a time and place. The prompt reply made me feel even more concerned about his plans for departure.

Champ

Connectrix, like much of the corporate world, I'd come to realize, was perpetually undergoing adjustments and realignments. Even when things were going well, there was restlessness for change, usually unrelated to specific need. Everyone was constantly craving advancement, even when it was clear that advancing would lead to arrival at a point of incompetence and misery. I was trying, for the sake of my own finances, to get past the idea that contentment was a valid goal, and to prepare for a more aggressive lunge for a higher salary and better benefits package.

Despite Lewis Hall's position in the control tower of the company, I saw little of him. He had one of the few completely private offices in the building, and it was never clear to anyone exactly how much time he spent on site. In mid-morning, I crossed several of the catwalks that connected one section of the upper floors to another, gazing down into the dizzying atrium where it was always a carefully controlled approximation of springtime. There was snow lazily falling onto the skylights above, but down there, the trees never lost their leaves, and something was always blooming. I knocked on Lewis's door. After a loud roar of laughter, he told me to come in.

"Richard Rossi," he said, hanging up the phone. Using full names was one of his friendly, prep-school affectations, but it was also a reminder of his position of authority. It would have been entirely inappropriate for me to call him Lewis Hall in a similarly ironic manner, as I'd discovered the one time I'd tried. "So we meet again. Take a seat."

He was sitting behind his desk, leaning back in his chair. Maintaining a look of relaxed calm, as if he was doing nothing, was among the incongruous ways he communicated that he was firmly in command of every facet of the company.

"I'm just passing through," I said. "I wanted to run something past you."

Lewis was a tall, handsome man, with the face and features of a long-lost Kennedy relative: thick swept-back hair, rugged, sun-damaged skin, a big white smile. He was from Chicago and had traces of that city's accent in his flat, Midwestern a's. The accent made everything he said sound, to my ignorant East Coast ears, sincere, sensible, and imbued with wholesome practicality. He had a lot of jocular sayings and mannerisms. He was always clapping you on the back and calling you "champ," a word that would have sounded even more unconvincing in my mouth than "dude." I admired his ability to maintain an iron fist of control over the company while still convincing the majority of the employees that he was at heart "one of the guys," but I always felt I was talking to an actor doing a good job of playing a role rather than a completely authentic person.

Given his position, no one trusted him, but as far as I could tell, no one disliked him, either.

"I'm all ears," he said. "Nice shoes, by the way."

I looked down. Lewis routinely complimented my uninspired wardrobe, his way, I suspect, of showing acceptance of my sexuality.

Lewis had been a venture capitalist for many years, and his main interest in Connectrix was the bottom line. All of his jocularity hid what I knew to be a mind for numbers and an ability to be ruthless when it was called for. Like a surprising number of the higher-ups who pulled all the important strings, he seemed to know only enough about our products to show off, for five minutes, how "cool" they were before going back to what really mattered.

He was married to an attractive and athletic woman, one of those handsomely aging tennis players, and when they appeared together at company gatherings, they seemed to have a close, physical relationship—there was always a lot of touching and teasing. And yet, according to rumors Cynthia claimed to have from good sources—Anne, no doubt—Lewis had had affairs with more than one of the young women who worked at the company, our sexual harassment policies notwithstanding. Although I'm usually eager to believe rumors of anyone's infidelity or graft, I would bet the source of the rumors was his office, the only one in the entire building without glass walls into the atrium. No one could believe that he wasn't making the most of the opportunities afforded by this architectural anomaly.

I told him about the Brandon Miller rumors, and he listened in his inscrutable and slightly distracted way—long fingertips tapping each other, eyes gazing off to the side of my face. Like a lot of successful men, he appeared to be always waiting for a more important person to walk in the door.

"I wonder if he's told his parents," he said. "Do you know what his plans are?"

"It's all at the rumor stage right now. I'm having lunch with him next week."

"Well, see what you can find out. If he's going on to something better, his folks would be thrilled and it would look good for me. If it's something crazy, talk him out of it."

Brandon's mother was an epidemiologist, an attractive African-American woman in her forties who frequently turned up on CNN discussing world health emergencies. His father was a judge, considerably older than his mother, from a Boston Irish family with money. Both had prestige and political connections, and it wasn't hard to guess why Lewis wanted to stay on their good side.

"Either way," I said, "I'm planning to make sure he stays."

"How are you going to manage that, champ?"

"Well, for the past eighteen months, Brandon's been helping me keep his peers around. Some of what he's taught me is bound to have rubbed off."

"He's a tough one to read. He's so open, you can't help but think he's hiding something. Gay?"

"I have no idea."

This ignited his full attention, and he looked at me directly. He had beautiful blue eyes, almost feminine in their prettiness, and they softened his weather-beaten face. "Really? I figured you'd know. Interesting."

"It's never come up in our conversations."

"No," he said. "I'm sure it wouldn't. I was just thinking that since he's an only child, the chances might be higher."

Lewis and I were more or less the same age, so even though he was my boss, I sometimes felt embarrassed by my desire for his approval and the lengths I occasionally went to to try and get it. But even I had to draw the line somewhere.

"That's the wackiest idea I've heard in a long while."

"I was just throwing it out there, Richard. See what you can find out about his plans. And take him someplace cheap. I want to start trimming the expense accounts."

"It'll be my treat," I assured him.

Caught

After a gym visit that evening, I went to an Italian restaurant on Beacon Hill for dinner. The food wasn't especially good, but it was close to home, inexpensive, and since I'd slept with the maître d' once, a million years ago, I always felt a little special when I walked in. We greeted each other with hugs and knowing looks, conveniently forgetting that we'd had no chemistry.

I chatted with Al for a few minutes and ordered my meal. It was a neighborhood kind of place, and many of the other diners were couples who lived nearby. One of the complications of my friendship with Benjamin was an inability to look at married heterosexuals in quite the same way I'd once been able to. If someone as decent and devoted as Benjamin could have an active bisexual side he kept hidden, then why not the guy at the next table who was clearly paying no attention to what his wife was saying to him? Why not the young man in scrubs—Mass General was a couple blocks away—holding hands with his girlfriend and glancing fleetingly at Al? Men, trained and encouraged to keep their emotions bottled up and to suppress their enthusiasm for anything other than contact sports, are often adept at compartmentalizing their lives, rationalizing their indiscretions, and, of course, lying. Looking at these men and fantasizing about the hidden corners of their lives made me miss Ben. I wished I'd been able to call him, but of course, it wasn't possible. Right about now, he'd be cleaning the dinner dishes or helping his daughter with her homework.

Midway through my meal, I took out my phone and called Conrad. I hadn't spoken to him since he left, and it was time to check up on him. It had once seemed rude to talk on a phone in public as I was about to do, but increasingly it seemed rude not to. Sitting quietly, reading the newspaper or a book as I'd done in the past, now looked suspicious and slightly pathetic. A friend of mine claimed that it was "unfair" to other people, since it made them worry about you—a solo diner tragically without friends or family with whom you could loudly discuss the details of your personal life in public.

Since Doreen had gone with Conrad, I assumed the trip to Columbus was for legitimate business reasons. Still, I was fearful that I might catch him in the middle of some moment of erotic excess that I'd prefer not to know about, although I did block my number before dialing so he wouldn't know who was calling and would be more likely to think it was a business call and pick up.

His hello was lively and enthusiastic, and when he learned it was me, he was effusive. "Doreen and I had a fantastic day," he said. "We met with three potential clients. We're sitting in a restaurant right now, going over the details of the day. Are you at the gym?"

"I've been," I said. "I'm having dinner out."

"You're not alone, are you? Poor Richard. He's eating alone," he said to Doreen.

I named the restaurant and described what I'd ordered. It was a place I'd introduced him to when we first met. He'd shown a certain amount of ironic appreciation for the place, undoubtedly trying to convince himself that my frugality was quaint, appealing, and temporary.

"I haven't been there in years," he said. "We'll have to go when I get back to town. And don't stay up too late reading that political garbage, sweetheart. Watch a movie or something."

After we'd hung up, it occurred to me that he sounded very much like someone who was relieved to have been contacted while he was engaged in legitimate business, rather than whatever it was he'd been engaged in earlier. Benjamin often sounded this way when his wife called as he was walking out of the Club and he could honestly report that he was heading back to work.

Probably, I decided, it was best to put off calls for a few days.

Discrimination

The discrimination lawsuit Anne had mentioned was taking up an increasing amount of my time. It wasn't approaching a settlement as rapidly as such cases usually did. This particular case involved a former employee—let's call him Z—who was suing Connectrix for discrimination after he'd been fired. It was a common enough occurrence, a lawsuit being the first line of defense for most employees who'd been let go. Everyone could come up with some reason they might have been discriminated against: age, race, sexual preference, marital status, even, in one case, an employee who claimed she'd been fired because she had bad teeth. I'm not suggesting such things never happen, but in that instance, the employee had shown up for work so infrequently no one had had the opportunity to notice her dental work.

Z had been let go because he had made wildly exaggerated claims of experience on his résumé and, for the eleven months he was at Connectrix, had done virtually nothing. His supervisor had made a convincing case for his firing and had assured me that he was keeping proper documentation of performance reviews and warnings. It had seemed such a clear case of incompetence that I'd taken the supervisor at his word and let him proceed with the dismissal. A younger, female replacement had been hired. Z was claiming age and gender discrimination, and almost daily I was discovering that his supervisor had not kept records or followed up with reports to the extent that he claimed. On top of that, the supervisor, thinking it was the most gracious way to let go of Z, had made the mistake of writing a favorable letter of recommendation.

The supervisor was Randy Trask, a lumpy member of the creative team in his early thirties who specialized in technical matters. There was something childlike and unformed in his appearance and personality, but I'd been told that he was a mathematical whiz, one of the people other employees went to to solve small but crucial problems involving numbers and complicated formulas. Unfortunately, he'd been promoted to a position in which he had to deal with people, an area where he was completely inept. There was something eerily robotic about Randy, but I was sympathetic toward him—he hadn't wanted his current position but hadn't been able to refuse the promotion either—and I'd developed a paternal sort of concern for him and a conviction that if I could get him past this problem, he'd become a more valuable employee and grow as a person.

When Z's lawyer called about the case the following day, Randy was in my office going over some largely irrelevant e-mail records he'd recently discovered. I didn't have the heart to kick him out, figuring it would make him more paranoid, so I let him listen to my end of the conversation. He sat across from me, winding a rubber band around his index finger. He had a round, fleshy face, often spotted with stubble, as if he hadn't yet mastered the art of shaving, and a thick mop of dark hair that he combed neatly over his forehead in a perfectly shaped flap. He had big brown eyes, but his face was oddly expressionless. I would never have had a clue what he was thinking or feeling if it hadn't been for the bouts of furious blushing and rapid blanching that gave clues to his emotional shifts.

He flushed red as I stonewalled for a few minutes, assuring Z's lawyer that I'd read his most recent batch of depositions. "Our lawyer," I told him, "wants to interview Randy Trask a couple more times. So far, it appears that everything's in order. I'm not sure what else we have to talk about, and I have a full plate today."

"Richard, my client is going through a severe depression right now. We all want to put this behind us, Richard."

The complainant's lawyer's annoying habit of repeating my name at least once every couple sentences was allegedly a show of respect, but really a form of condescension about the fact that he was a decade younger than me. Both of us knew there would eventually be a settlement, but he had to try to wear me down by calling me instead of the Connectrix lawyer, repeating my name too often, and talking about his client's damaged ego and life. I countered the lawyer by asking questions about the weather in Braintree (twelve miles south of the office), putting him on hold, and acting chagrined in a sarcastic way I didn't even attempt to make convincing.

"Mr. Trask is not exactly on top of the world either," I said. Randy's basset-hound eyes drooped. "Don't think the stress of your client's lawsuit isn't having an impact on his life, too."

Support

I'd barely put down the phone when Randy let the elastic band snap off his finger. It shot across the office and bounced off one of the glass walls. "You weren't supporting me," he droned. "What about our lawyer interviewing me? The lawyer knows the whole situation. No one mentioned that to me." Randy always dressed in a white shirt and dark work pants that were either too big or too small, making him look like a child in his father's ill-fitting and outdated clothes.

"Don't worry. It's just a ploy. No one blames you. Three months from now, no one will remember the entire incident. It's meaning-less."

"*I'll* remember it." Randy had the squeaky voice of an adolescent, not exactly pleasant to listen to, but at least it added some modulation to his otherwise flat tone. "And what do you mean I'm not on top of the world?"

"You're upset about this for absolutely no reason." I'm a big believer in people's ability to change, even if I've never been especially good at it myself. I wasn't deluded enough to think Randy would ever turn into a robust and exuberant person, but I was convinced that if I could see him over this particular hurdle, he'd at least become more recognizably human.

"You're implying I'm having psychological problems. You're telling the lawyer I'm on the edge of a nervous breakdown and I'm supposed to sit here and listen."

"To be honest, Randy, you're not supposed to listen at all. I just don't like saying things behind your back. This is a routine matter. You need to calm down and let go of it and let the lawyer and me handle it. I should have been paying more attention to the records you were keeping, so I'm not without responsibility either."

"The guy is blaming me for his fake résumé. I'd like to strangle the creep."

"You officially didn't say that. Your coloring's worrisome. Are you getting enough exercise?"

"I don't see how that's relevant."

"It might take your mind off things and help put this in perspective."

My belief was that most problems in most people's lives could be solved if they got more exercise. The fact that some of the problems in my life might have been solved by my getting less exercise was an exception.

"I don't have time for *exercise*," Randy said, uncharacteristically enunciating the word as if I'd recommended he take up macramé. "I barely have time for lunch. And this is the last thing I need to be dealing with. I need to feel supported here. How can I produce if I don't believe you're behind me?"

It amazed me that he was so unabashed about launching into this infantile rant, but it fit in with the rest of his marginally adult behavior.

"Let me give you some unsolicited advice. Take a few days off. Take your girlfriend away somewhere and put all this in perspective. It's not worth the high blood pressure."

"We broke up," he said. He stood and leaned his hand on my desk again. There was a ketchup stain on his shirt. Binging on French fries and fast food to deal with the breakup, no doubt. "She said I was too obsessed with this and claimed I was sucking her into it."

"Do you think she had any basis for saying that?"

"I called my father to tell him and maybe get a little consideration, and he said the same thing. 'She's probably right.' He's always been a bully. Nothing ever pleases him, anyway. He always said he couldn't understand why Sandra was with me, and all of a sudden he thinks I shouldn't have let her walk out. Well, just for the record, Richard, I didn't let her walk out. I got her in the car, started driving, and for four hours, I tried to talk some sense into her. I told her it would be her fault if I went into a big depression. I tried, Richard," he said, as if he was proud of the abduction. "It didn't work. Don't think I just let her go. It wasn't like that."

His complexion had become blotchy, patches of red and white on the uncooked dough of his face.

"If you change your mind about the exercise, I'll treat you to a free pass at my gym."

He offered a sarcastic "thanks" and padded out. I hated being lumped in with his unyielding father, but transference usually came in handy at some point in most of these situations. I tried to picture Randy holding his girlfriend hostage in his car, speeding down the highway, making a case for himself and doing what people who try to make a case for themselves always end up doing—confirming the other person's worst suspicions and justifying their reasons for wanting out. The biggest problem I had was imagining what kind of a person Sandra might be that she'd been with him in the first place.

Feminism

A little later in the day, I wandered into Cynthia Viano's office with my notes on Randy Trask. Although I was responsible for handling his case, I felt it was best to have backup support from her in case things got ugly down the line. Ordinarily, I was vain about my ability to judge character, but the information I'd gleaned from Conrad's cell phone had made me less sure than usual about my talent for reading people. If I hadn't spotted what had been going on with the person I lived with, how could I be sure of my perceptions of relative strangers? It was also a good way of discussing the Brandon Miller rumors with Cynthia without appearing to know less than she did. Cynthia and I were always dancing around each other in an amiable way that was loaded with veiled suspicion, like two friendly rivals having drinks together, each wondering if the other had slipped something into his martini.

She was talking on the phone when I walked in, and she motioned for me to take a seat. I pushed aside some papers and sat. Cynthia was meticulous in the way she dressed, cut her hair, and spoke, but her office was bursting with heaped-up papers and books, an assortment of sneakers, slippers, and comfortable shoes—she considered her tiny feet her best features and she pampered them, as if they were adorable kittens—and a jungle of overgrown plants. She kept the plants alive with a complicated system of miniature grow-lights and a rigorous watering routine. She was one of the most blunt and unsentimental people I knew, but she had names for all her plants (Susan, William, Ringo, that kind of thing) and frequently spoke about them in a cloying way that made me want to look away.

Cynthia was in her mid-forties and had been, for many years, a nurse. About eight years earlier, she'd become disillusioned with health care and had gone to a business school, although she hadn't finished her degree. She had about her the kind of no-nonsense practicality I associate with nurses, and although her techniques could seem, at times, a little undiplomatic, she had a way of getting problems solved quickly, especially when the problems involved potentially embarrassing personal matters. A surprising number of cases that crossed my desk had to do with inappropriate attire or awkward behavior that teetered on the edge of sexual harassment. When I got complaints that someone was dressing too provocatively (the term "low-cut blouse" was one I heard almost weekly), or had offensive body odor or offensive perfume odor (smells, good and bad, were always offending someone and setting off panic alarms about allergies, asthma, and lawsuits), I consulted Cynthia, even when the complaint involved someone from my creative team.

When she finished her phone call, I updated her on my conversation with Randy while she made motions of swirling something in her thermal coffee mug. I don't think I'd ever seen her without her mug—walking around the office, at meetings, on her way into work—but I'd never seen her drink from it. For all I knew, it could have been empty.

"He's troubled," she said of Randy. "I usually like troubled, but this guy makes me uncomfortable. I'm glad his girlfriend had the brains to leave him. To be honest, it's hard to imagine he had a girlfriend in the first place."

"I know what you mean. You don't think he's making her up, do you?"

"I don't think he's imaginative enough to invent a story like that. Or if he did, he'd be more likely to tack on a happy ending."

"He claims it was a serious relationship. What kind of woman—"

"You don't understand women, Richard. Women will fall for anything. She probably had a rescue fantasy, taking care of a wounded bird. It's a common female delusion."

Cynthia claimed to be an ardent and radical feminist, but she was constantly disparaging women's tact, judgment, and intelligence, making it hard at times to distinguish between her brand of feminism and misogyny.

Mother Issues

Cynthia was a petite woman who came up to the middle of my chest. She wore dark, pin-striped business suits and silky white blouses every day, no doubt in an effort to create a more authoritative appearance. All of her clothes seemed to be expensive, and they fit her perfectly, but something in the styling made them look as if they'd been designed for a larger person and then shrunk down. They emphasized her doll-like stature. She scoffed at my exercise regimen and frequently accused me of being neurotic (as if I didn't know), but she herself was such a compact bundle of nerves and energy, she stormed around the building at great speed with her coffee mug in one hand and stacks of paper in the other, burning up more calories than I could hope to in any hour-long workout. She once told me her mother had pushed her into gymnastics as a child, and given her body type, it was easy to see why.

"Maybe you should go talk to Randy in that soothing, gentle way you have," I said.

"It wouldn't work with him. His mother issues are bigger than I am. He's terrified of women, especially now that the alleged girlfriend dumped him. Then there's all that blushing or flushing or whatever it is. I never know whether to slap him or call an ambulance." She picked up her coffee mug, swirled it around and set it back down on a heated coaster. She loved gadgets and was always giving people little electrical trinkets and special cutting tools, the sorts of things advertised on late night television. Very late night. Cynthia was single, and it was unclear to me if she had a social or romantic life. "He hasn't threatened anyone, has he?"

"He made a hostile comment about the complainant, but there's no indication he's been fantasizing a specific plan. At least as far as I can tell. I'm considering recommending him for anger management."

"I'm guessing he's too passive for violence." She gazed over at a tall, spindly avocado plant near the door. I was afraid she was about to begin a long digression on the subject of Melanie—or whatever the plant's name was—but after a moment, she turned back to me and said, "The last two times I referred someone to anger management, it made them more paranoid and hostile. If you want my opinion, I'd wait. I don't know how you deal with those goofy people anyway. They're all so awkward. From what I can tell, Randy's one of the more normal."

It was clear that Cynthia considered herself above me in some sense because the people she dealt with wore suits and neckties and could, if called upon, summon up a few social graces. The marketing department traveled to cities around the world convincing multinational companies to buy our products or upgrade them if they already had. They had more frequent flyer miles than Neil Armstrong and looked you in the eye when they talked to you. Overall, they were undeniably more sophisticated than the eccentrics I dealt with, but I found them aloof and condescending and was happy to have minimal contact with them. I was always discovering oddball habits and interests that endeared my group to me—they belonged to ukulele orchestras and contra-dancing clubs, they collected baseball cards and held potluck dinners at each other's apartments. I was tempted to point some of this out to Cynthia, but I knew she'd think I was grasping at straws.

"You're insecure about the way you're handling this," she stated. "That's not like you."

"Really? I thought it was perfectly in character." I shrugged it off. "I'm getting tired of the case. I want to get it behind us and get Randy back on track."

"Are you sure that's all? Have you been sleeping?"

"Reasonably well."

"If you want something, I can get it for you." Cynthia had maintained her connections in the medical world and was always offering Ritalin, painkillers, and antibiotics. It was tempting to take her up on her offer (I like the idea of stockpiling pharmaceuticals, even though I'm not big on taking them), but I resisted the temptation, figuring it was the kind of detail she could use against me at some point. "You look gaunt," she said. "Not that that's unusual."

While it would never occur to me to randomly comment on someone's weight gain or obesity, there are no social taboos against disparaging someone for being too thin.

"How are things at home?"

"Things at home are fine."

She nodded as if she'd hit pay dirt and patted down her hair. She had thinning hair she wore in a short, Peter Pan cut that made her look even more diminutive. "Something's going on with Conrad?" she asked.

"He's in Columbus. Everything's fine." Cynthia was capable of shrewd insights, and because she was so blunt, she could make insulting but surprisingly good suggestions. I was tempted to tell her about the text message, but it was another piece of personal information that would give her the upper hand.

"You left a message for me a couple days ago," I said. "What did you want to talk about?"

"Brandon Miller. There are rumors going around that he wants to leave."

"Obviously, I've heard all about it."

"Oh really? Did Anne tell you?"

"I have my sources."

She went over to an overgrown fern and pulled off some brown fronds. I'm no fan of houseplants in general, but ferns have always struck me as especially pointless. "Ginny's been a little under the weather the past few weeks," she said. "I guess the winter's hard on everyone."

"Please don't start with the plants," I said. "You know it disturbs me."

"Maybe I need to vary her diet a little. I was only trying to be helpful, telling you about Brandon."

"I made an appointment to talk with him," I said. "As far as I know, he hasn't turned in his resignation, so there's no need to jump to any assumptions about this. I'd appreciate it if you wouldn't spread the news around. The fewer people who know about this, the better."

"We'll do our best," she said. Exactly who the "we" referred to was not clear, but for the moment I chose to assume it referred to her and her little family of plants. "And if you change your mind and want to talk about Conrad, you know where to find me."

Something's Brewing

Depending on the size of the project they were working on, Benjamin's architecture firm employed between ten and fifteen people. In his self-effacing way, he made disparaging comments about what he did—the dull buildings, the emphasis on bland utilitarian design—but underneath that, I could tell he loved his job and took pride in his success. My sense was that he enjoyed working through problems of space and organization with mathematical formulas and without the ambiguity of emotions and human behavior that brought so much confusion to his personal life.

Ben had been a history major in college. He still read a great deal, but when I tried to get him interested in Trollope, he'd returned the books to me, claiming he'd found the complicated lives of the characters disturbing.

Based on the details I'd harvested over the years, he was doing well. And yet, he always talked about his finances warily. "Something's brewing," he'd moan, referring to an unspecified pending crisis. I shared his sense of doom, and undoubtedly he had more insight into the world economy than I did, but his anxiety was clearly bound up with his worry that someone was going to discover "something" about him that he preferred to keep hidden.

Fearful as he was of his own situation, he was consistently reassuring to me about mine. He had a blind faith in my competence that I found comforting, no matter how baseless it was, and a touching belief that what I did was interesting and important, not as a cog in the corporate world, but because I was making a difference in people's lives. When I felt myself getting worked up about an incident at Connectrix, I could give him a call and he would talk me down.

"You have to follow your instincts on this," he said, referring to Randy. "You know what you're doing. If you think he's a threat, get him into treatment. Don't worry what Cynthia thinks."

My co-workers and his comprised another large cast of players that figured prominently and invisibly in both our lives. In contrast, I'd dragged Conrad to numerous company outings, and he still couldn't remember anyone's name.

"She's been right about this kind of thing before," I said. "Maybe I'm just overreacting."

"For Christ's sake, Cynthia has an obsession with plants. You can't base your actions on anything she says. I've never really trusted her. Go with your gut on this."

I proposed we meet for lunch the next day. "Conrad's not coming home until Friday," I said.

"Have you talked with him?"

"Only briefly, but that's not unusual. He left less than a week ago."

"But now you know more than you usually do, so you should call again. I don't think we should meet until you've discussed this with him. It wouldn't be right."

This comment rankled me, especially since his marriage to Giselle was in a perpetual state of uncertainty, as far as I could tell. But it wouldn't help me any to bring that up.

"I'm planning a big dinner for Conrad when he returns. A nice meal for the two of us. Good food—with sentimental overtones as value-added. I bought the ingredients and everything. Doesn't that count for something?"

"It's a start," he said. "Let me know how it goes. Give me the recipe and I'll make it for Giselle over the weekend."

Normalcy

The problem with trying to lead a sensible, upstanding life is that the choices you make and actions you follow on a regular basis quickly become part of your definition of normalcy. You meet a friend at the Club, you discuss the weather and fuck, you take a shower, you prepare a meal for your partner, you add another item to the At Least List.

- *At least I used a condom.*
- *At least no one else knows.*
- *At least it's an organic chicken.*

I worried that I was capable of justifying and assimilating any behavior, no matter how egregious, once it became routine. Fortunately, I have enough impulse control to stop the worst of it (raiding colleagues' retirement funds? physical violence?) before taking the first step and having to line up the justifications.

Although he'd been loath to admit it to me initially, over time I'd learned that Benjamin had recognized his attraction to other men early in his life. As with most people, me included, it had caused him confusion and uneasiness. Among other things, he'd been brought up in a nice Catholic French-Canadian family to believe that homosexuality was evil, disgusting, and a lot of other adjectives used by Catholicism to describe most pleasurable activities. Because he had just enough wherewithal to know that he himself wasn't bad and evil, he figured, through some convoluted deductive reasoning, that therefore he must not be homosexual. He had enough experience with girlfriends to know he could enjoy sex with women, even if he sometimes thought about Calvin Klein underwear ads while engaged in it.

Early in our friendship, he told me that Giselle had been everything he'd always wanted—beautiful, cultured, talented, and intelligent. "The girl of my dreams," he'd said, apparently forgetting that he'd already told me his erotic dreams often involved being gang-raped by the Russian Olympic wrestling team.

And yet I was certain his marriage hadn't been one of convenience for him or a way to step into a more secure closet. He had been in love, and like most married men in his situation, he'd believed his marriage would turn off the wrestling-team impulses and the other assorted lustful urges that made him uncomfortable anyway. In that respect, he wasn't so different from anyone who marries. Everyone pledges fidelity and believes in the moment that they're capable of adhering to it; then they hit their seventh anniversary, meet the baby-sitter, and start hunting for ways to forgive themselves for their hoped-for transgressions.

(At least she's almost in college. At least we're paying her more than minimum wage.)

He wasn't so different from me, either, although Conrad and I had never made any pledges more solemn than mumbled words in moments of passion that we both understood were to be considered aphrodisiacal rather than taken literally.

Benjamin's kids had come along, and whatever his problems with his son, he was one of the most devoted fathers I'd ever met. For the sake of his family, one might argue, he might have resolved to keep his wayward urges more tightly bottled up forever, but such resolutions usually start in church and end in a sting operation at a highway rest stop bathroom.

A Bookcase

As Ben described it, six years earlier, someone had propositioned him on a street corner, and he'd followed him home, as if in a dream, not fully aware of what he was doing. It had been a fumbling, moderately satisfying encounter, neither shatteringly good nor discouragingly bad, and afterward the man asked Ben to help him move a bookcase from the living room to the bedroom. According to Benjamin, he was so terrified of having sex with another man, he never would have repeated the experience had it not been for the cordial normalcy of moving the bookcase. This was just an average person, another man who needed help moving furniture and was not, as far as Ben could tell, evil or more disgusting than most human beings. The sex got connected to the bookcase and that, too, began to feel like two men helping each other out with something they couldn't quite manage alone.

Six months later, it had been Benjamin who did the propositioning, and a few years after that, we met.

- *At least he was the one who placed the ad.*
- *At least I wasn't his first.*
- *At least we aren't in love.*

Family Matters

Since the death of my parents, more than a decade earlier, my sister, Beth, and I have routinely spoken on the phone once or twice a month. She is my only sibling and still lives in the house where she and I grew up in Buffalo. She is an intelligent, energetic woman who does a large number of good deeds, including donating many hours of legal work to the local Democratic Party and taking in dogs from a rescue network until they can be placed in permanent homes. I've always thought of her with warmth and fondness, and I admire her generosity and hard work, both of which far outpace my own. But whenever we talk on the phone, some stubborn piece of unresolved family business or sibling rivalry surfaces, and the conversation ends in harsh words or tears. It probably would be better for both of us to carry on our relationship through e-mails and the occasional holiday visit, but the truth is, she is the only family I have, and I often find myself missing her—right up to the moment I hear her voice. I have a theory that both of us long for a closer relationship and are frustrated by the fact that we don't have all that much in common. Unless it's frustration over how much we do have in common.

I returned her call from earlier in the week one night as I was sitting in my apartment watching a light snow falling outside. Her son answered.

"Nicholas," I said, "it's Uncle Richard."

"Oh, hello. How are you?"

"I'm doing very well. How's school, young man?"

"School is quite interesting. I'm enjoying it."

"I'm glad you are."

"Yes. So am I."

Nicholas had recently turned nine. His sister was seven years older than him. Beth maintained that Nicholas had picked up his spooky maturity in speech and mannerisms from his sister, but Laura was a high-spirited and giggly teenager who seemed, in many ways, younger than her brother. Nicholas spent the majority of his time diligently but mechanically practicing the clarinet or locked in his room (my childhood bedroom) making carefully organized lists of people and cities. Beth would sometimes tell me she was proud of his maturity and his organizational skills and then burst into tears.

"Have you started the book I sent you?" My Christmas present had been a copy of *David Copperfield*. Nicholas was an advanced reader with a special affinity for long adult novels, many of which he found on the shelves of the room my mother had designated the library and had stocked with books she'd randomly picked up at church sales. It's not that I had anything against the works of John O'Hara and Allen Drury, but Dickens seemed more likely to be within his emotional grasp.

"I'm planning to begin on February 16. I should finish it by the middle of April."

"I see. I hope you enjoy it," I said, although it was pretty clear that his chief pleasure would come from keeping to his schedule. "Is your mother home?" I asked.

"Yes, she is. Would you like to speak to her?"

Nicholas had an uncanny ability to distinguish between truth and lies, so I tried to be as precise as possible: "I'd appreciate it if you'd tell her I'm on the phone."

"I'll do that. It's been nice talking to you, Uncle Richard."

It sounded as if Nicholas had dropped the receiver to the floor. There was, as usual, a lot of barking and snarling in the background.

Most of Beth's foster dogs were from a dachshund rescue group, and whenever I visited, there were several traumatized dogs battling for her affection. Nicholas paid no attention to them, and they ignored him as if he were invisible.

"At last," Beth said. "I thought you'd vanished from the face of the earth."

"It's been a hectic week," I said. "I meant to call earlier, but—"

"It's all right, Richard. I don't take things personally anymore. I just called to check in. We missed you at Christmas."

"The snow," I said.

"Lucky for you we have such bad weather here. Even so, it wouldn't hurt to make more of an effort."

Beth considered me selfish because I'd moved away from Buffalo, because I was gay, because I didn't have children, and because I never gained weight. She sometimes acted as if I led a glamorous life filled with travel and adventure. I'd have welcomed the flattering misperception, but she seemed to resent me for it. I'd planned to spend Christmas with her, but Conrad had balked at the travel and prospect of so much bad food.

Beth had chosen a life for herself that was almost identical to that of our parents. She'd taken over our father's small, modestly successful law practice, married a silent, emotionally distant man who bore a striking physical resemblance to our father, had two children, and lived in our parents' large uncomfortable house. The fact that she was following a pattern that hadn't made our parents especially happy didn't seem to have crossed her mind.

We'd never been an especially close family. My father had rarely been in evidence, and my mother had invested all of her energy in her own siblings, especially her younger sister, a short, accident-prone woman who had a tumultuous marriage to a drunken bully. I sometimes felt that Beth was waiting for me to confess a secret misery to her so she could assume the role our mother had played with her only sister. Growing up, Beth and I had lived separate lives in our rooms on different floors of the house where she now lived. I missed my parents from time to time, but the sad truth is, I thought of my childhood dog—a small brown mutt who'd been deaf in one ear—more often and with more emotion. I was secretly hurt by the fact that Beth never suggested I take in one of her homeless dogs, but I never brought it up since I almost certainly would have refused the suggestion.

"Was it a fun holiday?" I asked.

"Karl's family was here," she said, referring to her in-laws. "That gives you some idea. They go out of their way to make snide comments about everything, and I'm supposed to ignore them. You would have been a good buffer."

"Now that you put it that way, I'm especially sorry I missed it."

"Oh, don't get sensitive. I'm too tired for that. Thank you for the presents. Karl's family kept asking why you hadn't sent Nicholas Harry Potter books. They don't know what to make of him."

"Well . . ." Since Nicholas had an alphabetized filing cabinet in his bedroom filled with school papers, grade sheets, and birthday cards he'd received beginning at age four, I didn't really know what to make of him either. "I suppose they could have bought them for him, if they feel so strongly about it."

"No, they have to give him presents they know he won't like, just to point out to us how unusual he is. In the meantime, they have three of the dullest children I've ever met." I could hear a little catch in her voice and sensed that tears were coming. "He's a lot like you, you know."

I didn't say anything. I'd noticed that, increasingly, the fallback explanation for most studious or socially awkward behavior in boys was budding homosexuality. It had never been clear to me if Beth wanted me to confirm her suspicions or assure her that she was wrong.

"I'll try to come out for his birthday," I said.

"No, you won't. Don't say that when you know you won't."

"I'm sorry about Christmas, but December was a bad month at work, and—"

"A minute ago it was the weather. Just don't bullshit me, okay? I don't know why you stay at that job anyway."

"It has its satisfactions," I said.

The comment sounded grimly unconvincing even to my ears, and I suddenly felt a strong, not entirely unfamiliar emptiness open up around me. The apartment was chilly, I was alone, and the snow had started to come down more heavily. My books, the items I had once valued most highly, had been judged by their covers and put into storage. I felt strangely detached from the place I considered home.

"Why don't you and Nicholas come here this spring?" I said. "He hasn't been since he was four."

Beth seemed as surprised by the invitation as I was. She said nothing for a moment and then said, "True, but he remembers everything we did, right down to a clam roll we ate at some takeout place by the water." She attended to the yapping of her foster dogs and seemed to be mulling over the invitation. Although I'd made the suggestion without thinking about it, I began hoping she'd agree to the idea.

"Karl and Laura can handle the dogs," I said. "We can go on a whale watch. It will be fun for just the two of you to get away."

"Whales aren't Nicholas's thing."

It was such a minor and specific objection, it was clear she wasn't ready to turn down the idea completely. When, a few minutes later, I ended the conversation, she accused me of having other, more interesting things to do. But really, I just wanted to get off before she refused the idea of a trip out of hand or one or the other of us started shouting.

Is That All There Is?

The gym I belonged to near the office was in a new building on the river, a ten-minute walk from both Connectrix and the Club. Looking out from the bank of cardio machines in front of one of its glass walls, I could clearly see the concrete tower of the apartment building. I sometimes found myself exercising especially aggressively when I noticed it, but I wasn't sure if the sight inspired me or made me feel guilty.

I went to this gym—Fitness Works, a borderline clever name— about four times a week. Once or twice a week, I met my friend Jerry Weinberg there.

The day before Conrad returned, I walked into the gym in the middle of the afternoon and saw Jerry standing at the reception desk chatting up one of the staff members, a statuesque twenty-something woman with green eyes the color of rhododendron leaves. Plastic rhododendron leaves. Like most trainers of both sexes at this gym, she seemed to equate fitness with a lot of cosmetic adjustments—hair extensions, the tinted contact lenses, frighteningly white teeth, an unnervingly even, mud-colored "tan," and breasts that were impossible to imagine as original to her otherwise fleshless body. Jerry waved at me and continued to listen to her with the earnest, rapt attention men his age feign when they're flirting with a woman they know is out of their league. I stood at a discreet distance as he nodded and made an effort to appear amazed by what was probably a discussion of a new membership drive or one of the vast drums of powdered nutritional supplements the staff was constantly promoting. I didn't suspect Jerry of trying to pick her up—Jerry was one of the few genuinely faithful men I knew—but it's always flattering to act as if you think someone's up to no good, as long as you know they're not.

Eventually, he came over and said, "You're early."

"I apologize. I hope I didn't break anything up."

"Oh yeah, it was a real romantic interlude. She was trying to talk me into joining a weight-loss seminar she's giving for post-natal women and post-prime men. Great pickup line, isn't it?"

"You're post-natal?"

"Nice try, Richard. Let's just get this show on the road."

We went into the locker room, a glittering fantasy of polished marble and bleached wood that smelled of the eucalyptus from the steam room and a reassuringly unpleasant antiseptic cleanser. Unlike the basement dungeon near my condo where I did my most neurotic exercising, this gym was an overpriced fitness palace that had opened a decade or so earlier, when everyone still had money and felt optimistic about their finances and their ability to maintain their level of old-fashioned American excess forever. I always ended up feeling better when I left the place, if for no other reason than because the thick towels and the expensive shampoo made me believe I deserved to be pampered.

Jerry and I had been friends for years; he was one of several people whose friendship I'd inherited from my late lover, Samuel, who had been Jerry's college roommate. Samuel had died a dozen years earlier, but my friendship with Jerry continued to feel as if it were mediated through a third person, rather than being solid on its own. We met at the gym, I socialized with him and his wife a couple of times a year, and he and I occasionally had decent political conversations over lunch; but there was always the feeling, no matter what we were doing, that we were making small talk, waiting for Samuel to get back from the men's room.

Jerry was an affable man who, in his younger days, had had a long string of successes with women. He'd been a track star in college and—according to pictures I'd seen—had looked like a Roman athlete, lean, long-muscled, taut, and bursting with barely suppressed sexual energy. Now, decades and a few pounds later, he still had the healthy look of one of those suburban guys who have a lot of used gym clothes stashed in the back of their cars. He'd lost most of his curly dark hair and, after dabbling with embarrassing comb-overs, sported a shiny pate. The hair loss had been a blow to his self-esteem, but I was of the opinion that the baldness enhanced his appearance. It made him look, as bald men sometimes can, exces-sively clean but still capable of debauchery, should the opportunity present itself.

The most remarkable thing about Jerry was that he did not have any cruel or malicious intentions, and when you talked with him, he seemed to be sympathizing with you, even if the news you were sharing was good. Jerry was famously helpful, stepping in to lend a hand when and wherever he could, but he was notoriously unhandy at practical things like changing tires, fixing faucets, and replacing batteries in his kids' toys.

He and Sam had been roommates freshman and sophomore years, and owing to a bullying incident Sam had faced back then, Jerry had developed a protective, brotherly feeling toward him that had never faded. Even now, all these years after Sam's death, I could hear it in his voice when he talked about him.

The triumphant culmination of Jerry's early womanizing was his marriage to Janet Braine, a younger, beautiful former dancer who was enough outside of his league to be a score but not so far outside that the marriage looked ridiculous. He and Janet had three daughters, and so Jerry lived, as he'd always longed to do, in a king-dom of pretty blond women.

In the past five or so years, sadness had crept into Jerry's face and demeanor, as if he was exhausted from the assorted travails and complications of actually having found the life he'd looked for. This cloud of melancholy hung over a lot of happily partnered people I knew, especially if they were committed to being faithful. It wasn't that they didn't love their spouses, it was just that they no longer had anything to strive for. I'd occasionally catch Jerry gazing off into the distance as if he was hearing the faint strains of "Is That All There Is?" playing and was trying to figure out where the music was coming from.

Health

"I have no idea why I'm here," he said as we were getting changed. "I have more work than I can handle and no energy for this crap."

"Maintenance," I said.

He slapped at his hairy stomach. He'd always had the physique of a soccer coach, but increasingly, he looked like the coach of the losing team. "Why the fuck would I want to maintain this?"

"You're here for your health."

"My health. There's a joke. The best thing I could do for that is work through the pile on my desk."

"You should hire Walmi," I said, referring to my personal trainer. "Or the girl at the reception desk."

"The last thing I need is someone looking over my shoulder. I suppose you're working out with him today? Come over to the bikes when you're finished, okay? There's something I need to talk to you about."

Jerry was a former journalist, a once-upon-a-time idealistic lefty. Just before marrying Janet, he'd taken the practical and more lucrative step of quitting his political beat for a management position in the business office of a chain of suburban newspapers. It was a sacrifice of a job he loved, not to mention of his principles, but a sacrifice he was happy to make for the sake of proving his commitment to Janet and his willingness to enter a new phase of his life. Janet had sacrificed her dancing career so they could have kids; it was the least he could do. It had been typically selfless on his part, but where once he'd been driven by a passion for the stories he was investigating, he now was consumed by anxiety related to pushing papers. The wear and tear was showing in subtle ways on his body. For years I had aspired to Jerry's level of fitness. Now that I'd passed him, I wanted to make sure I stayed one step ahead.

Training

Walmi, my personal trainer, was waiting for me outside the locker room, sprawled on a padded bench. He reached out a hand, either to shake mine or to be pulled up. "Richard," he drawled. "You looking good today, man."

I thanked him and left it at that. In the past I'd tried self-deprecation as a way to elicit a second compliment, only to have him respond with mournful comments such as, "Well, for your age, you not looking so bad," or, "Oh come on, what do you expect, my friend?"

Walmi was a languid Brazilian beauty of indeterminate age. He was so perpetually laid-back and enervated, it was almost impossible to imagine how he maintained his flawless physique—the broad chest and the perfectly shaped calves. By contrast, it was not impossible to imagine how he maintained the smooth, hairless skin, the platinum crew cut, and the perfect tan.

"What are we working on today, Richard?"

"Upper body," I said. "You told me you'd show me a new routine for my shoulders."

"I did? Well, we'll see what we can come up with. I'm tired today. I was up all night."

"Marco trouble?"

"Nothing but trouble with him, Richard. I can't do it any longer."

He led me to a corner of the weight room, took a seat on a bench, and directed me to pick up some weights as if merely lifting his hand was an effort. "Do fifteen of the fly things," he said, gesturing in a way that loosely suggested the moves I was supposed to make.

I'd first hired Walmi about eight months earlier to help work around an injury I'd sustained to my knee. He was knowledgeable about musculature and anatomy, and he'd offered a lot of sound advice, albeit in his lazy drawl. Since I tended to overdo things in this compartment of my life, his languor was useful to me. The mistake I'd made was telling him I'd once had a private psychology practice. He took this as license to fill me in on the travails of his love life with the mythic Marco, Italian stallion with a housecleaning business and, reading between the lines, what was clearly a secondary income stream as an untrained, unlicensed "masseur." It was bad enough that I was paying Walmi for the privilege of listening to his problems, but worse was his occasional comment clearly indicating that he assumed my age and appearance removed me from the complications of love, sex, longing, and all expressions of passion. "You lucky you don't have to worry about any of that." "I can't wait to be quiet like you." "Quiet" was his synonym for asexual. When I mentioned that I lived with a partner, he responded with a cloying, "That is so cute," as if Conrad and I were five-year-olds playing house.

"Pull in the elbows like this," he said, and gave himself a sleepy hug. "Yeah, okay. It's okay."

I was addicted to the Marco soap opera as the perfect inconsequential background music for exercise, although it distracted Walmi and made his instructions infrequent and insubstantial. Initially, I'd made the mistake of giving Walmi advice about organizations he might contact for help with Marco's apparent alcohol and drug problems, a lawyer he could call when Marco had taken his car and sold it to one of his clients, and so on. All the advice had been rejected. I'd thought at first Walmi had some objection to the expense of these measures, but after a while it became clear he was insulted that I viewed his problems—for example, Marco burning all of Walmi's clothes in the bathtub one night when Walmi had forgotten to pick up Marco's shirts at the dry cleaner—as anything other than normal lovers' quarrels. Now I listened, attuned to the beauty of Walmi's hazel eyes and expressionless face, titillated by his unqualified devotion, and evident addiction to the nonstop battle. As for his sleepiness, why wouldn't he be tired when, by his own account, the only sleep he got was the two or three hours a night when he wasn't fighting with or getting fucked by his lover?

I'd been tempted to tell him about Benjamin, but despite having a drug-addicted boyfriend who worked on the fringes of the sex trade, Walmi was devoutly Catholic and almost violently disapproving of anyone's infidelity. He was suspicious of Jerry in this regard and had taken an intense dislike to him. Equally inexplicably, he felt the need to complain constantly about my friend to me, as if Jerry was a corrupting influence.

"I saw your friend with Paris just now," he said.

"Paris? I thought her name was Tammy or something like that."

"That wasn't working for her."

I nodded. A lot of trainers were drawn to cities and cars as inspiration for names.

"I hate how your friend is always flirting. He has children. I hate that. Paris is a young girl for him. It isn't right."

"He's not really flirting," I said. "He's just talking. I keep telling you, he wouldn't do anything."

"He would. You don't know, but I can see. Do not hyperextend like that. Bad for the joints at your age. I can't wait for the age when Marco and I can retire and have a nice quiet life."

The idea that Walmi and Marco could live a quiet life was preposterous, but Walmi's longing for it and belief in it seemed so genuine, I'd bought into the fantasy. For Walmi's sake, I sincerely hoped that it would happen one day.

No matter how lethargic Walmi was on any given day, he was always able to rouse himself to full consciousness when exactly thirty minutes had passed. The former shrink in me admired his professionalism in this matter.

"I'll see you next week," he said. And then he added, "You stay out of trouble," with a yawn and a frown, as if he was contemplating the next set of trials in his own life.

Fitness Works?

Since the housing market had started to soften in Boston, the gym had become noticeably less crowded. Businesses in the neighborhood had begun to downsize, and I'd heard that many of the luxury condos overlooking the river were sliding into foreclosure. Although I no longer had to wait to use the machines and dumbbells, there was a chilly, party's-over atmosphere in the air, made more pronounced by the loud, upbeat music.

I took my place on a bicycle next to Jerry and gazed out at the view. The apartment building that housed the Club rose above the lower buildings of MIT. It was that view that had caused me to tell Jerry about Benjamin, over a year ago, and to give him occasional updates when Benjamin was in retreat or when things had started up again. If he was at all homophobic, Jerry never let any indication of it slip out. He had a satisfying way of being interested in the prurient details of Benjamin's sexual confusion without seeming judgmental or queasy. It wouldn't have surprised me to learn that Sam and Jerry had had a fleeting spell of drunken intimacy in the confines of their college dorm room, although Sam had denied it and I'd never felt comfortable asking Jerry.

Jerry's reading glasses were sliding off his nose as he restlessly turned the pages of the *New York Times*. He nodded as I filled him in on the latest chapter in the Walmi drama, but I could tell his interest was minimal.

"What is it you wanted to talk about?" I said.

"How do you mean?"

"You told me to come find you, that there was something you wanted to talk about."

"I did?" He wiped off his bald head with a towel. "Well, yeah, I guess I did. You're good at giving advice, Richard, right?"

"*I* think so, which doesn't prove anything."

"You have to help me with something." He stopped pedaling altogether, and I slowed down. He gave me a sympathetic look, as if he felt bad for me, owing to the favor he was about to ask. "You don't have to slow down. In fact, I'd prefer you didn't. It'll make it easier to spill my guts here."

I wondered if my faith in Jerry's fidelity had been misplaced, although I found it hard to believe Walmi had spotted something I'd missed. Still, I was so prepared for a confession of that sort, or of financial mismanagement, that I was shocked when Jerry told me he was having health problems.

"What kind of health problems?"

He gave me a serious glance over the top of his glasses, almost as if he was trying to evaluate how trustworthy I was. "I have to go in for some surgery."

"Anything serious?"

"A valve," he said. "And don't ask me for more specifics than that, because my brain froze when the doctor started telling me about it."

"Valve? You're talking about heart surgery?"

"Exactly. Cracking the rib cage, the whole fucking nightmare."

"Jesus, Jerry. How's that possible? Look at you: young, incredibly fit. You're my role model."

"Well, apparently I'm not as young and fit as we thought. And you should start looking for a new role model. Don't worry about me collapsing, by the way. The doctor said I could keep doing light exercise. He wants me to keep working out until they saw me apart."

These announcements of health problems related to organs that had started to deteriorate with use and time, like sets of tires or sofa springs, were happening more and more. The people I knew seemed to be gradually eroding. Samuel, my connection to Jerry in the first place, had been HIV positive, but he'd dealt with that only to die of what the doctor said was an unrelated melanoma. Samuel had been a caustic, shrewd little man who'd suffered more than his share of indignities and traumas and had risen above them all. He'd insisted, in a typically cheerful, ironic way, that he was lucky to be dying before turning forty. "You'll see," he said. "You'll all go in this same direction, only more slowly and miserably."

All the expensive, underused equipment in the gym, the soaring windows giving way to a view that fewer and fewer people could afford to enjoy, began to seem even more pointless and sad. Snow was predicted for later in the day, and the sky was gradually turning a sodden shade of gray.

Yes, he told me, he'd had a second opinion and had had the diagnosis confirmed. No, he said, alternative treatments were not an option. Yes, he nodded, he trusted the wisdom of his doctors.

"How's Janet taking it?" I asked.

"I haven't told her yet. I've known for two weeks and I can't bring myself to do it. You know how high-strung and sensitive she is." I'd always considered her shrill and self-absorbed, probably the same thing, although "high-strung and sensitive" sounded more artistic and interesting. "That's where you come in, my friend."

"You're not suggesting I tell her, are you?"

"So you won't do it?"

"Janet doesn't even like me."

"Well . . . she doesn't dislike you either." He took off his glasses, and I could see the worry and fear in his big dark eyes. "What do I do? What do I say?"

"You tell her, that's all, just like you told me. She'll react and then the two of you will decide how to tell the girls."

"I haven't mentioned this to anyone. You're the first."

"Maybe your real problem is admitting it to yourself. Telling Janet makes it too real."

"I hate that kind of analysis. It's so demeaning."

"Go home, make a nice dinner, put the kids to bed, and sit her down. The two of you can have a good cry, and you then can start dealing with the practical details. I know it's horrible, but you're going to have to get it out there."

He hooked his glasses over the neckline of his T-shirt. "You make it sound simple."

"Isn't that what you want me to do?"

"I want you to tell her for me, but I'll take what I can get."

"It's going to go fine, Jerry. I'm sure of it. Send me a text message after you've told her. I'll expect to hear from you by ten o'clock."

"A deadline. I'll do my best."

"You're a journalist. You guys love deadlines."

Routine

Despite the fact that we rarely did more than shake hands, I gave Jerry an awkward hug on the icy sidewalk.

"I'm not so bad off," he said, "that we have to start getting sentimental. It's a pretty routine matter these days."

I noticed, though, that he didn't pull away. "Even so," I said. "Not your usual routine."

"You've got a point."

He yanked a woolen cap over his smooth head and gave a depressingly cheerful little salute goodbye as he wandered off.

Important Ghosts

Later that afternoon, on my walk home across the bridge, I was struck by a desire to call Benjamin and tell him about Jerry. He knew of Jerry, of course, as one more important ghostly figure, and since he was probably driving home, he wouldn't mind the distraction. But any discussion of illness tended to throw him into a crisis about the meaninglessness of life mixed with paranoia about his own well-being. It didn't take much to link general concerns about illness to the idea not too deeply buried in his consciousness that his sexual impulses were "sick." There were also the more legitimate worries about the whole cavalcade of sexually transmitted diseases to which he might be exposing himself and Giselle, despite rigorous protection. It wouldn't do to start telling him about someone getting his chest opened up.

I called Conrad instead. He was sympathetic to other people's problems but so fundamentally wrapped up in his own life that they didn't disturb his sleep. He wasn't especially fond of Jerry, but I figured he'd at least offer me some warm, rote words of comfort. There was a rehearsed quality to a lot of Conrad's reactions, but they were well rehearsed, making them satisfying, if not always convincing. I have no objections to acting, even in the most intimate circumstances, as long as it's good acting.

Conrad's business partner answered his phone and uttered a crisp, professional greeting. "Mitchell and McAllister."

"Hi, Doreen," I said. "It's Richard."

She repeated my name with the bored surprise that seemed to

be her perpetual response to me. Her tone said: How unexpected that you called and how disappointing.

"How are things going out there?" I asked.

"A little more slowly than I'd hoped, in terms of the project. Otherwise, fine." She let that sit for a few seconds, and then added, "I suppose."

She and I had never been close. I considered her cold and aloof, and she clearly thought I was a boorish prole who lacked either taste or enough money to buy taste. I sometimes wondered if she looked down on me for having Italian roots; she'd also come from a working-class family, but she had the good sense to pretend otherwise. She clearly felt I was unworthy of Conrad, which, if you factored in Benjamin's attitude, was something of a consensus. But the little pause and the sarcastic lilt with which she said "I suppose" made me think she was opening up a tiny door of détente.

"Is our mutual friend anywhere in the vicinity?" I asked.

Another pause. "He went for a walk."

"Without his phone. How atypical."

"We're expecting some calls, and, at the moment, it's easier if I respond. Shall I tell him you phoned?"

"That would be nice. Are you still coming back tomorrow?"

"Those plans have not changed. What's that horrible noise?"

"Wind, I'd guess. I'm walking home and it's snowing again."

"Well, it's very difficult to make out what you're saying."

"I'll get off, then. Have a good trip home. Tomorrow's supposed to be clear."

"I heard. We have the Weather Channel here, too."

Cooking

I decided to stay home that night, avoid sinking into despair and delight at the latest political outrages of the administration, and prepare for Conrad's return, something I'd given up doing years earlier, after his fifth or sixth business trip. I'd tidy the apartment and prep the chicken so it would be ready to toss in the oven when I got home from work the following day. Once upon a time, I'd been a fairly imaginative and enthusiastic cook, spending hours chopping and slicing and slowly simmering the garlic so it didn't brown, but then I cut back on drinking and discovered that without a layer of wine-induced languor, shelling peas isn't that appealing. Now, most often, I found myself sticking everything in a pan at high heat, sloshing it around until it didn't appear to be a health threat, and hoping for the best.

I tried to do better that night, treating the chicken to a bath and massage, as you might give a favored pet. I stood at the sink, looking out across the back alleyway to the brick row houses of Beacon Hill as they were gradually covered over with a fresh layer of fluffy snow. I'd bought the condo more than a decade earlier, back when there were still a few bargains to be had in the Boston housing market. Its value had increased to an almost comic level. But the numbers were theoretical and represented financial security for me that was equally theoretical.

I was waiting for Jerry to call or send me a message letting me know he'd told his wife about the surgery, and the longer I waited, the more slowly I worked in the kitchen and the more satisfying the process became. I was certain the meal would be a triumph. The apartment already smelled warmer and more welcoming. I felt lucky to own a place that was increasing in value, to be in the kitchen preparing a meal, to have as problems not the threat of pending heart surgery but a certain amount of waning influence at work and, at home, a partner with a little out-of-town distraction.

Bounce, Bounce, Bounce

I didn't hear from Jerry that night. It wasn't until the following day that he called, and then I was in the middle of a meeting.

I was interviewing a young woman who'd been part of a team that had worked with Z. Cynthia and I were trying to get some specifics about his incompetence, since Randy's record keeping on Z's firing had turned out to have been so incompetent. Ellen was a thin, fidgety person with spiky dark hair and what appeared to be a leg-bouncing compulsion. I found the latter tic unsettling both because it made her seem unbalanced and because I had the feeling I was watching her in the midst of some masturbatory act she couldn't control. I'd asked Cynthia to sit in on the interview with Ellen, hoping that the presence of another person would underscore the seriousness to the process. It didn't seem to have worked.

Prior to this meeting, Ellen's supervisor had told me she was consistently late for work, that she'd missed meetings and was falling behind on deadlines. She was a month away from a review of her own job performance and, thus far, had used this interview with me and Cynthia to hurl criticism at her supervisor in what I suspected was a preemptive strike. Since the advent of reality TV shows in which competitors strategize to boot each other off islands and out of group houses, cutthroat behavior in corporations had become much more common and sophisticated.

Ellen's criticism of her supervisor amounted to a lot of complaints about the supervisor's lack of specificity and clarity in directives, all delivered in unclear and nonspecific ways. She kept repeating, "Okay, and then, for another example," to introduce yet another vague criticism: "She just doesn't get it." "She's so random." "She says something, and we're all, like, 'What?'"

Although the employee made me uncomfortable, I had been hoping for more helpful concrete details regarding Z. Five minutes into the meeting, Cynthia had stopped asking questions and was listening with a wide-eyed fascination that crossed over into irony.

Bounce, bounce, bounce. "Okay, and then, for example . . ." *Bounce, bounce, bounce.* "Okay, and like, for instance . . ."

Ellen had a small, pale face, and the spiky hair made her look like an art student who was trying to make up in personality what she lacked in talent.

It was a relief when my cell phone rang, and I saw Jerry's name pop up on my screen.

"I'm in a meeting," I told him. "But briefly . . . how did Janet react?"

"I didn't get a chance to tell her. She had a bad day with the kids, and it just didn't seem fair. Plus, to be honest, she's been crankier than usual lately. Are you sure you can't help me out with this?"

"Tell her this weekend. Take her out to dinner. Or get a baby-sitter and go for a drive. I have to go," I said. "Just make a plan and follow through on it. You'll feel better as soon as you do."

We were sitting at a table in a small glass conference room, and I turned back to face Ellen. "A friend with some medical problems," I explained.

She gave me a blank stare. "Okay, and then, to give another specific example: She tells me something and half the time, I'm thinking, 'Did she just say what I thought she said?'"

It seemed like the right moment to cut my losses and try to save face with Cynthia. "I'm interested in hearing what you have to say about this," I told Ellen, "but this other matter is a little more urgent right now, and if you don't have anything else to say about that, we can make another appointment to discuss your supervisor."

The relevant background information, known only to Cynthia

and me, was that based on the most recent financial reports, Ellen's department was probably going to be cut by 40 percent or more anyway, and it was unclear if Ellen or her supervisor would survive the purge.

Piece of Cake

I ushered her out and sat down at the table, discouraged. "Sorry for wasting your time with that," I said to Cynthia. "What's your impression of her?"

"ADD, obviously."

"Do you think drugs are a possibility?"

"I think they're a necessity," she said. "Not one word of substance. Who's this sick friend of yours?"

Increasingly, I found something suspicious in almost everything Cynthia asked me. Even though this question was a perfectly reasonable one, I couldn't help but wonder if Cynthia was trying to find information she could use against me down the line.

"I don't think you know him. We're old friends and we meet up at the gym a couple times a week."

"Ah, right. The gym friend. Jerry?"

I looked at her. I was almost certain I'd never mentioned Jerry to her. Given the way she felt about the rigors of my fitness regimen, I'd stopped discussing the gym. She must have heard about Jerry from Anne. "He has to have open heart surgery," I said. "Jerry."

She waved this off. "Piece of cake. My father had it twice."

Her father, as far as I knew, had died at age sixty-five of some coronary crisis.

"Weekend plans?" I asked.

"My mother and I are going to do some pop visits at the buildings." In addition to working at Connectrix, Cynthia and her mother had inherited two small brick apartment buildings in an outlying suburb when her father had died. She was a strict, no-nonsense landlady who was always evicting tenants for some minor lease violation.

As we were getting ready to leave the conference room, Brandon Miller stuck his head in. He was somewhere in the neighborhood of too-tall, which gave the move an Alice-in-Wonderland aspect. He had a big grin plastered on his face, displaying, as was always the case with his generation, perfect teeth. "Looking forward to the lunch next week, Richard," he said. "Take me someplace pricey!"

With that he disappeared, and without looking at her I said to Cynthia: "Don't worry, I'm paying out-of-pocket."

A Brief, Blurry Sketch

Having dabbled on the fringes of literature and, more recently, at the center of psychology, I liked to consider myself a humanist, perhaps another way of saying I imagined myself something of an *artiste manqué*. I was too old to believe that I was one day going to wake up and compose a symphony or sculpt marble, but I hadn't let go of the belief that what made me professionally successful, even in the glass and steel world of business, was an appreciation of human foibles and a capacity for empathy that amounted to artistry of some kind.

I was always tempted to explain this to Conrad, since he had, on the whole, a grim view of my professional life, but I'd come to realize that once you step out of your thirties, no one—not even the people with whom you're most intimate—is interested in learning how you got to where you are. (I've been told that by the time you reach sixty-five, no one's interested in where you are, either, but I still had time to put off worry about that phase.) When you're post-forty, a period that Conrad himself was about to enter, people assume you're lugging around a substantial amount of heavy baggage and are content with a brief, blurry sketch of your background.

In my case, the professional sketch involves the turn away from literature and toward a social work degree, followed by a number of years of doing not-all-that-much-good in state-funded educational programs, brought to a halt by budget cuts, complicated by a bout of unemployment and depression, exacerbated by the death of Samuel. There was a get-yourself-together return to school for an advanced degree, which gave way to a private counseling practice with shared office space, sluggish referrals, and a group of clients that, on the whole, were more interested in discussing medications than problems.

I was saved from drowning in the swamp of that unhappy period by a friend's suggestion that I segue into HR. After initially dismissing the idea, it had begun to look logical and appealing. Three consulting gigs and one headhunter later, I ended up at Connectrix, happy for the see-through office and the substantial salary.

In many ways, I was more able to be the kind of shrink I wanted to be at Connectrix than in my private practice. When, at the latter, I could steer my clients off the topic of Zoloft, they talked about their work problems to excuse the mistakes they made in their personal lives. At Connectrix, people talked about their personal problems to excuse the mistakes they made at work. I felt a moral responsibility to deal with employees as people first and help them make decisions that benefited them as individuals. But sometimes I worried that this conflicted with an implicit moral responsibility I had to the company paying my salary to help them make decisions that benefited Connectrix.

The name Connectrix was an amalgam of "connection" and "matrix" and undoubtedly had been concocted to evoke images of effective, lightning-speed communications, a mysterious network of wires, and Keanu Reeves in a black leather trench coat. To my ear, it had a clumsy, elusive sound that made me think of a prescription drug for joint problems.

When I told people where I worked, they usually asked, out of politeness, what the company did. I'd noted, however, that politeness only goes so far. Specifically, up to the edge of listening to an answer.

Connectrix maintained an atmosphere of austere luxury—the striking architecture, the excessive perks, the large number of people employed to accomplish ill-defined goals. Much of it was beginning to feel like anachronistic vestiges of a different time, and even the pretty, impractical walls and beams of the building were beginning to look fragile.

Conrad's Wife

I was expecting Conrad to arrive home at eight o'clock. I left work early and walked into our condo to find Doreen McAllister sitting stiffly in the living room. I greeted her with a warm and affectionate hello, which, given the way she felt about me, amounted to a form of aggression on my part.

"Richard!" she said, as if she was surprised to see me in my own apartment. "I'm waiting for *Conrad*."

"Yes, I figured."

"He's in the *shower*."

"Ah. How are you, Doreen?"

"I'm fine. How are *you*?" She had a funny way of pulling back her head slightly and looking at me with a distrustful gaze, as if she wouldn't believe me, no matter what I told her. In general, I tried to reveal as little as possible.

"I'm keeping my head above water," I said. "A little too much going on at work, but what can you do?"

"I have no *idea*," she said, clearly trying to distance herself from my loathsome career in the world of technology.

"I thought you and Conrad were landing shortly after seven." I'd left work early so I could have the fragrant dinner ready and waiting for him when he arrived. Doreen had not appeared in any of my fantasy scenarios of the evening.

She tucked her chin. "Change of plans?" she said, letting her tone add the unspoken, "Ever hear of it, moron?"

If Benjamin was my husband, then Doreen, a severe and stylish woman he had met more than a dozen years earlier, was Conrad's wife. I suppose because she'd known Conrad for longer than I had, she tended to treat me like an interloper, and had since the very early days of our relationship. At first, I felt that she judged me unfairly, but I had to acknowledge that as is usually the case with a partner's good friends, she knew more about Conrad's life, and possibly my own, than I knew myself.

She was sitting in a black leather Le Corbusier chair—Conrad's idea of shabby chic—with her legs crossed and her head pulled back in that appalled and condescending way. She was a tall woman of extreme slenderness that seemed to be her natural body type exacerbated by an apparent belief that there was something lower-class and demeaning about eating in front of other people. In the years I'd known her, I'd seen her nibble and pick at food, push it around on her plate and fold it onto her fork, but I had no memory of seeing her do anything you might consider actual eating. Her face was angular and pinched in the dramatic way that's often mistaken for beauty, with a lot of shadowy recesses she emphasized with makeup. She had a flair for clothes and accouterments that gave all of her features a stylish glamour. Big earrings that drew attention to her long neck, Bakelite bracelets to adorn her slim wrists, and heels that made a statement out of her thin legs. Her overall appearance was so carefully but unnaturally arranged, like a composed salad, that it was hard to imagine her walking in the outdoors or getting any regular exercise. I was shocked when Conrad told me she was a strong, determined swimmer who often spent forty minutes or more doing laps in the pools of the hotels where they stayed.

I went into the kitchen, turned on the oven, and took out of the fridge all the food I'd prepared the night before.

When I met Conrad he was working as a curator at a local art museum and Doreen was a partner at a gallery in Boston. Both were looking for something else to do, and two years later, they joined forces to form their consulting business. I'd encouraged Conrad in the endeavor and had bankrolled him a significant amount of money. It was the perfect job for him and his wife. They both had excellent taste, a thorough knowledge of the art world, and an attitude toward the opinions of others that was scathing without being overtly insulting. People didn't object to being told they had bad taste as long as they were reassured that underneath it ran a reservoir of artistic savvy, which Doreen and Conrad were going to help them tap.

They both had similar degrees in art history, but Conrad had a bag of conversational tricks for making it known that his was from Harvard.

An Opening

I went into the living room and sat in a chair opposite Doreen and made strained conversation with her about a job she and Conrad had recently completed in Atlanta. I'd seen photos of the immense, newly constructed house and the paintings and sculptures they'd used to fill the soaring spaces. They were discreet about their clients, many of whom were apparently "known," although I usually had to feign recognition when I learned their names. Doreen accepted my compliments with a tentative smile. She had a habit of lightly touching the corners of her mouth with a finger and thumb when she smiled. Probably it had something to do with her lipstick, but it always looked to me as if she were manually stretching her lips for the desired friendly effect.

She asked me a few questions about Connectrix, but in a way that indicated she wasn't really interested in the answers—"Things are going well at the company, I assume?"—and then picked up a magazine.

"Conrad should be out in a minute," she said. "Don't feel you have to entertain me."

"Are you two going out tonight?" I asked.

"An opening. We're not expecting much, but it's one of those obligations. I know the gallery owner, so we can't *not* go. The reason for our early return?"

This habit of stating what she considered the obvious in the form of a question was something she had, alas, picked up from Conrad. It was annoying, but objectively, I had to admire how effectively one little punctuation point recast a word or phrase into scathing condescension.

"It was pretty snowy while you were away," I said. She was wearing high heels with elaborate straps and toe cleavage. "I don't suppose you have winter boots with you."

"Winter boots," she said, befuddled, as if I'd suggested she get shoed. "Did Conrad buy you that tie?"

My tie had been a birthday present from Benjamin. Since he had an aversion to shopping, I suspected it was a regift of something given to him by one of his colleagues. (*At least it probably hadn't been a gift from Giselle.*) "I think I picked this out myself."

She pulled her head back. "Good choice," she said. She touched the loose chignon at the back of her head and then returned to her magazine.

I should have left the room and gone to find Conrad—it was what both she and I wanted, after all—but for some reason, I felt it would have been rude to walk out on her. Despite her hauteur, Doreen exuded an air of loneliness that came off of her in little waves like a faint, slightly tired perfume. A sad sidelong glance, a too-tight clench of her fingers. As far as I knew, her friendship with Conrad was her main romantic attachment. She had had an early, failed marriage that Conrad knew little about. She carried herself with a brittle aloofness that made her seem older than she was— apparently, she was teetering over the brink of forty—and made it impossible to ask her about her personal life. I was always im- pressed by the ability some people have to build a wall around themselves that protects them from direct questions. When I'd had my private practice, some of my patients had the ability to steer me away from questions related to important but shameful aspects of their private lives for weeks or months.

In addition to not wanting to abandon her to her solitude, I had a lingering question about the brief pause in the conversation we'd had on the phone. It was inconceivable she wouldn't know something about Conrad's Insignificant Other, and I had a strong suspicion she wanted to discuss it with me.

"Are you getting sick of all the travel?" I asked.

She gave me one of her quizzical looks and tossed the magazine onto the coffee table. Now that I'd interrupted her, there was no point in going on with her reading. "Not especially. As long as we stay organized, it's relatively easy."

"Yes," I said. "Conrad has that tidy little suitcase at the ready all the time."

This topic was of no interest to her. "There's something exhila- rating about being in new places, even if they're not especially excit- ing," she said.

"Like Dallas?"

"Dallas is a fascinating city."

"I've been," I said. "Frankly, I didn't find it so."

"In that case, I suggest a return visit. Of course, when we visit anywhere, our hosts try to show off their town at its very best, so my view might be skewed."

"What about Columbus?" I said. "You seem to be spending a lot of time there."

"It has its high points, but I wouldn't call it fascinating."

"Conrad seems to find it appealing. I'm surprised at how appealing he finds it."

She looked toward the bedroom. I could hear the faint hiss of water.

"He's still in the shower," I said. When she didn't respond to this, I added: "He can't hear us, so if there's anything you wanted to tell me—about Columbus, for instance—now would be a good time."

"I know you think I support Conrad's every whim, Richard, but we have different opinions of some things. There are some things he finds fascinating and attractive that I consider a waste of his time and talents."

Doreen and Conrad talked a lot about each other's "talents," but they used the term loosely. I didn't discount the value of their knowledge of art, but these days they mostly used "talent" to refer to the ability to bully someone into shelling out a six-figure sum for a work of art they didn't like.

"Really?" I asked.

"Yes. *Really.*"

"In that case, maybe you could exert some of your influence over him. Try to redirect his attention away from projects in Columbus?"

She slipped back into her withering mode quickly and said, "Please. I would ask the same of you. I think you know enough about the dynamics of our friendship to realize that I have no influence. And I know enough about the dynamics of your relationship to know you have some, if not a lot."

"I appreciate your honesty," I said.

The hissing of the water stopped and Doreen handed me one of her business cards. "That's my cell number." She shrugged. She was wearing a black woolen dress, and there wasn't a stray hair, fleck of dandruff, or hint of makeup on the shoulders. "Call me if you like." She rolled her eyes—at herself this time, not me—and said in a milder tone, "What I mean is, I'd like you to call."

Blameless and Dashing

A few minutes later, Conrad strolled in, blameless and dashing in a white shirt, slipping a cuff link into his starched cuff. He was the kind of guy who looked entirely in his element wearing expensive cuff links and stiffly starched shirts, as if he was always preparing for a dull but important cocktail party. These clothes looked natural on him, not affected or pretentious. His blond hair, wet from the shower, was combed back off his face. Whatever had happened in Ohio had been washed down the drain.

He stood behind my chair, draped his arms over my shoulders, and rested his chin on top of my head. Doreen looked away. He smelled of the ridiculously overpriced Italian shower gel he bought over the Internet. It was his signature scent, bitter limes, bracing and masculine, if perfume can ever be said to be masculine. He was big on his signatures—the shower gel, the crisp white shirts, the floppy blond hair that magically seemed to remain at exactly the same length at all times, the mail-order shampoo that was the only substance that ever touched his scalp, an expertly executed foxtrot he hauled out at weddings that made older women swoon, and an astonishing ability to sit down at a piano and play with great feeling the first three bars—but only the first three bars—of "Moonlight Sonata."

"Did you miss me?" he asked. It was a question that was impossible to imagine him asking if the two of us had been alone.

"Desperately," I said. "How long were you gone?"

He rapped my head lightly. "Were you two having a nice conversation?"

"We were talking about you," Doreen said. "But we hadn't arrived at the interesting parts."

"Interesting parts? I'm happy to hear there are some." That said, he straightened up and went back to his cuff links.

"Oh yes," she said. "You're endlessly fascinating."

"Did you tell Richard about the opening?"

"We discussed it," I said, wedging myself into the conversation.

When the three of us were together, I usually had the feeling, even in my own living room, that I was a houseguest who'd long overstayed his welcome. Since I'd just taken the unprecedented step of making an alliance of sorts with Doreen, this bothered me less than it usually did.

"We're not planning to stay late. Although we might go out for dinner with someone afterward."

"Anyone I know?" I asked.

"I doubt it. But it could be a good contact for us."

Doreen made a disparaging moue.

"I hope it works out," I said. "It's all about contacts, isn't it?"

"These days, we have to follow every lead. Are you sure none of the well-paid kids at that company of yours is interested in art, sweetheart?" He smiled at me in a tender way that recalled something from the early days of our relationship.

"All they're interested in is Japanese cartoons," I said.

"I'm sure we could make it work."

"I'm sorry to hear about the dinner," I said, trying not to sound sorry at all. "I was planning to cook."

"I wondered what all that food was in there. You should go look, Didi. You've never seen so much food."

"I'll pass," she said.

"Go ahead with your plans, Richard. You still have to eat, even if I'm not here."

That settled, Doreen rose from her chair, and her wool dress fell into place on her narrow body. Conrad went to her and adjusted her collar. She smiled at him as he pressed its points against her collarbone. There might have been something sad in Doreen's love for Conrad, but I had the feeling the relationship involved about as much intimacy as she could tolerate.

Conrad slipped into his long blue coat—cashmere with a silky lining. "I suppose you'll go to the gym and come back exhausted," Conrad said. "No need to wait up for me."

At the door, he looked back over his shoulder and said, "Although I wouldn't object if you did."

Two Toasters

A couple of years earlier, when I'd told Jerry about my arrangement with Benjamin, he'd listened with nonjudgmental curiosity and asked some questions, most of them of an oddly practical nature: Did Benjamin shower at the Club before leaving? (Usually.) Did he answer calls from his wife and kids when we were together? (Always.) How much was he making a year? (Had never been specified and seemed irrelevant to my concerns.) Who paid rent on the Club? (I did, with occasional cash reimbursements from Benjamin.) What kind of car did he drive? (No clue. I'm hostile to people who take note of that kind of thing, along with those who identify themselves by the kind of computer they use.)

On one point, Jerry was genuinely confused. Since I'd told him that Conrad and I continued to have reasonably passionate sex on a regular basis, why did I feel the need for someone else? He'd said this the way one might say, "But you already have a toaster. Why buy another?"

While it's true that all toasters do pretty much the same thing, my experience is that every sexual encounter functions on its own terms, fulfills a particular need, comes with its individual pleasures, thrills, and frustrations. Just because you own a toaster doesn't mean you might not want a blender or a microwave or a food processor.

My sex life with Conrad had always been a complicated battle of wills, and the undercurrent of hostility was what kept it vital. I've never had great faith in the possibility of sustaining sexual heat in an atmosphere of unchecked tenderness; love, it seems to me, is what kills the passion in most relationships. In essence, Conrad needed to submit to a bullying will and, at the same time, to make you feel that he was doing you an enormous favor by letting you touch him.

The Intensifier

The night of Conrad's arrival from Columbus, I was dismayed enough about his abandonment of me and the chicken to forgo the whole cooking routine. The poor chicken had been languishing in the fridge since I'd bought it and probably qualified as hazardous waste anyway. I tossed everything into the snow-covered Dumpster behind the building and headed off to the basement gym near the apartment.

If the place I went with Jerry specialized in the fantasy of wealth and borrowed luxury, this place specialized in icy reality and mildew. The smell of mold and stale basement air hit me as soon as I opened the door on street level, and got stronger as I descended into the depths via a narrow, winding staircase. No faux-tanned, surgically enhanced front-desk employees here, just a bunch of stern men and women in red T-shirts. They were mostly post-thirty-five and looked as if they'd struggled with fitness for years (high school and college athletes with joint problems and drinking issues), had fulfilled their exercise quotas for life, and were now officially done. An attitude of disapproval radiated off them toward those of us who came to work out, as if we were lazy slackers who were still sending in checks on a mortgage, while they'd had the good sense to pay off theirs years earlier.

The men's locker room reeked of the ubiquitous mildew. Scattered throughout were a number of battered lockers with old padlocks on them that appeared to have been left unopened for years. No one ever used adjacent lockers due to a smell of rot and the vinegar scent of sweat-dirty laundry that emanated from their perennially locked chambers. You'd never find yourself referring to this place as a health club.

No one in the gym ever talked to anyone else. We walked around with grim determination, as if we were all in a clinic, waiting to be hooked up to a machine for an unpleasant but necessary treatment. There was one man I saw every time I went. The fact that I'd never once been to the basement gym when he wasn't there led me to believe he was always there, always on one of the elliptical machines, forever pumping his arms and legs in a weary, grinding rhythm, with his eyes straight ahead, as if he was staring at an uncertain and unobtainable goal. Naturally, I'd never spoken to him, but I referred to him in my mind as the Intensifier, and I sometimes carried on long, imaginary conversations with him as I went through the paces of my own desperate regimen.

I guessed him to be about my age. His body looked like a cable of wires wound together so tightly they were about to snap, and while he might at one time have been handsome, he appeared so thoroughly exhausted and hollowed out, he'd moved well past the point at which his looks were of any relevance. It was impossible to guess his motivation for the exhausting gym ritual, but unfocused anger certainly appeared to be part of it. Something in the set of his jaw, his glazed eyes, and his hairy shoulders made me think that his life had a deeply unwholesome element in it somewhere. A vaguely incestuous relationship with an overbearing mother? A tormented friendship with an underaged girl he invited to sunbathe in his backyard? Religious convictions? Naturally, my favored theory was a stifling combination of all three, held together by the defining tragedy of repressed homosexuality. This, I sometimes liked to think, was what Benjamin would look like if he didn't have the solace of his safe sexual outlet with me. *(At least I'm saving him from this.)*

I took the elliptical machine one down from him and, gazing straight ahead, carried on an imaginary conversation with the Intensifier in which I presented myself as the long-suffering, endlessly patient partner of an unfaithful and inconsiderate man. I tossed in a few unkind words about the president running the country into the ground, even though I suspected the Intensifier of listening to talk radio and voting Republican just to spite Massachusetts liberalism. His imagined responses to my list of grievances consisted of a lot of nondescript, angry grunts that displayed disinterested agreement with my position. It didn't take much insight to conclude that he dealt with all the problems in his life by bottling up his rage until it was allowed to simmer on one of these machines and fuel the compulsive exercise that was probably killing him.

Luther

Conrad still hadn't returned when I got back home, so I went to bed and read for a while. For several weeks, I'd been trying to make headway in *Luther's Commentary on St. Paul's Epistle to the*

Galatians, a slim volume I'd found abandoned at Fitness Works and was reading in an attempt to understand the national obsession with Jesus and perhaps to get a more empathic understanding of my secretary, Anne's, religious beliefs. In terms of clarifying things, it wasn't proving useful. There were a lot of lurid descriptions of Jesus that bordered on fetishism and descriptions of God that made him sound like my uncle Hank, an overbearing boozer who'd made a fortune in real estate and was always smiting people in the most capricious ways—driving them into bankruptcy, outbidding them on purchases just because he could. Since everyone was afraid he'd turn his well-funded, well-connected wrath on them, they were always praising him for his judgment and fairmindedness. He'd appear at family functions and talk about having evicted a family of five from one of his buildings because they'd complained about an annual rent increase, and everyone would shake their heads in awe and commend his generosity for giving them two weeks' notice. Thus, in *Luther's Commentary,* there were sentences like: "By this we may plainly see the inestimable patience of God, in that He hath not long ago destroyed the whole Papacy, and consumed it with fire and brimstone, as He did Sodom and Gomorrah." As for Paul, it didn't take much reading between the lines to see that he was probably one of those self-righteous preachers who make themselves feel better about their transgressions by making other people feel worse about theirs, a syndrome I suppose I knew well.

All of this, combined with my imaginary conversation with the Intensifier, put me into a bad mood. I threw the *Commentary* to the foot of the bed, and then, ashamed of how childish I was being, kicked it onto the floor through the sheets.

I didn't understand why I tormented myself reading this kind of tract or poring over demoralizing political news when ten pages of Trollope would have been so much more edifying about the human condition. I contemplated tromping down to the basement to haul out my copy of *The Warden*, but my quadriceps were already aching from my earlier workout and I couldn't face the stairs.

I wished I had a sleeping pill. I love the idea of sleeping pills— even the words are comforting—but I considered the desire for them a sign of weakness and effeminacy, so I'd never asked my doctor for a prescription. Cynthia undoubtedly could have supplied me with some, but that would have involved revealing more about my private life than I cared to.

I turned out the light and did my best to will myself to sleep.

A Proper Hello

I was in a state of semiconsciousness when Conrad opened the bedroom door and let in a corridor of light, thin and blue, like skimmed milk spilled across the taupe carpet. He sat on the edge of the bed to take off his shoes, and I smelled a faint combination of winter air, Conrad's bitter-lime shower gel, and alcohol. Conrad was a connoisseur of fine wines. He was under the common delusion that you can't really be said to have a drinking problem as long as you get sloppy on expensive reds.

I grumbled something about trying to get to sleep, a complaint that made me feel old and cranky as soon as the words left my mouth. I sat up in bed, making a bad-acting attempt at looking wide awake and scrambling to find nouns. "How was your thing?" I asked, too loudly.

"Thing," he said, emphasizing the stupidity of my comment by leaving off a question mark and speaking at an appropriately soft, midnight volume.

"Opening. Dinner. Whatever."

"It was fine," he said. "Let's talk in the morning." He looked over his shoulder at me and smiled. "When we're both awake."

Without Doreen to perform for he seemed considerably less happy to see me.

"Let's not," I said. "Anyway, we haven't properly said hello yet, with Doreen around and all."

We were headed into dangerous territory. If I displayed any eagerness for Conrad, it gave him too much power, in which case either refusing me or giving in to my demands would hand him an easy victory. But if I showed no interest, it might appear that I had been defeated or depressed by his absence and was punishing him.

He sighed and stood to undo his cuff links and slip out of the still crisp and noisy white shirt. "What is a proper hello, sweetheart?" he asked.

"Why don't you come here," I said, "and find out?"

He had his back to me, and with his shirt off, I could see his silhouette, gratifyingly less shapely than my own. He tossed his blond hair off his forehead, an unconscious gesture that I knew, after all these years, to be a small indication of blossoming desire. Like most overbearing and condescending people, Conrad responded well to being bossed around, especially by someone he considered to be beneath him intellectually.

"Couldn't you ask more nicely?"

"I suppose I could, but I'm not inclined to. Come here."

He turned around and faced me with a withering, annoyed look, the corners of his mouth turned down. But the fact that he'd done as directed was a point in my favor. He was pouting, another sign that, Insignificant Other or not, he was responding to me.

How Cute

Conrad was one of three children, the baby of the family and the only boy. His place in his family had been an inverted image of my own. He was the puffy, pretty blond son with the big blue eyes. He'd grown up being carted around by his sisters as if he were a porcelain doll, being told how cute he was, how bright, how full of promise. His parents—financially comfortable Californians going back a couple of generations—loved each other with that combination of outdoorsy wholesomeness and sexual profligacy that is endemic to certain upper-middle-class neighborhoods in Southern California and ski resorts all over the world.

When they came to visit their son in Boston, it was usually a stopover on a return from an adventure vacation that involved acts of physical endurance—hiking, climbing, deep-sea diving—and, you got the feeling, partner swapping. Their child-rearing philosophy had revolved around the disastrous, increasingly common belief that chanting "You're Perfect!" was the best thing they could do for their kids. This had relieved them of the obligation of making corrections or spoiling their perfection by getting too involved in raising them.

When Conrad was twelve, his parents had faced a marital crisis of some kind. Since there really is only one kind of marital crisis, it was safe to assume it was an affair. They decided that they had to do everything they could to save their marriage, "for the sake of the children." What this involved was taking leaves from their jobs (his father was a dermatologist and his mother managed his office), dumping the children on assorted resentful relatives, and going off on a series of intimacy-building trips that lasted for almost a year. Eventually they came back, their marriage so successfully rescued they had even less time for or interest in their kids. By that point, Conrad's sisters were involved in the usual teenaged pursuits—boyfriends and bulimia—and the golden childhood Conrad had been led to believe he had, along with the family as he'd known it growing up, were gone forever. There were moments when I looked at him across a room or when we

were sitting in a restaurant, and I saw on his face some of the befuddled desperation he must have felt at that time. In those moments, when I saw behind the haughtiness that often rankled me,
he became most dear and adorable to me.

Tenderness

He stood facing the bed, the arrogance in his expression starting to
melt around the edges. I tossed the sheets off, just to let him know
that whatever he had going on elsewhere, he still had duties at home.

"I've had a long day," he said without looking away.

"I'm sure you've had many this week."

He didn't respond to this, but I could see he was contemplating
his next move, trying to figure out the best way to get what he now
wanted without appearing to give me what I wanted. We exchanged
a few more sentences, all of them laden with cliché innuendos and
double entendres. Verbal clichés are never more useful than in sexual
situations where they function a little like ambient music in estab-
lishing a mood with almost embarrassing efficiency. I grabbed his
belt and pulled him down onto the bed. I had a great deal of stamina
and strength, thanks to all the compulsive exercise, so despite the
fact that Conrad was heavier than me, it was easy to overpower him
in a way that made it look as if I was punishing him rather than satisfying my own desires. It was exhausting but gratifying work, and
when it was over, there was a fleeting moment of the gentle insults
that had come to represent tenderness in our relationship.

"You certainly woke up for that," he said.

"I had some pent-up energy to burn, dear," I told him. "As did
you, apparently. Which is surprising."

"Oh, I'm full of surprises."

"I'm finding that out."

There was enough ambiguity in that comment to silence him. He curled against me, and I raked my fingers through his pretty, light hair.

"Any leftovers from dinner?" he asked.

"I never got around to it. I felt abandoned by you, and instead of cooking, I tossed everything out in a fit of pique."

"Aww. That's sweet. I'm happy to hear I can still throw you into a fit of pique. It shows you still care."

"Don't let it go to your head; partly it had to do with the age of the chicken. There might be some ice cream in the freezer, and I can make you an omelet if you like. I thought you and Doreen went out for dinner."

"We planned to, but we ran into the boys and we all went out for drinks instead."

"The boys" were three single men who ran a very successful gallery in Boston. They were all smart, well read, and attractive with impeccable taste and enormous wardrobes. Conrad and Doreen were honorary "boys" since they all socialized together so often, even though Conrad wasn't single and Doreen wasn't a boy. The boys were all swirling somewhere around the drain of age forty and thus none of them had been a boy, by even the most generous definition, for at least a decade. They were in that awkward in-between stage of life in which they hadn't quite found new identities for themselves. The days of being invited everywhere as ornamental guests were gone. "Partying" was too exhausting, and, at their ages, promiscuity required a lot more creativity and Photoshopping to arrange than it once had. The business of not quite having settled into new identities caused them to drink too much and then, as the central topic of conversation, discuss other people's drinking problems. I enjoyed their company, primarily because they flirted with me and made me feel attractive, even though I knew they flirted because I made them feel young by comparison.

"Did you all have a nice time?"

"Timmy had too much to drink, and Billy had to see him home. As soon as they left, Robby started unloading his latest heartache."

"The usual?"

"The usual." He yawned and punched at his pillow. "I'm too tired to eat anyway. I wouldn't mind losing a couple of pounds. I've been indulging all week, or being indulged."

On that note of ambiguity, we turned out the lights and he went to sleep.

Together Again

My sister, Beth, had once asked me why Conrad and I stayed together. It was a reasonable question, but I'd been annoyed by it even so, probably because I had no quick, easy answer like "Because he makes me happy," or "I can't imagine living without him," or the ever-popular "I love him"—even though, to one extent or another, all three things were true.

It's always seemed to me that you form attachments to people based on small incidents that appear insignificant at the time but create an indelible impression through which you then view the rest of their behavior for as long as you know them.

Conrad and I had met on the ferry to Provincetown, the scene of many great romances, most of which last about thirty-six hours. It was one of the old ferries that took three hours and sloshed over the waves like a sloppy drunk. But it was a hot day in late June and the water was eerily calm. Almost everyone on board was up on deck, eating and baking in the sun. But Conrad, covered in a loose, long-sleeved shirt and pants, was huddled in the shade, reading *The Portrait of a Lady*. He had on a pair of round, horn-rimmed glasses and he seemed so completely absorbed in the book, I was intrigued. He was handsome enough to be doing, in this setting, whatever he wanted—by which I mean, whomever he wanted—so the fact that he'd chosen to read Henry James made him appear doubly intellectual. His blond hair was blowing in the breeze in a careless way, and even when a whale was spotted off the side of the boat, he didn't move from his spot.

I made sure I was behind him in line as we were disembarking, and I pointed to his book and said he seemed to be enjoying it.

"As much as I'm enjoying anything these days," he said. It sounded less self-pitying than it might have if he hadn't been smiling. "I just hope it has a happy ending. I really can't take any fictional unhappiness right now."

"Ah, well," I said. "I won't give it away. But you might start thinking more about artistic perfection than happiness per se."

After we'd been seeing each other for a couple of months, I learned that the eyeglasses were a fashion accessory, that the trip to Provincetown had been to meet someone he'd been flirting with online, and that later he'd gotten drunk and left the book in a restaurant and never bothered to replace it. But none of that registered in the same way the false first impression had.

On that day in June, he'd just been dumped by Mort, an older man he'd been with for nearly a decade. Given the twenty-year age difference, Conrad had assumed he had the upper hand with Mort, a lumpy ophthalmologist, as he described him. But in what—with hindsight—should have been a predictable twist, Mort had discovered the virtues of online pharmacies and found himself a man who was exactly the same age Conrad had been when they'd first met. It was hard to imagine that Conrad and I would have clicked if we'd met at any other point in either of our lives. But Conrad was reeling from Mort's dismissal in a way that knocked down his defenses and exposed his most vulnerable and true self. Once he'd thrown himself under the oncoming bus of my middle age and felt secure in our relationship, the defenses and the hauteur all began going back up. But that didn't matter so much because I'd already seen what was behind them. All I had to do was read between the lines, something I'd been trained to do.

As for me, I'd finally accepted that Samuel, the love of my life, was really dead and was never going to reappear as he so often did in my dreams.

Now, no matter how many problems there were in my relationship with Conrad, I still felt most at ease when he was at home. It was as if a troublesome child had returned from a long absence and, for the moment, the whole family was together again.

Good Game?

Since Brandon Miller was rumored to be on the verge of quitting Connectrix, I let him choose the restaurant for our lunch meeting. The restaurant was, at first glance, a simple sandwich joint with rough-hewn furniture and an open kitchen where a group of hyperactive, long-haired men in painters' hats were joking and tossing around rolls and enormous bags of salad greens. But since I arrived ahead of Brandon, I had time to observe that the casual sloppiness of the place had been carefully selected by a masterful architect or designer. The primitive dog paintings on the walls had obviously been mass-produced, and the food, prices, and presentation had the unmistakable look of having been run past a marketing consultant and a series of focus groups. The clientele was mostly young and loud, and the plates in front of them were heaped with big sandwiches with their guts spilling out, as if they'd exploded on the way to the tables.

Ten minutes after I arrived, I looked out the window and spotted Brandon sauntering along the snowy sidewalk in khaki pants and a polo shirt, topped off by a huge fur hat you'd expect to see on a Russian diplomat. I'd noticed that Brandon and most of his peers rarely dressed according to the season or the weather. They were as likely to wear shorts in January as in July. Theirs was the first generation raised in the full flowering of global warming, and they'd learned that unpredictable weather patterns had made seasonal outfits irrelevant. It was best to dress for the climate-controlled indoors. He had a bag of golf clubs slung over his shoulder.

According to his personal information, he was six foot five, and because he was thin in an almost adolescent way, he looked even taller.

He swept through the front door and started joshing with the guy who was acting, more or less, as maître d'. The golf clubs were whisked off to a remote corner of the restaurant and the two new best friends roared with laughter.

Brandon waved at me and made his way to the table, his walk erect and confident.

"Good game?" I asked as he lowered himself into his chair.

He shrugged and smiled. "I did all right."

I'd meant the comment ironically—who plays golf in the snow?—but I should have known better. Brandon was spectacularly earnest, and I always ended up feeling I'd been trumped by his sincerity. Of course he'd been playing golf in January.

"Where do you go to play in this weather?" I asked.

"It wasn't really a game. Golf lesson with my trainer at a building downtown they converted into a driving range and virtual golf course."

"Interesting," I said. "You'll have to take me sometime."

"Are you kidding? I would love to."

"I didn't know you were such a serious player."

He eyed the menu and said, "It's all part of the master plan, Mr. Rossi. All part of the master plan."

"I didn't realize you had one. I counted on you being Mr. Spontaneous."

"The idea of making plans came to me spontaneously."

WATERFORD TOWNSHIP PUBLIC LIBRARY
5168 Civic Center Drive
Waterford, MI 48329

Mom and Dad

Brandon Miller had come to Connectrix about six months after he'd graduated from one of Rhode Island's lesser colleges. "I have no idea what he studied," my boss, Lewis, had said, "but he's presentable, and you get the feeling he'll stumble his way into doing something worthwhile at some point. He says unintentionally smart things in the middle of discussing snowboarding. His parents want to keep him out of trouble."

When I first met Brandon, I was appalled by almost everything about him. He came for his interview dressed in khaki pants and a green sweater that looked as if he hadn't taken it off in a month, possibly because it was so flattering. Despite his ridiculous height, he carried himself without a self-effacing slouch, as if he wasn't even aware of his towering stature or, worse still, was proud of it. He had a long, narrow face with a smooth, warm complexion. He was handsome and sexy in the way everyone under thirty is handsome— the unspoiled look of a piece of fruit that hasn't yet started to rot. He always had an expectant look in his large eyes, as if he were staring at a blank screen, waiting for a video clip to download and begin playing.

Even though I had the advantages of age and authority, his casual manner—and connections—intimidated me right from the start. He made it clear he wasn't especially eager to be hired. He'd moved back in with his parents after graduating college, had few expenses, ill-defined ambitions, and was making an income of sorts through Internet poker games, the legality of which was questionable.

I was amazed by the confident way he announced his "job," and even more amazed by the happy way he described his living situation. Moving back with one's parents would have been the source of misery and shame to anyone of my generation. But many of his peers, even some who were gainfully employed at Connectrix, lived with their parents. They didn't talk about them as authority figures, but made "mom and dad" sound like a pair of agreeable older siblings. Taking up residence somewhere in the vast, five-bathroom houses where they all lived was a favor to the parents, nothing more. When I asked Brandon why he'd moved back in with them, he said, "They've got a lot of space they don't know what to do with. Plus I think Mom misses doing my laundry."

If he wasn't exactly polite, he was genial. Somewhere in the middle of the time I spent with him—"interview" isn't the right word since there was no possibility of not hiring him and he didn't seem to understand the concept: at one point he said to me, "You ask a lot of questions, don't you?"—I realized that I was learning more from him about the attitudes and work ethic of his peers than I'd learned in months of studying the situation on my own.

As an entry-level employee, Brandon didn't make a lot of suggestions or take the initiative on proposals; he took directions well and strolled around the stupendous building as if he owned it, spreading a lot of good cheer and fulfilling the largely clerical assignments that had been given to him. Because he was handsome, sexually ambiguous, and had a title—HR Coordinator—his peers looked up to him, even before he was given the role of helping to prevent them from leaving the company as soon as they had a more appealing offer or an opportunity for fun.

He'd been studying the menu with a bemused and perplexed look—as far as I could tell, he and his peers lived on burritos and anything else that could be wrapped into a tubelike package and eaten while on the go—but he put it down and folded it up neatly. I found it almost impossible to imagine what he would look like in thirty years; there was something about his great height and his rangy, hollowed-out body that struck me as perpetually postadolescent. Women found him irresistible, largely, I suspect, because of his childlike sincerity. I pictured him as one of those playful lovers you could probably get a good time out of, provided you were willing to do all the work.

His Perspective

"Okay, Richard," he said. "I know you've heard the rumors about me, so let's get to it." His voice had the narcissist's unmistakable mixture of annoyance and excitement at imagining himself as a topic of conversation.

"Listening to rumors and gossip is 90 percent of my job," I said. "And not all of them, believe it or not, are about you. Which ones are you referring to?"

"I can understand if you're upset about it, but you just have to see the whole thing from my perspective."

I was a little taken aback by the word "perspective," which struck me as more carefully considered than most of his vocabulary. "What do you understand me to be upset about? Specifically, I mean."

"I was talking with Cynthia and she told me what you guys had heard about me leaving. I want you to know I'll definitely give two weeks' notice."

"Considerate of Cynthia to have prepared the way," I said.

"My point is, I know you want to discuss the poker thing," he said, and picked up the menu. "It wouldn't bother you if I ordered the pulled pork, would it?"

"Not in principle."

"I thought you were vegan or something, being so skinny and all."

The idea appalled me; it certainly wasn't an image of myself I was trying to project. Next he'd accuse me of being a Christian Scientist.

"I hope that's not another impression you picked up from Cynthia. But let's get back to poker. You told me you were done with that. It's officially outlawed anyway."

"It is, but that's just the tip of the iceberg. You know I still play."

"You've mentioned it."

As an undergraduate, Brandon had made a significant pile of money playing online poker. I gathered it had been a dorm-room obsession around the world. Several of his friends had been tossed out of school and into clinics for gambling and Internet addictions. That was what happened when you lost a lot of money. If, like Brandon, you had restraint and had made money, you went on to play face-to-face with other unrepentant addicts. While Brandon could be vague about a lot of things, he tended to turn excruciatingly specific when discussing poker. I knew nothing about the game and found the particulars confusing and boring. In fact, I find most games confusing and boring—another way of saying I always lose.

"Here's the thing," he said, moving his long face a little closer to mine. "I have a chance to go out to Vegas with a friend of mine. He knows a group of people who've been making an incredible living for the past few years on the poker circuit. A lot of private games."

"Sounds seedy," I said. Almost anything connected to Las Vegas sounds seedy to me, especially the recent attempts to turn it into a family vacation spot.

"I'm not saying it isn't. Maybe that's part of the appeal."

Now or Never

If there was one thing you couldn't take away from Brandon, it was his well-scrubbed wholesomeness. He was very much the latest model of the All-American Boy—multiracial, bright but far from intellectual, athletic in a random, casual way, excessively tall. I assumed that he, like everyone, had inner demons, but guessed that his were along the lines of a need to call his sexual partners "Mommy."

"So let me get this straight," I said. "You're thinking about quitting a job at which you've had two promotions only a few years after graduation, and are not, I might add, exactly drowning in work, and going out to Las Vegas to start life as a poker player?"

He leaned in again, as if he was about to divulge a great secret. "These guys have been making fortunes, Richard. I'm talking about millions."

"All of them? Where are the millions coming from?"

"It's a risk. That's part of the fun. Sure things don't interest me much. It's been one of the problems with this job. It's too stable."

"Don't be so sure," I said. And then, intoning Benjamin's favorite catchphrase, "Something's brewing."

"No kidding. And your way of preparing for it is to burrow into the bunker and try and stave it off. I'm trying to adapt. Anyway, if you think about it, it's one of those now-or-never deals. Once I hit thirty, I won't want to go through with something like this out there. You must have had some now-or-never moments in your life, Richard, haven't you?"

"Why is it," I said, "that in these now-or-never situations, people always assume 'now' is the best choice. Isn't there a 50-50 chance that 'never' would be the better option?"

He seemed frustrated by this comment and picked up the menu again. "I don't especially care about being sensible right now. On top of that, I'm not even hungry."

"In that case, the pulled pork might not be the right choice."

"And I'm not planning to have a career as a poker player," he said. "It's a diversion. Just like this job has been a diversion."

After we ordered, we spent a few more minutes sitting in awkward silence, looking out at the snow. He told me about his golf

lessons. Apparently, while was my attention was directed somewhere else, golf—along with ballroom dancing, collecting vinyl records, and playing the accordion—had become a hip pursuit.

Benjamin was a golfer, but in his case, the game seemed to be less
a hip hobby and more social climbing, an affectation he'd picked up
at boarding school. He'd confessed to me he found the game almost
painfully dull and hated spending so much time in the sun, but continued to play because it was "centering." What he meant was that it
helped anchor his public identity as a heterosexual, in the same way
that holding an annual Oscar night party anchored my friend Kenny's
public identity as a homosexual. Benjamin had kept his golf a secret
from me for the first six months we'd known each other, accurately
guessing that I'd take a dim view of it. He preferred to keep almost
everything secret until he figured out what other people's reactions
would be. Probably, it was this touching but sad desire to please that
had prevented him for so long from revealing his true self even to
himself. I'd kept my mild disgust with the sport a secret, too, although whenever I felt the need to distance myself from Benjamin
emotionally, I conjured up an image of him in a pastel jersey and
plaid pants, driving a cart around a sun-blasted golf course.

For some reason, though, I liked the idea of Brandon playing
golf somewhere in the desert, perhaps with a hangover after a long
night of drinking and poker. But I wasn't about to tell him that.

"Just out of curiosity," I said, trying my best to sound disinterested, "what do your parents make of this plan?"

"My parents have always been great. They'll be totally behind
me on this."

"In other words, you haven't told them yet."

He shrugged, as if it was of no immediate concern. "They're
busy all the time, so I haven't had a chance. My mother's been at a
lot of conferences lately."

I nodded. Although Brandon knew that Lewis was casual
friends with his impressive parents, it was obvious he assumed they

had nothing to do with his hiring. Ordinarily, I never brought them up in conversation, and Lewis had made it clear that Brandon should be led to believe that he'd been promoted due to his own accomplishments, which was partly true.

"I should warn you," I said, "that I'm going to try very hard to get you to stay at your job. I'm going to make promises of salary increases, and benefit packages."

"I'm flattered," he said, "but if you'd been able to keep people on at Connectrix, you never would have needed my help figuring out how to do it."

"A valid point," I said.

When the waiter arrived with the exploded sandwiches, Brandon looked at me and said, "You know, Richard, maybe you should see this as an opportunity to learn from me."

"Really," I said. I was appalled and delighted by his audacity. "How so?"

"Don't you have any now-or-never opportunities in your own life you can take advantage of? You're not too old, you know."

Since I'd brought up his parents, I probably deserved the reference to my age, but when people say you're not too old to do something, it usually means you are. I didn't mind telling myself I was too old to change, but I certainly wasn't interested in hearing it from another person. "I've spent a few decades trying to get my life where it is right now," I said. "Ideally, I'd like to enjoy it in its present state for a while."

He dug into his food so lustily, it was as if the question of now or never applied to eating, too. "Almost sounds as if you believe that," he said and mopped at his mouth.

Violent Movies

Among the many hundreds of items related to Benjamin I'd added to the At Least List over the years was that while we usually talked several times a week, *at least I always waited for him to call*. If he was feeling a need to be sequestered with his family or focused on his kids or wife, I never interrupted him with any untoward sexual demands or emotional distractions. Sometimes, I had the sense that he didn't want to be reminded of the contradictions that a message from me might raise.

Typically, I didn't have to wait long for his calls. Whether Benjamin and I were in a sexually active phase of our friendship or not, he usually phoned me on Mondays. After a weekend of immersion in his heterosexual life, he needed to touch base with someone who knew his true self so that he wasn't completely undone by isolation. I didn't know a whole lot of people with more packed schedules than Benjamin's, or a more extensive list of friends, co-workers, and family. Even I sometimes got them confused, not surprising since he seemed to have trouble keeping track of them himself at times. But I suspected him of suffering occasionally from profound loneliness as a result of being surrounded by people who had limited knowledge of his life and the full range of his interests.

So when Thursday rolled around and I still hadn't heard from him, I began to worry. I played out a series of doomsday scenarios. Most of them involved Giselle's discovery of some piece of incriminating evidence, which spiraled into accusations and confessions and ended with death threats. Particularly worrisome was the thought that I would be implicated and be forever connected in Benjamin's mind to the dissolution of his marriage and his family life as he knew it.

I'd already thought up a lot of advice for him about how to respond to any accusations that might come up, explanations for untoward discoveries and responses to unwanted questions. For someone who lived the bulk of his waking hours deceiving the people he was closest to, Benjamin was curiously guileless and an inept liar. When he had to change our plans at the last minute, for example, he frequently offered way too many details: there was a crisis at his son's school or Giselle's mother was visiting.

I completely rejected the idea that if confronted by Giselle, Ben should simply come clean and let everyone get on with their lives. This is what I had advised all of the clients who'd come to me with issues of sexual confusion back when I'd been a practicing therapist, but in this instance, I had scores of well-articulated reasons for protecting the innocent party from the truth, so I could continue to have my share of the guilty party. I'd gone as far as making an actual list of excuses Ben could give Giselle and attitudes he could take ("appear hurt but downplay it," "don't get angry") that I kept in a misleadingly named file on my computer: Dessert Recipes.

By Thursday afternoon, I was sufficiently distracted and worried to break with tradition and make a call to him, placed dangerously closed to the end of business hours.

When he picked up with an elaborately cheerful hello, I felt both relieved and cheated that he wasn't in the midst of an emotional meltdown and resorted to asking him if everything was all right, a passive-aggressive way of chastising him for not calling.

"Of course," he said. "Why wouldn't it be?"

"I haven't heard from you," I said. "I was starting to get worried."

"It's been a busy week. And by the way, I followed up on your suggestion for taking Tyler to a movie. It was a perfect idea. I wasn't sure what the movie was about, but someone was blown up at least once every five minutes in a graphic, disgusting way, and it gave us a lot to talk about. Tyler was deeply disturbed by it."

"I'm glad to hear it was such a success."

"To be honest, Richard, I was relieved to see he wasn't completely immune to that kind of violence, despite the video games and the rest. Afterward, I took him out to eat, and reassured him that the world really isn't the chaotic, out-of-control mess it was in the movie."

I remained silent long enough to let him know what I thought of that comment.

"Look," he said, "if you had kids, you'd try to be a little more optimistic, too."

I hated when people acted as if I was less human than they were because they'd decided to have children and I hadn't. Particularly galling was my sister, Beth's, attitude that childlessness was selfish; it was hard to imagine anything more selfish than adding to the world's disastrous overpopulation by deciding, sometimes repeatedly, to replicate your genes.

"How are things going at home for *you*?" he asked. *Now that things at home are going so well for ME*, his tone implied.

"Things are going fine," I said. "Conrad is home all week and we've been having a nice time."

"Really? I'm glad to hear it. What have you been doing?"

"Long walks, romantic dinners, hours of intensely personal, intimate conversations, a couple of group-sex scenes with some BU students."

"It was an honest question, Richard."

A Slight Advantage

Because he was in a more thorny position than I was, I'd always felt I had a slight advantage. I often ended up consoling him and, better yet, reading into his feelings in ways he wasn't quite able to read into his own. But I felt as if he was turning the tables on me, identifying me as the one with relationship problems that needed to be addressed. That whole possibility made me feel so lost that I said, in a more plaintive tone than I'd intended, "Things have been fine. Maybe there's a little more distance between Conrad and me than usual, but it's not grave. Mostly, I've been missing you, Ben."

I realized almost immediately that I hadn't made such a brusque pronouncement about my feelings for him in the years we'd known each other. It made me feel exposed and vulnerable, but since it was too late to put my guard back up, I went on. "You haven't even sent any e-mails."

Ben had a distinctive writing style that involved an amazing number of misspellings and malapropisms, so that while reading his e-mails, I had to guess my way through much of the text, as if I were reading a foreign language or deciphering someone's illegible handwriting. Since, as an architect, he had to be precise and clear in most things, I felt privileged that he allowed himself to expose this carelessness to me. It was like a private language between us, just as so much of our connection was private.

"I guess," he said. "I just haven't had a whole lot to report."

There was a long stretch of uncomfortable silence. I was walking to the gym near the office, and across the river, I could see the muted skyline of Boston and the back end of the neighborhood where Conrad and I lived. It was unfortunate that I'd told him I missed him during a period when Conrad was in town and even more unfortunate that I actually did miss him during a period when Conrad was in town.

"Since when do you need to have something to report to call and say hello? Saying hello is enough news."

There was more silence, and then he said, "Well, maybe we'll see each other next week."

The "maybe" was a dead giveaway that he had no intention of even trying to get together and was, in all likelihood, lurching toward a period of retreat. I offered a chilly goodbye and got off the phone.

Broken Window

"Lower the shoulders," Walmi drawled. "Not good to strain the joints at this age. I keep trying to tell you this."

"I'm sorry," I said. "I'm a little distracted today."

"It's no need to apologize. I am in the same condition. Marco broke a window last night. No sleep with the police and the fire department coming to the house at midnight. It was a very long night, Richard."

"Oh." By now, the police and fire department probably knew as much about Walmi's domestic life as I did. "Did he . . . throw something through the window?"

"Marco is not an animal. I keep telling you this. The window was not his fault. It happened when he drove his car against the house."

"I see. That is different. I suppose it was an accident."

"Please, not so much talking. Concentrate on lowering the shoulders." He pushed my shoulders down, leaned against a wall lazily, and began picking at a pimple on his smooth, tanned forearm. "He was in the driveway. Angry I was late coming out of the house and hitting the horn. His foot slipped and . . . bang."

"I hate when that happens," I said.

"Very sarcastic, but it was an accident. Stupid landlord does not understand."

Having finished the prescribed number of repetitions, I put down the weights and waited for Walmi to finish excavating his pimple. He was clearly charmed by every pore of his beautiful body, and he managed to make this picking and popping look like loving ministrations.

"Where were you going at midnight?"

"Shopping. Marco got home late and wanted me to make him dinner. Midnight, the store isn't crowded. I recommend going then."

He and Marco lived on the bottom floor of a three-family house in Revere, not far from the beach. I tried to picture the mechanics of this accident, but didn't want to raise his ire by asking for the relevant details. Had Marco smashed through a wall? Was there structural damage? Was anyone hurt? Not that the answers to any of those questions would alter Walmi's perceptions of the incident, and asking them would probably provoke more resentment toward me.

"Why are you so tired today, Richard? What is the distraction? Your life is very settled. You shouldn't be distracted."

"You're absolutely right. I shouldn't be. But sometimes the most settled lives have the biggest distractions."

"Only when they are unsettled. You should just relax into everything. This is what I am waiting for, when the hormones stop."

"Have you seen my friend Jerry here recently?" I asked.

"No. Not once. It is obvious he is busy with other things."

"He's dealing with some big matters in his life right now," I said. Jerry hadn't been in touch with me and had stopped answering my calls. I took this to mean that he hadn't made any progress in telling his wife about his pending heart surgery and was embarrassed to admit it.

"I do not doubt that. It happens when you make trouble. I would kill Marco if he was thinking about cheating on me."

I nodded. The important thing was to establish rules. If Walmi's rules allowed death threats, drunken blackouts, sex for hire, and driving the car into the house but *not* a flirtation on the side, who was I to criticize?

"Should we move on to the next station?" I asked.

Walmi checked his watch. "You are so stressed," he said. "We have only eight minutes left and you want to go to something else. Okay, I'm tired, but it's okay. Let's lie down and do some stretching."

Baby?

Lying beside him on a mat on the floor, I tried to sneak in a few ab-
dominal crunches while he performed a series of sensual, catlike
stretches punctuated by yawns, and told me that if things didn't improve soon in the U.S. he would go back to Brazil. If it weren't for
Marco, he probably would have left already. "The dollar is worth
nothing now," he said. "Everyone at home thinks I am crazy to be
here still. I send money and it's worthless there. Plus they think
your president is a madman. They don't understand why there isn't
a revolution."

"You send money to your parents?"

"No. Why does everyone think this? They are okay. They don't
need money from me. I send it for the baby."

"I see. Whose baby?"

"It is mine, of course. My wife works, but the extra I send helps
out. The baby is almost five now. I miss him, but that is life. So you
can see that I have distractions, too."

Among the many things I loved about Walmi was his ability to
pull one revelation out of another, so that almost any topic he raised
proved to be a Russian doll of surprises, each one opening up a
multitude of new questions and possibilities. The announcement—
eight months into my knowing him and listening to nothing but
Marco and gay drama—that he had a baby and a wife was so incongruous it struck me as close to insane. And yet, it was no longer
shocking to me in the way it would have been a few months earlier.
If I asked him for further clarification, he'd have a long list of explanations and justifications that would open up doors into a whole
other wing of his loopy funhouse. And since my thirty-minute ses-
sion with him was nearly at an end, I preferred to delay the gratification of heading in that direction.

"I have a small favor to ask, Walmi."

"For you, Richard, anything."

"If you see Jerry here, I'd appreciate it if you'd tell him to get in touch with me. I'm a little concerned about him."

"Even though I don't approve," he said, "I'll do that. Except we both know we are not going to see him anytime soon."

Ambitions

Unprompted, Conrad sometimes hinted at dissatisfaction with his business. He felt that since it was essentially a limited kind of interior decorating, it was a waste of his talents. It provided no security whatsoever, and it wasn't what he wanted to be doing in ten years. Although I thought what he did for a living was perfectly suited to his interests and personality, I sympathized with his anxiety about it not being what he'd imagined for himself.

Whenever I asked him direct questions about how things were going, he responded with optimistic and evasive answers, as if he was pitching a narrative of success to a potential client.

Did they have a lot of projects lined up for the remainder of the winter? "This is New England, dear. You never know how long winter is going to last."

Did their clients talk much about fear of a pending economic downturn? "We're not paid to listen, we're paid to talk, sweetheart."

Would they be traveling a lot in the upcoming months? "Enough to do the jobs we have to do."

When he and Doreen were in town, they met at a small office they rented in a loft building that housed galleries and used furniture stores that specialized in mid-century pieces with a pedigree. Their work involved a lot of phone calls and high-end, carefully structured socializing. They were always going to lunches and cocktail meetings with wealthy people as a way of getting to even wealthier people.

Conrad was haunted by the belief that there was a big piece of unfinished business at the center of his life. He had gone to art school to study painting but, as he reported, had been so discouraged by the harsh criticism of several teachers that he'd lost confidence in his own talent. He'd destroyed his canvases, put away his paints, and had gone in a more academic direction. I'd encouraged him to start painting again—as a hobby, if nothing else—but he'd been insulted by the tone of the suggestion. If he was going to do it, he was going to do it right, which apparently meant renting a studio and devoting all of his time to it.

I said nothing about this, but given the expectations he'd built up for himself and the fact that he hadn't picked up a paintbrush in over twenty years, it didn't seem realistic. We all have a central fiction about ourselves, a favored delusion about talent or untapped potential. Most of us hang on to it as if it were a lifesaver, even though the obsession with it is often the very thing that drags us down and prevents us from fulfilling some lesser but more obtainable goal. I knew I had a treasured delusion about myself lurking somewhere in my background, but I hadn't been able to identify what it was.

Conrad and Doreen had been back in town for a couple of weeks before Doreen was able to see me. I was curious about any information she might have on Conrad and his Insignificant Other in Ohio, but I was also eager to tell Benjamin that I was doing some investigative work into Conrad's indiscretion. A perfect excuse to call him, something I was looking for since I hadn't heard from him in almost two weeks.

Doreen invited me to her apartment for a drink on a Wednesday night, and although it meant missing the most odious and therefore favored spinning class of the week at my underground gym, I went. She lived on the opposite side of Cambridge from where I worked. The harsh, wintry weather, uncharacteristic in the warmed-up new atmosphere, had persisted right into February, but I walked from Connectrix anyway, taking the long way along the windy banks of the Charles. I love the bleak misery of early evenings deep in winter, the wind off the water, and the crystals of ice tinkling along the shoreline, lights in the distance a faint promise of remote and unobtainable warmth. It had been years since we'd had such a severe and prolonged bout of cold weather, and the novelty of it was appealing, even if the fact of it was uncomfortable.

It had been a difficult day at work, and I was happy for the opportunity to clear my head. I'd been avoiding talking with Lewis about Brandon Miller's crazy plans, but he finally summoned me to his office to find out what I'd learned. I told him that Brandon hadn't settled on a date to leave, a sign of uncertainty, and that I was doing my best to convince him to stay.

"Does he have another job lined up?"

"He has plans," I said.

"Plans? What does that mean?"

While I'd always found Lewis's use of my full name, terms like "champ," and general frat-boy affability affected and annoying, I found the absence of them in this particular conversation worrisome.

"He's a pretty serious athlete," I said.

"Since when?"

"Well, he golfs. And he wants to be in a climate where he can play year-round. He's thinking of Las Vegas."

"Is this about the poker bullshit?"

"Partly."

"In other words, entirely. This isn't what I want to have to tell his parents."

With Lewis's calculated good cheer gone for the moment, his finely chiseled features looked hard and sharp, as if all the softening social skills had been sanded off.

"I don't see why they'd hold it against you. They know how strong-willed he is."

"Strong-willed? There's a laugh." Lewis drummed his fingers on his desk, an unusual show of impatience. "I'll lay it out for you, Richard. Brandon's mother has ambitions. Health and Human Services in the next administration, assuming it's a Democrat, and maybe after that, the Senate, for all I know. His father made an investment in this company when Brandon got hired. They need to keep him out of trouble for the next few years. It wouldn't look right for Dr. Miller's son to be holed up in a casino or tromping around a golf course like a spoiled prick. She'll get her appointment and Brandon will age out of this nonsense, settle down with whoever he's going to settle down with, and live a life of quiet desperation like the rest of us."

Las Vegas was starting to sound better all the time.

As I was leaving his office, Lewis clapped his hand on my shoulder and said, "I want this to work out for everyone, Richard. That means for you, too. Get working on it, okay?"

I couldn't tell if he was wishing me well or threatening me.

Too Early?

Doreen lived outside Harvard Square in a building that was famous for its pampering services and views of the river. As I stepped into the lobby, I was greeted in polite but discreet manner by a uniformed concierge who made a big show of calling upstairs and announcing my arrival. "Go right up," he said, making me feel I'd passed a test. "Eighth floor."

I rang the buzzer outside Doreen's door, and after a moment she opened it. "You're extremely prompt," she said.

"I'm sorry," I said. "Am I too early?"

"Not at all. I'm fanatical about time, something for which Conrad frequently takes me to task. Let me have your coat."

Given the size of Doreen's apartment, the pomp and circumstance in the lobby below was false advertising. It was a single, modestly sized room with only one window, but a large one that faced the river and took up the bulk of one wall. The place was as tidy and carefully organized as a ship's cabin. Standing in the tiny entryway, Doreen carefully put my coat on a thick wooden hanger, draped my scarf around the collar, and slid it into place in the little pocketlike closet.

"That's a wonderful scarf," she said, something in her tone suggesting that she was asserting her own authority in matters of taste rather than complimenting mine. As with the tie she'd complimented, the scarf had been a present from Benjamin, something I didn't enjoy being reminded of at that moment.

"I'm glad you approve. You look lovely."

She appeared shocked that I'd said so, and reared back her head as if I'd insulted her. She was dressed in a pair of slacks that billowed out around her thin legs, and a black angora sweater, the softness of which was in striking contrast to her rigid posture and personality. She did look lovely, albeit in a cold-blooded way that matched the weather outside.

The apartment was arranged to give the illusion of space—open but with the suggestion of distinct areas—and since there was no bed, I assumed she slept on a pullout sofa of some kind, a depressing thought. Everything in the place was white, a light and elegant choice that made sense for a small space, but emphasized the fact that Doreen's life was so carefully controlled she could live in an all-white environment. It was certain that no one ever fucked or ate pizza in this room.

Don't Touch

Doreen waved at a low white cube, and I sat. On a little table in front of me, she'd placed two small white bowls, one heaped with tiny cornichons, the other with thin matchsticks of carrots. The colors were startling in the all-white room. She slipped into the kitchen alcove and emerged carrying two wineglasses with a shallow serving of white wine in each, handed me mine, and sat opposite me on another white cube. She dipped her legs to one side gracefully, while I struggled to settle in and figure out what to do with my knees.

"Cheers," she said. She raised her glass and appeared to wet her lips with the contents.

There was something in the very hostesslike way she was dressed and the careful way she'd put on a layer of dark lipstick that made me feel almost as if we were on a first date. Since I couldn't think of anything else to ask, I asked her how business was. She smiled wanly and looked out the window. "Conrad could tell you as well as I could," she said.

"You're probably right. Although it isn't something we discuss very much."

She shrugged. "Perhaps you should then. Assuming you're genuinely interested?"

"That could be the problem. The genuine interest."

Lurching toward another scrap of small talk that might make me feel a little closer to her before we began on Conrad's sex life, I said that Conrad had mentioned awhile back that she was dating someone. I did have a distant memory of this, but had no idea how far back he'd said it.

Her face was completely expressionless, her red lips perfectly still, and she didn't seem to react to my question at all. "That was a long time ago," she finally said. "And it didn't work out."

"That's too bad."

"I have a history of failed relationships, including one failed marriage, so at this point in my life, it's what I expect." She pulled her head back, that odd and confrontational gesture of hers, as if to say "Do you have a problem with that?" and took a sip from her glass, a real sip this time. "On top of that, I've come to the conclusion that I'm the kind of person who doesn't especially like being touched."

This was the variety of intimate information I'd wait months to hear from a patient. The fact that she was delivering it to me so unexpectedly and so unapologetically instantly made me like her more. Self-awareness and confession make up for almost any flaw, in my book. "I don't think that's all that uncommon," I said. "Although most people wouldn't admit it."

"Most people resist admitting anything about themselves that contradicts their fantasy of who they are," Doreen commented. "I'm a mass of unappealing quirks, but I'm a realist and past the point of making excuses for them." She pushed the two little bowls closer together on the low table. It was clear the food in them was meant to be ornamental. "I just finished reading a biography of Frank Sinatra, and he also didn't like to be touched. I'm in good company—assuming you consider crass, brutal men with organized crime connections good company."

There were no bookcases anywhere in the room. To the extent that I'd given the matter any thought at all, I'd always imagined Doreen reading *Art Forum* and design magazines. It was hard to picture her listening to Sinatra—or any music—never mind reading an entire book about him. Perhaps she had a dark attraction to disreputable men. "I thought Sinatra was an infamous womanizer," I said.

"One thing doesn't exclude the other." She said this with such dry finality, I began to wonder if she, like everyone else on the planet, had a secret life stashed away somewhere.

"Are you a big fan?"

"Not especially. Not at all, in fact. I find his early recordings generic and his later ones so specific in style, they're embarrassing. Hipster with a hairpiece. My father was a fan, so I'd guess I read the biography as a way to feel closer to him. The lurid tidbits about Sinatra himself were unexpected bonuses."

A few years earlier, when Conrad and I were more in the habit of discussing the secrets and psychologies of our friends as we lay in bed at night, he'd told me that Doreen had been an only child, the adored daughter of her gruff and physically imposing widowed father. According to Conrad, he had been the love of Doreen's life, the standard against which she measured all other men, even though she had done everything possible to erase the traces of her working-class roots and, by implication, her father. As to this makeover project, her father had been in full support of it, sent her off to the best schools he could afford, and set her up in this well-respected apartment building many years earlier.

"Are you and your ex-husband still in touch?"

She stared at me with such an icy gaze, I wanted to look away. Somewhere along the pathway of life, she'd apparently picked up the unnerving ability to keep her eyes from blinking. Finally, she said: "He's dead. He's been dead for many years."

"I had no idea. He must have been very young." She didn't respond to this. Her face had become immobile, but beautiful in its frozen, challenging way. "I'm sorry," I said.

"Initially, *I* wasn't. Which has only made me more sorry and guilty ever since." She looked around, almost as if she was checking to make sure we were alone. "He was gay. As it turns out."

"I see." Based on the sequence of the revelations, I wondered if he'd died of AIDS, but it seemed inappropriate to ask just then. "A lover of mine died young, too. I'm not sure I've ever really gotten over it."

"There was a lot about the marriage—and about him—I've

never gotten over. And in case you're wondering why you didn't hear about this before, it's because I've never mentioned any of the details to Conrad. Given that he is who he is, it isn't as if he'd ask for more information."

I liked that she didn't feel the need to ask for my discretion, that it was understood to be between us, and that she trusted me enough to not demand a vow of silence. I was still in the habit of asking for someone's silence, even though I knew that since the advent of cell phones, text messages, and the forward option on e-mails, discretion had pretty much gone the way of phone booths.

Clarke

She set down her glass and crossed her legs. "Sooner or later," she said, "we're going to have to come to the point, which we both know has nothing to do with Frank Sinatra or my past."

"True. Would you like to begin?"

She balked at this suggestion, and then said: "Why not? I'd love to. I've always had the feeling that you were good for Conrad in a number of ways. And since I have a great deal invested in him, professionally and personally, I've been pleased that things have been stable between you two. In that way, I very much approve of you."

"I'm happy to hear that."

"Really? My opinion counts for so much?" She closed her eyes and shook her head, as if she was trying to shake off a chill. I was used to seeing her with her hair pinned up, but tonight she had it pulled back into a very tight ponytail that tugged a bit at the skin around her eyes and swung back and forth as she shook her head. It made her look like a girl, albeit a forty-year-old girl. "I'm sorry. It's easy for me to get snappy and unpleasant, even when I don't mean to. I'll start over: I gather you know about Clarke. With an *e*."

Clarke. A silly name, one that conjured up images of privilege. I told her that I'd suspected for a while that Conrad had an outside interest in Columbus (the term "fuck buddy" didn't seem appropriate around the all-white furniture) but that I didn't have any details. "It doesn't come as a shock," I said. "Conrad and I have an unspoken agreement about that sort of thing."

"'Unspoken agreement.' There's an interesting concept. A little like an imaginary friend. Am I snapping again?"

"Not too badly," I said. "And it doesn't matter anyway. Conrad and I haven't discussed this person, so I'm assuming he's a minor distraction who will fade out of the picture soon enough. At least that's what I'm hoping."

"I see. And the reason you came here is for reassurance that that's the case." To my astonishment, she picked up a cornichon, tapped it against the side of the bowl, and popped it into her mouth. I could see the muscles of her jaw snapping at it through her pale skin. "I hate to disappoint you, but in my opinion, that's not going to happen. Clarke is an attractive older man."

"Older than me, do you mean?"

"I haven't checked his passport, but I'd guess early sixties. He has money, a certain amount of charm—of the most obvious variety—and *way* too much time on his hands. He owned an auto rental company or something equally practical and lucrative. Ten years ago, he sold it for a small fortune. I find his focus on Conrad worrisome. First of all, it interferes with our business, then it makes me feel ignored."

From this I gathered that Conrad was possibly spending time on a number of their business trips, in and out of Columbus, with his new friend. "This . . . Clarke is getting attached?"

"I'm sure you think I'm in love with Conrad, Richard. I'd say I have a mild, harmless infatuation with him, the main advantage of which is that it will never go anywhere. When you have to spend as much time with someone as I spend with Conrad, it helps to be a little infatuated, especially when you have no interest in touching each other. I have no illusions, but it's true, I am somewhat jealous. It's always easier to accept a friend's long-term relationship than his love affair."

I was unsettled by the word "affair" and even more so by the word "love." I preferred to think of my relationship with Benjamin as a "situation" or a "complicated friendship" and I hadn't even put Conrad's Insignificant Other into that category.

"Do you know how long this has been going on?" I asked.

"That's another item you should take up with Conrad. What I do know is that he'd like Conrad to move to Columbus."

"That's an amusing thought," I said. I reached into the bowl on the table and stuffed a few carrot sticks into my mouth.

"He's offering to set Conrad up in his own gallery."

"It's sounding more and more absurd. We have nothing to worry about," I said, putting the two of us, I realized later, in the same category with regards to an investment in Conrad.

"You haven't met Clarke."

Open Sky

This was more information than I had been prepared for, even if it was just by implication, and I was surprised at how much it wounded me. I suppose it showed on my face, because Doreen softened her tone and asked me if I'd like more wine. When I refused, she said, "Good. I don't have more. And all I meant was that Clarke is one of those manic-depressive, bullying types who's had a lot of success in business and is used to having his way. I suspect he's on a variety of mood-altering pills. There's no other way to explain his energy. At the moment, it's all directed toward Conrad."

I sat in silence for a moment and looked out the window. I could see the lights of the cars passing on either side of the river, and a pink glow of lights in the winter sky over Boston. The view was too open and windswept for my tastes. I prefer obstructed views and nearby rooftops, which make me feel enfolded and less lonely. One of the reasons I love living in Beacon Hill is the claustrophobic proximity of neighboring buildings.

I wasn't sure how to assimilate this new information about Conrad. I'd come to expect and even enjoy the fact that there was a lot we didn't know about each other. It made for the possibility of fresh discoveries at unexpected turns and kept at bay the asexual sibling dynamic that a lot of couples lapse into. It was one thing to learn that he was having sex with someone else—life is short; why not?—but quite another to be told that he was planning a change of career, location, and partner. Yes, I had Benjamin but *at least the whole basis of that complicated friendship was to preserve both his and my primary relationships. At least he wasn't setting me up in business. AT LEAST I WASN'T MOVING TO OHIO.*

"Do you like all the white in here?" Doreen asked, sounding as if her voice came from a great distance.

"The furniture?"

"That and the walls and the rugs and the pillows."

"It's beautiful," I said. "Maybe a little formal."

"Does that mean you find it unwelcoming?"

"It's welcoming up to a point."

"Good. That's exactly the message I hoped to send." There was something about her composure, her rigid posture on the low little cube that was impressive but unnerving. I suppose there's always something a little grotesque and inhuman about perfect posture, just as there is about perfect diction outside of the theater. "I'm about to be indiscreet," she said. "I appreciate if you'd listen so I don't have to repeat myself."

"Yes. With pleasure."

"Conrad is planning to go to Columbus again soon, probably for an extended time. He's going without me, although he's not planning to tell you that. I think you should make sure he doesn't go."

I told her I'd do my best, but we both knew that Conrad was stubborn.

She gave me a piercing look, one that suggested a good deal more curiosity about me than I would have guessed. "I suppose your lack of anger about all this has something to do with the wonderful unspoken agreement."

"I'm trying to put it in perspective. All the talk of same-sex marriage and everything aside, I think the best relationships between men are the ones that are handcrafted. Do you know what I mean?"

"Not in the least."

"They're outside of tradition. They take into account the particulars of men's sexual needs and attitudes, which are different from women's."

She mulled this over for a minute while finishing her wine. "I'm happy to learn I'm not the most emotionally cut-off person in this town."

Unsure Footing

I found I was a little wobbly when I left Doreen's cosseting building and stepped into the cold. Even though I'm not much of a drinker, it seemed unlikely that my unsure footing was due to half a glass of wine. It was dark now, and the appeal of the winter twilight had vanished. The night felt merely cold. I decided to forgo a long icy walk home along the river and headed into Harvard Square. If I nurtured my incipient anger toward Conrad a little while longer, I would start ranting aloud on the subway, probably more healthy in the long run than channeling it into a stationary bike.

As I was walking past a noodle restaurant crowded with students talking on cell phones, I saw Billy—one of "the boys"—coming toward me. He was a thin man with a distinctively erect walk and a habit of always patting down his pockets, as if he'd misplaced his keys. This habit was, Conrad had told me, the last vestige of an obsessive-compulsive disorder that otherwise had been effectively treated with drugs. He stopped and said hello and introduced me to the scowling older man at his side. "John Loggern," he said. He paused for a moment while he tapped at the pockets of his leather jacket. "The artist," he added.

I pretended I recognized the name and asked Billy what he was doing in Cambridge. "John lives here," he said, as if that answered it. John was a good-looking man, but in the blue light spilling out of the restaurant window, he appeared to be in his eighties. Was Billy suggesting they had a romantic attachment of some kind? "And you?" he asked. "What are *you* doing here?"

I told him I'd just had a drink with Doreen. Billy had a droll, flirty way of opening his eyes wide when he listened, so that I always felt I was saying something surprising or shocking when I talked with him. "I didn't know you and she were *friendly*," he said, stunned.

I explained it had been a brief, impromptu visit.

"Richard," he explained to the artist, "is Conrad Mitchell's partner?" The little question mark he put at the end and the way a light bulb seemed to go off over the artist's head ("Oh, ah! I see.") made me suspect they both knew more about Conrad's life than I'd known an hour earlier. And given the boys' penchant for discussing the most intimate details—real and invented—of their sex lives with each other, he probably still knew a thing or two I didn't. It made me feel even more betrayed and angry than I had when I left Doreen's. It went without saying that the boys would have heard an exaggerated version of Conrad's out-of-state adventures, but their elderly cohorts? That struck me as too much.

I asked Billy how business was, trying, out of sheer pettiness, to make it sound as if he ran a card shop. "We're thriving," he said. "You never come to our openings. Make Conrad drag you along. Come next week. Will Conrad be in town?"

"The last I heard, yes."

Billy's eyes popped open. "Then, I'm sure he will be. Come!"

"I'm cold," the artist said, clearly intending it to be an order to his companion.

Billy shrugged, and the two of them went off down the street.

When I got home, Conrad was working at the dining table. I tried to initiate an argument, which, given what I'd just learned, seemed the responsible thing to do.

"I hate having these photos scattered all over the table," I said.

"I'll have it cleaned up soon," he said. "Did you have a nice time at the gym?"

He clearly wasn't interested in taking the bait. I hate to lie, but I've never had a problem making broad statements that are intended to be misleading. "I don't go to the gym to have a good time."

"Oh, Ricky, life's too short for self-flagellation. You should cancel one of those memberships."

"I'll take that into consideration. Where are we supposed to eat if you've set up shop here?"

"I made reservations at a place in the South End. My treat. As long as you promise to cheer up."

Anger over what I'd heard from Doreen made me want to refuse to go, but he'd chosen a place I was especially fond of, and all the walking in the cold had made me hungry. In the dim light of the restaurant, we shared a bottle of wine and psychoanalyzed his parents. We'd covered this territory dozens of times, but I always found it amusing, especially when Conrad did imitations of his mother. I was swamped by a pleasant sort of laziness about my relationship that was made even stronger by the wine. Conrad would have his fling and that would be that. We'd carry on our life of quiet contentment, which was not even close to the same thing as quiet desperation. Most relationships thrive on inebriating effects of love, but when you've built up a tolerance to that, the inebriating effects of alcohol and familiarity can work nearly as well.

Good News

A few days later, I had a breakthrough of sorts in the Randy Trask discrimination case. I managed to track down a former freelancer who had worked with Z, the complainant, on a project and she was happy to testify to his ineptitude. She, unlike Randy, had kept extensive records of the e-mails she'd sent to Z and the ones he'd sent her in return. It was clear from the messages back and forth that Z didn't understand the most basic technical terms, had refused offers of help, and had never completed the assignments he'd been given. As a freelancer who'd had a frustrating experience with Connectrix, she had no particular loyalty to us, but she was meticulous and had an idea that it would be fun to testify in a trial. I refrained from telling her that her information made it more likely that there would be a settlement before it got to that point.

I decided to share the good news with Randy in person. As I was leaving my office, I asked my secretary, Anne, if she'd seen him around.

She looked up at me from behind her big eyeglasses. "I never see him around," she said. "And if I did, I'd run in the opposite direction."

"I can't imagine that would be necessary. He's a little confused, but I have some news that will cheer him up."

She took off her glasses and began polishing them with a little green rag. "Really?" she said. "It must be very good news to cheer *him* up." She held the glasses to the light, as if all her attention was focused on them. "I suppose it must be about the case."

Even though I didn't entirely trust Anne, I had a sudden urge to tell her about the e-mails. Nothing's more effective for getting information out of people than pretending you're not interested in hearing it. I resisted. Anne put her glasses back on and changed the subject.

Religious Principles

"There's something I need your help with, Richard. It's about the yoga teacher you hired."

I nodded. A year earlier, I'd taken Brandon's advice and had hired a young woman to offer a yoga class at 5:30 daily. A large number of employees came to work with yoga mats slung over their shoulders and half of them left the office early to make a class in some other part of the city. Why not have in-house classes? Employees would appreciate the convenience, and by scheduling it for 5:30, we'd keep a few people at their desks past five instead of having them skip out. Anne had objected to the hiring, claiming it was a class in religious instruction, but had never pressed the matter.

"I thought you'd dropped your objections to that," I said.

"She's getting married," Anne said. "She announced it several weeks ago, and one of the tech people took up a collection for a gift."

"Well, that's pretty much standard procedure, isn't it?"

"It is. I contributed twenty-five dollars."

"Generous of you." I usually gave ten. I'd never asked anyone to celebrate my relationships, so I didn't completely understand the expectation that I'd celebrate someone else's.

"What I didn't know," Anne said, "is that she's marrying another woman."

"Ah. Well, as you know, that's legal now."

"I asked for my money back, and Sarah refused to give it to me."

Offhand, I had no idea who Sarah was, but I immediately approved of her tactics. "I'm not sure this is the kind of thing I need to get involved in, Anne. It seems like it's a more personal matter."

"It's a matter of religious principle."

There was something large and vulnerable about Anne's eyes, wobbling behind her glasses. I was insulted by her position, but having spent the bulk of my life feeling like an outsider, I sympathized with her minority status as one of the few loudly religious people in the company. As far as I could tell, Anne's religious principles were focused almost entirely on controlling the behavior of other people. Considering the state of her own marriage, she might have directed her energy a little closer to home. Still, I couldn't rule out the possibility that she'd make a cause out of the incident. It had the potential to develop into the kind of messy, emotional conflict that made everyone feel attacked and unhappy on some level and that Lewis in particular hated to have surface.

"Speaking of religion," I said, "I've been reading *Luther's Commentary on St. Paul's Epistle to the Galatians*. Interesting stuff."

Anne was unimpressed. "I'm not a Lutheran."

"I'll tell you what; I've been meaning to donate to the fund, so why don't I give you the twenty-five dollars instead? You get your money back, the fund ends up with twenty-five dollars less than it would have had, and we cut out the middleman."

She looked up at me as if I'd just insulted her. "That's unacceptable. I don't want your money, I want Sarah to give me back mine. It's my right as a religious person."

"Well, as you know, I'm gay, so at least you'd be taking money from another homosexual."

She didn't see the validity of the comment, and I promised her I'd look into it.

Randy was not in his office, and I strolled along the metal staircases and the catwalks suspended over the atrium without bumping into him. I poked my head into a few doorways, but at the mention of his name, everyone launched into an abrupt denial of having seen him, almost as if the question had been an accusation. *Nope, not all week. Why would I have seen Randy? Randy? I just try to mind my own business.*

I decided to give up and wait until later in the day. I walked into one of the bathrooms off the mezzanine and there he was, standing in front of a sink, meticulously combing the thick flap of hair across his forehead with a black plastic comb. He had on his uniform of a white shirt, dark tie, and dark pants, and today he looked like a Mormon missionary.

"Randy," I said. Instead of turning around, he made eye contact with me in the mirror and continued to run the comb through his hair. "I have some good news. We've had a big breakthrough in evidence. We're nearly done with this whole chapter. I told you it was just a matter of time."

Given Randy's blank expression, I felt as if my voice was swimming in the air between us struggling, unsuccessfully, to reach his ears.

Eventually, he put the comb into the pocket of his shirt and turned to me slowly. "So my word wasn't good enough? You need evidence?"

I felt cheated by his lack of enthusiasm. If he couldn't be pleased about this, what could he be pleased about?

"There's a certain protocol for these kinds of cases and some of it involves evidence. It doesn't really matter whose it is. Now we have some. That's what matters."

His eyes and voice registered nothing, but his face flushed a dark, angry red. "It matters to me, Richard. It's still a black eye on my review and someone else gets a pat on the back for having kept records."

"You have to let it go," I said. I put my hands on his shoulders to emphasize the point.

"From my point of view, this is just another insult." He knocked into me as he walked past. "Thanks for nothing, Richard," he said, and let the door bang behind him.

I was left looking at my reflection in the big wall of mirror over the sink. I'd put on a dark green shirt and a brown tie that morning, and in this light, both appeared to have been mistakes. I looked pale and drained under the energy-saving fluorescent bulbs and almost as green as my shirt. Years earlier, when my hair had started to go gray around the ears, I'd gone to an expensive and needlessly discreet salon in Boston to have it "fixed." But after a while, keeping up with it didn't seem worth the time and effort, and I'd just let it take its course. I didn't mind that it made me look old, which is to say, my real age, but I hated that it, along with the droopy eyelids, made me look perpetually sad, as if I had a wire implanted in my ear that was always feeding me little updates of insignificant but unhappy news.

At least I don't feel as tired as I look. At least I don't need glasses to see how bad I look. At least some people still find me sexually attractive.

On that note, I took out my cell phone and sent Ben a text message: "Lunch at the Club?"

I waited a couple of minutes for a response, but when none came through, I washed my hands and left. It's never a good idea to spend too much time in the men's room.

Good Grammar

A few days later, when Conrad and Doreen were in Atlanta, I called my sister, Beth. As usual, Nicholas answered the phone. He told me he had begun *David Copperfield* on schedule and was seventy-four pages ahead of where he expected to be at this time.

"Does that mean you're enjoying it?" I asked.

"I am enjoying it," he said. "It's easier to read than I expected, so I've adjusted my timetable. Except the writer uses commas in a strange way, I'm finding."

"Really? You've studied commas in school?"

"Not as much as I'd like. I think punctuation is very interesting."

At this rate, Nicholas would fit in well on the creative team at Connectrix. Despite his eccentricities, he was more socially adept than Randy Trask and good grammar was always in short supply. I was disappointed that he hadn't mentioned the trip to Boston, but I didn't bring it up in case Beth was planning to surprise him with it.

When Beth came on the phone a few minutes later, she expressed concern that I was calling without provocation. "You're not *always* the first one to call," I reminded her.

"As a matter of fact," she said, "I am. Is everything all right?"

"I didn't hear back from you about the hotel suggestions I e-mailed you. Did you follow the links?"

"I've been busy, Richard. I haven't had a chance yet."

"Well, I'd like to make the reservations," I said. "I've been looking into getting tickets for some offbeat museums I thought Nicholas might enjoy, too. There's a horology museum at Harvard he would probably find fascinating. I take it you haven't mentioned it to him."

"No, I haven't," she said flatly.

I felt such an unexpected stab of disappointment, I sat down on one of Conrad's leather and steel armchairs. I had just returned from a spinning class at the basement gym, and I felt the combination of clean and desperately in need of a shower I always felt after sixty minutes of intense sweating. I had the warning signs of a headache, too, possibly from mild dehydration.

"Does that mean you've decided against it?"

"You don't understand Nicholas at all, Richard. He takes things seriously. If I tell him you've invited us to Boston, he'll put it on his calendar and start planning for it."

"I'm hoping he will."

"Yes, except there's a 75 percent chance you'll cancel at the last minute, and he'll be upset in that cut-off way of his." I could tell she was starting to get tearful. "He has feelings, you know. He's not a robot."

I was stung by the number she'd assigned to my unreliability. It was true I did back out of our plans with some frequency, but I would have thought it was more like 60 percent of the time, a number that, in the current context, didn't sound very promising either.

"I'm the one who suggested this," I said. "I'm looking forward to it."

"The last time you came out here," she went on, "you spent half your time at the gym. What's to say you won't do the same thing when we're in town?"

I'd found a very nice gym in Buffalo, and the last time I visited Beth, I probably had spent a few more hours there than I should have, rationalizing that it made me more relaxed in the time I did spend with my sister and her family.

"I'm trying to change all that," I said.

"Oh really? You used to do more worthwhile things with your time, you know. You read books and went to demonstrations and got involved. I always admired your activism."

What Happened

My involvement and her admiration were news to me. I'd noticed among a lot of my friends a fairly recent tendency to claim a past filled with political activism, most of the time without presenting much evidence to support it. War rallies, marches on Washington, ACT UP demonstrations. It was a given that every gay man of a certain age had been at the Stonewall bar the night of the riots, and that every left-leaning person had been dragged to civil rights marches by their parents. The fact that a certain number of these self-professed activists had been toddlers in the late sixties was of little import. I'd begun to exaggerate my own involvement in politics as well, although I wasn't aware of having done so with Beth. I wasn't trying to take credit for having had a hand in changing history, but given the grade inflation of sorts that abounded, you sounded like a right-winger if you didn't lay claim to a few radical acts or at very least having smoked pot at Woodstock. It was related to the feeling that the country was in decline. Everyone wanted to claim they had, at some point, lent a hand before the ship sank.

"I think you're giving me more credit than I deserve," I said.

"Not really. You took me to things as a kid. You were my inspiration. You send Nicholas books, but as far as I can tell, you don't read them anymore. I'm not sure what happened."

I had a vague memory of seeing a black and white photo in her house of the two of us, younger and more round-faced, at a rally in Washington, but I had no memory of having been there. It was unrealistic but pleasant to imagine that life was one upward trajectory with improvement following improvement. *I'm not sure what happened* suggested a more downhill slide, exactly the kind I preferred to avoid thinking about. I was tempted to bring up Luther again, but reading that seemed to impress no one.

"Just look at the hotels," I said. "See which one looks best to you. Or you can stay here if you want."

"Conrad's too particular," she said. "I'd be too nervous about spilling something."

I considered this progress.

After we'd hung up, I went to my computer and began perusing one of my favored political blogs, but midway through a long

entry detailing a conspiracy about the ways in which Christian fun-
damentalists had engineered the election of George W. Bush as a
step toward ending civilization to fulfill a biblical prophecy, I got
distracted. It was a theory I only partly believed, and wasn't all that
concerned about. I didn't understand the obsessive fear of the world
ending: death has always seemed less frightening to me than slow,
painful decline. More to the point, it occurred to me that reading
this kind of tract night after night wasn't the same as doing something in the way that Beth had meant it, and it wasn't enhancing
my understanding of people in the way reading literature did. It
was neither fact nor fiction, but that peculiar and fluid amalgam referred to these days as "truth."

I went down into the basement of the building, and opened up
the little storage unit Conrad and I had packed with castoff pieces
of furniture, dishes we had no use for, and crates filled with records,
CDs, videocassettes, and other cultural artifacts. The boxes of my
books were located in the farthest reaches of the space, indicating, I
guess, that they'd been the first things to get stowed away. I managed to dig out one box. It was covered in a thick layer of dust, and
the sides felt damp, but I lugged it upstairs and dumped the contents onto the living room floor. The room filled up with the smell
of mildew and some other odor probably related to mice. But the
books looked reasonably intact. I decided to spread them out and
give them a chance to dry.

Another Basement

At least once a day, my secretary, Anne, asked me if I'd made any
progress in getting back the twenty-five dollars she'd donated to the
yoga teacher's wedding fund. I'd been hoping it was one of those
petty matters that get forgotten and die, but it didn't seem to be

headed in that direction. I told Cynthia that I was worried about Anne.

"Worried how?" she asked.

"She seems more focused on this than she is on work. She's fallen behind on a couple of requests I've made, and she has a self-righteous attitude about it, as if she shouldn't be expected to get anything done because of this. How is she with you?"

"No different from always." Cynthia's most recent purchase from a home shopping network was a boxy foot massager. Whenever I walked into her office these days, she was sitting at her desk with her feet resting on it and a far-off look in her eyes. She'd offered to let me try it, but it seemed like such an intimate item, I couldn't imagine sharing it with her. It would be like using a co-worker's toothbrush or trying on his underwear. "I'm not having any trouble with her."

"On top of everything, her objections to the marriage are a little insulting to me."

"You and Conrad planning on getting married?" she asked.

"Certainly not." Since I'd always associated weddings with tacky ceremonies and bad food, I was offended by this question whenever I was asked it.

"With the glasses and the hideous husband, Anne makes for a more convincing victim than you," she said. "Don't take it personally."

"I'm planning to go strong-arm this Sarah into giving the money back and put the whole thing behind us. Do you know who she is?"

"She works in the basement on electrical wires or cables or something. I've never been down there."

I'd only been in the basement of the building a few times in the years I'd been at Connectrix. There was a grim lunchroom that few people ever entered, an ersatz gym that was half the size of my living room, and behind a wall of thick glass, a big cavern housing the guts of the company's computer and telephone systems. As I walked through the glass door to the cave, I felt as if I'd smacked into a wall of heat and noise. There was a heavy, unpleasant smell of chemicals and hot electrical wires, and the sounds of blaring rock music. I asked a young man with a sallow complexion if he could direct me to Sarah, and he pointed into the nether regions of the room silently, as if he spoke a different language or couldn't speak at all.

Sarah turned out to be a short, plump young woman outfitted in overalls and a long-sleeved T-shirt that seemed completely inappropriate for the heat. She had a round, freckled face that made her look fourteen, and she had her hair pushed off her face by a woolen headband, the kind you might wear skiing. As I introduced myself and described the problem, she gazed at me with huge green eyes, as if expecting me to scold her for not having put her toys away tidily.

"The point is," I said, speaking loudly enough to be heard above the blaring music, "that while I completely understand your point of view, politically and in other ways, it would be easiest for everyone to give Anne back her twenty-five dollars."

Sarah had her head tilted to one side and her tiny mouth pursed into a surprised O. She looked so intimidated, I wondered if anyone from the upper floors ever came down to visit. It's always the childlike romantics that collect money for wedding presents and baby showers.

"Shall I tell Anne you'll have the money to her by this afternoon?" I shouted.

She appeared to think it over and said, "I'd rather you tell the fucking cunt to go eat shit."

She blinked her round eyes once. I looked to see if there was anyone I could ask to turn down the music, but the few people in the room were busily at work.

"I tend to be a little more diplomatic than that," I shouted. "Since I'm planning to contribute twenty-five dollars to the fund anyway, it all comes out evenly."

"Give the bitch your own goddamned money. I'm not moving my fat ass one step to hand that homophobic cunt a fucking penny."

"Can you get someone to turn down the music?" I asked.

Without turning away from me, Sarah stretched her hand back and flipped a switch on the wall. The music died completely, making the clatter and clicking of the machinery and computers seem that much louder.

"Thank you," I said. "I gather you're friends with the yoga teacher?"

"If that's your way of asking me if I'm a dyke, it's none of your goddamned business. I take her yoga class here, which sucks, by the way. She seemed so fucking proud of herself for having found someone who'd actually put up with her New Age energy bullshit, I figured I'd take up a collection. Plus her family is a bunch of ass-holes who disowned her."

A red light started flashing on a panel in front of her. "Crap," she said, and attended to what appeared to be a minor crisis involving wires and Ethernet cables. Her cell phone rang and without stopping what she was doing, she picked it up and cradled it against her shoulder. "Hi, Mommy," she said. "I can't talk now, I'm kinda busy. No, I brought my lunch today. Okay, I love you, too."

"Are you and your mother close?" I asked.

"She's my mommy, isn't she? And I'm not changing my mind about the fucking money, so there's no point in wasting more time."

The Wrong Things

In contrast to Lewis's office, Brandon's was one of the smallest and most exposed in the building. But if this bothered him, he gave no indication. I don't think he or his peers related to their physical surroundings the way I did. The most important space they inhabited was defined by their gadgets—laptops, phones, iPods, and tiny, ill-defined electronic devices they were always peering into. These small virtual worlds were where they held conversations, played games, read the news, and made social connections. The three-dimensional rooms that I considered reality were of less importance to them and were filled with inconveniences like traffic and weather.

When I walked into Brandon's office later that day, he greeted me in a friendly, enthusiastic way, but without looking up from his computer. I'd learned not to take this kind of behavior personally. I sat in front of his desk and looked around. His small space was cluttered with golf clubs, baseball caps, and a sprawl of magazines related to extreme sports, technology, and the electric guitar, which, as far as I knew, he didn't play. I knew I couldn't talk Brandon into staying by being direct, so I had decided to try to meet him on his own turf and see if it earned me some credibility.

"I need your help with something, Mr. Miller," I said, aiming for nonchalance and some of Lewis's jauntiness.

"That's what I'm here for," he said. "For now."

"I've been giving a lot of thought to golf."

"No kidding?" It was nice to see I could surprise him. "How come?"

"I don't know. Maybe I'm just looking for a form of exercise I can take with me into my final decades. I was hoping you would bring me down to your golf center one of these days. It's easiest going to a place like that when you're with someone who's familiar with it, don't you think?"

"Absolutely. And I would love to. I didn't figure you for the type, to be honest."

"I'm trying to change my type," I said. "Or maybe I'm not as predictable a type as you assume."

I noticed that he had a framed photo of his parents on his desk, both of them looking glamorous and windswept, seated on a bench

with a waterfall behind them, smiling at the camera in a proud be-
neficent way that made me certain it was Brandon who'd taken the
photo.

"You have very attractive parents," I said.

"Yeah, I got lucky in the looks department."

The stunning lack of humility made me want to take back the
compliment, but they were a good-looking trio.

"You must be very proud of them," I said.

He looked up, a little dumbfounded by the idea. "I'm not
ashamed of them, if that's what you mean. When do you want to
play golf?"

"Anytime that works for you. Make it during the day and we'll
take a long lunch."

He finished whatever it was he was doing on his computer, and
as if to challenge my assumptions about his relationship to the
physical world, rose up out of his chair and shut the door to his
office. I felt as if the two of us were sealed into a silent, cluttered
aquarium. He pulled a golf club out of his bag and began pacing,
using it as a cane of sorts.

"How often do you see Randy Trask?" he asked.

"Not very," I said. "Especially now that we're making real progress in his case."

"You'd never know you're making progress from the way he
talks about it. He wanders around the building all day, complaining
to people about this case. Complaining about you, if you want to
know the truth."

"I'm used to people complaining about me. It doesn't bother
me." This was a lie. It was especially bothersome to me that Randy
didn't understand I'd been working in his best interests all along.

Brandon turned his handsome face away from me. He had an
excellent profile, with a strong chin and a well-defined jaw line. I'd
begun to notice things like jaw lines and necks, brows and eyelids,
now that my own were beginning to sag and collapse. "I feel

weird saying this to you, Richard, since you're older than my father."

"That is an unpromising opening." Increasingly, people seemed to believe they were morally obliged to remind me of the fact that I was getting older.

"I think you're trying to change him or save him or something, and you'd be better off figuring out a way to get rid of him."

"You don't like him?"

"I don't care one way or the other. It's just that he's making people uncomfortable."

"I'll talk to him," I said. "Let me know about the golf school." I stood and handed him an envelope with twenty-five dollars in cash folded inside. "Do me a favor," I said, "and give this to Anne. Tell her it's from Sarah."

Surprised?

A few days later, I walked into our condo to find Conrad in the kitchen, kneeling on the counter and reorganizing the upper shelves. He had a mania for organization, tidiness, and prepared-ness, but he hadn't spent time in the kitchen in months, and there was something about his sudden decision to start housekeeping that infuriated me. Since my conversation with Doreen, almost everything he did infuriated me. A distraction, even an affair is one thing, but plans to change his life around? Infuriating. I always assumed that we had an agreement that our domestic ar-rangement was set, no matter how many problems and disap-pointments. Most infuriating of all was his apparent inability to see how angry I was.

He looked over his shoulder at me and gave me one of his sweet, closed-mouthed grins, adorable although increasingly age-inappropriate. He pushed his blond hair off his forehead with his wrist. "Surprised to see me here?" he asked.

"As far as I know," I said, "you still live here."

"I mean in the kitchen, sweetheart."

"It is a little out of character, isn't it?"

"Don't be silly. I'm a big fan of cleanliness."

"Yes, but that's not the same thing as being a fan of cleaning."

He chuckled at this, missing whatever nastiness I'd hoped to inject into the comment. I leaned against the doorway and studied his back as he reached up to a shelf. Conrad kept in shape casually by walking most places and doing a little ten-minute routine of calisthenics a couple times a week. He dismissed lifting weights and the other gym-related exercise I was addicted to as "unnatural" and thus unhealthy in an ill-defined way, something I'd begun to ponder seriously myself since Jerry's medical news.

Conrad's disapproval of "unnatural" activities did not extend, however, to cosmetic and chemical improvements; I was almost certain that he and Doreen had started visiting a dermatologist for injections to freeze or fill in their wrinkles, and I sometimes overheard him on the phone grilling friends about the details of their laser procedures or liposuction experiences.

I wasn't eager to know the whole truth, partly because I knew it would make me feel even more haggard. I had no principled objections to cosmetic adjustments, but I felt abandoned by friends who'd been surgically and chemically refreshed. The people who opted for surgery in its more extreme forms looked to me as if they belonged to a separate race. You could easily imagine them, with their similarly puffed lips, pulled eyes, and shiny, immobile foreheads lumped together in a separate chapter of an anthropology text, or about to step onto a spaceship to return to their native planet. Yet I couldn't help but wonder if they weren't having a more rollicking alien time in outer space than I was on planet Middle Aged.

A Little Talk

Conrad climbed down off the counter and pulled a carton of orange juice from the fridge. He shook it, and then, instead of pouring it out, stood holding it pressed against his chest. "Business is a little off," he said. "One big job we thought was a sure thing just canceled. It's beginning to make me nervous. I suppose I'm trying to keep busy."

"Everyone's a little skittish these days. The country's sliding, and what are we, sweetheart, once we're not the world's reigning economic superpower? Canada minus the clean water?"

He frowned. There was an element of ambiguity in Conrad's politics. He rarely discussed current affairs or political campaigns with me. I initially thought it was because it went without saying that we were on the same page on most issues, but that was no longer clear. He may have wanted to be an apolitical, bohemian artist, but he was increasingly in thrall to his Republican benefactors and the ease of their elaborate purchases and buffered lives. I suspected that by smiling benignly through their political diatribes over dinner, he'd become more sympathetic to their point of view.

He had on a dress shirt in an expensive shade of blue and a pair of wool slacks, the tightness of which was on the border between sexy and don't-bend-over. He looked at the floor and he said, "I think we should have a little talk."

We sat on opposite ends of the sofa in the living room, and he took off his shoes, put his feet in my lap, and leaned against the arm, surveying the room. Thanks to his work, he had temporary access to a lot of art and assorted *objets*. They came and went from our apartment, and given their high quality, I never complained about the comings and goings. But it was a little like living in a bed-and-breakfast—you were never sure what you'd be sitting opposite over coffee in the morning. I noticed a small painting on the wall behind him, a blue and green field of watery color that I'd never seen before, which is not to say it hadn't been hanging for a while.

"You brought some of those books up from the basement," he said.

"I did. I even started rereading them. I thought I knew them, but it's amazing how much more there is to learn from them than I realized. I put them all on the bottom shelves. I didn't think you'd mind."

"I'm adjusting," he said, and then fell silent.

The silence lasted a few minutes, and I said, "The little talk?"

"I know, but . . . it's not as easy as I thought it would be."

"You who have such strong verbal skills?"

He pulled his hair back with both hands and scowled. "You've been awfully testy lately."

"I was hoping you'd interpret it as caustic wit."

"Don't flatter yourself. It's very unbecoming."

At least he knows me well enough to aim for my vanity. "Would you like me to try and help you out?" I asked. "With the talk?"

"Well, yes."

"Let's see. It's obviously something of a serious nature. Work-related?"

He shrugged. "Not exactly."

"You're not asking me for another loan are you?"

"No. But I wish you didn't sound so appalled at the idea."

"There are a few things going on at work that are making me uneasy about finances," I said.

He tipped his head to one side, about as much sympathy as he was ready to offer. I always marvel at couples who have their finances commingled and sit around the dinner table discussing their investment plans. Then again, these days I marveled at couples who sat around the dinner table together, period.

"I'll take a wild guess, all right? I have a feeling this talk is somehow or other connected to Columbus."

Like most people whose secrets have been uncovered, he was more interested in the fact that he'd been found out than in the implications of the discovery. "Why would you say that?"

"I'm amazingly intuitive. On top of that, you've been hinting."

"Not intentionally."

"One never does it intentionally. Just a few breadcrumbs dropped along the path."

"And where do they lead?"

"Don't expect me to do all the work here, Conrad. You might start with a name."

"That's irrelevant."

I liked the sound of Irrelevant much better than the sound of Clarke. "Irrelevant, then. Undoubtedly not the first person you've encountered in your travels."

"Mostly, I'm busy on my travels. And I suspect you're not in a position to judge."

"I don't drop hints. I'm never late for dinner. And I've slept every night in our bed since you moved in."

"Now you're trying to make me feel guilty."

"I'm reminding myself of my own limited virtues."

He sprawled back with his head leaning against the arm of the sofa and his soft hair hanging down. His feet were still in my lap, and I liked that, even with the anger between us, we could still have some physical contact. I started massaging his instep, and in a slightly peevish way, he told me he was planning to spend some time out in Columbus. "I was going to pretend it was a business trip," he said, "but I want to be honest with you."

I hate when truthfulness is offered up as a sign of love and friendship, especially when it's truthfulness about betrayal. "I appreciate that," I said.

"There's some work involved, and besides, it's only for a few weeks."

"A few weeks?" This timeline was so unexpected, I felt my entire body stiffen. "You must be joking!"

"No, I'm not. That would be the outer limit, depending on how things go."

"It's out of the question," I said. "I'm supposed to sit around here like a fallback position, waiting to see how relevant Mr. Irrelevant turns out to be? Absolutely not. Call him up and tell him you've changed your mind."

"I think we need to have a little more discussion about this."

"I don't. If you want some privacy to make the call, I'll go for a walk. But it's best to get it over with."

Ben, I inappropriately thought, would be proud of me for taking such a firm stand.

A Huge Favor

I was so caught up in my anger, it took me a moment to realize the itch I felt on my leg was my cell phone vibrating in my pocket.

"I was just about to give up," Jerry said. "I called twice earlier."

"Are you sure? I didn't hear a thing."

"Maybe I dialed the wrong number. I'm all fucked up, Richard."

"What's going on?" Conrad had moved his leg and was now sitting upright at the far end of the sofa, his eyes focused on some undefined point in the distance. Probably figuring out how to describe the latest wrinkle to Irrelevant.

"I have a huge favor to ask," Jerry said. "I know it's a pain in the ass, but I'd really appreciate it if you could come out here tonight. I have to tell Janet about this surgery now, and I don't want to do it alone. She's been saying I'm not myself for weeks, and this afternoon she accused me of having an affair. Apparently, she's been obsessing over this for ages, which is why she's been acting so strange, which I thought was because she'd found out about the surgery."

"For Christ's sake, Jerry, that was the perfect opening to tell her the truth."

"Well, I didn't take it. Look, I know it's a rotten invitation, but I'm cooking, so the food will be good. And if it was going to be a rollicking good time, it wouldn't be called a favor, right?"

"Conrad and I were in the middle of a very testy conversation," I said. "This isn't the best moment."

"Bring him along. You know Janet is crazy about him. Seven-thirty all right?"

Tact

When we were halfway to Jerry and Janet's house, Conrad became restless and started complaining about the fact that he'd agreed to come.

"Heart surgery trumps infidelity," I said. "Besides, you were feeling guilty about Columbus so this will assuage your guilt."

"I suppose so," he said. "I didn't expect you to take it like that. I should have been more tactful."

"People always blame a reaction on the way they break news like this instead of on the news itself. It's the substance not the style that upsets me."

"I suppose I was being naive. I thought you'd understand."

I did understand, but clearly there was no advantage in admitting that.

Fatuous

I hadn't been to Janet and Jerry's house in well over a year, and I was surprised, as I often was when I pulled up in front, by how attractive it was. It was a New England farmhouse that had had a lot of wings and porches added over the years, destroying its architectural integrity, but adding to its rambling charm. It was painted in the classic style—white with green shutters—and looked as if it had been designed to be surrounded by piles of snow, as it was that night. Although their town was only fifteen miles west of the city, it felt as if we'd entered a different climate zone; snow was banked up on the sidewalks and blown in drifts against the house.

"Currier and Ives," Conrad said. He unbuckled his seat belt and looked out the passenger side window. "How many kids do they have?"

"Three. And the word is, they love you, so at least pretend you remember them."

The front door was opened by the eldest daughter, a seven-year-old named Elyse who carried herself with adult composure. She was dressed in a Christmas-y outfit of red velvet trimmed in white lace. Every time I saw Jerry's three daughters, they were dressed as if they'd just come back from a performance of *The Nutcracker*, which, given Janet's background in dance, was often the case. There seemed to be a lot of romping around in tights and princess outfits in that household, and I often wondered if Jerry didn't feel like an outsider in this kingdom of women walking *en pointe*.

Elyse had long, honey-blond hair, and tonight she had the flushed cheeks of a child who was either very happy or running a fever.

"You're looking all grown up," I said.

It's pretty much a given that you can compliment all children by assuring them they are not especially childlike. I wasn't entirely sure Elyse knew my name, so I wasn't about to hug her, but shaking hands with a girl in a red velvet dress seemed inappropriate, too, so we stood there at an awkward impasse. She did look adult, blocking the door like a sentinel and appearing to enjoy my discomfort. Conrad laid a hand on top of Elyse's head and said, "You're Elyse and I'm Conrad. We've met before."

"I remember you," she said. "You taught me how to play a folk song on the piano."

"I know. Are you still playing the piano?"

She shook her head from side to side violently, and her long hair swung around her face. "I'm playing the violin now."

I knelt down and looked her in the eyes. Perhaps if I won her over, I could introduce her to my nephew when he came to visit. It wasn't likely they'd hit it off, but they might learn something from each other. "In that case, maybe you can teach *him* how to play a song. And maybe, since we all know each other, you could let us in? It's cold out here."

She pulled the door open and in we went.

"That is a very pretty dress," I said, making another effort.

Elyse knew a consolation prize when she heard one, and stared at me warily. Without averting her eyes, she called for her mother.

"That didn't go over," Conrad said to me quietly. "Sounded a little fatuous."

"What does that mean?" Elyse asked.

From what I can tell, the chief distinguishing factor between children and adults is that children hear everything while appearing not to and adults hear nothing while pretending to listen.

Janet came into the entryway with another child in her arms. Irene, the youngest, I guessed, although all three girls were close in age and almost identical in appearance. Elyse attached herself to her mother's leg and Janet hobbled over to give me a perfunctory kiss and to hug Conrad with more genuine warmth. She did a little balancing act with the two children as she took our coats and draped them over a bench.

"Jerry's cooking," she said. She put the mystery child on the floor and gave the two girls a little push toward another room. "It's the first time he's been focused on anything around here in *weeks*. I'm glad you could come."

"It's our pleasure," I said. "We were arguing and didn't have any dinner plans, so it was a welcome invitation."

"Really?" Janet said. "Jerry told me he invited you weeks ago."

"I'm bad at remembering appointments."

She frowned at me. "I won't hold it against you for trying to back up his lie, Richard. It seems to be the main purpose of male friendships."

"Versus women's friendships," Conrad said amiably. "Which are all about discussing the lies the men in their lives tell them." There was nothing complimentary in this, but he'd delivered it in such an agreeable and benign way Janet appeared to be charmed. When you have a crush on someone, or God forbid, are in love with them, you're powerless to view their worst traits as anything other than indications of innocence and wit.

Janet had grown up in a Midwestern family with good bone structure and the remnants of industrialist money. Her parents, whom I'd once met, were a cheerful well-heeled couple who'd been supportive of Janet's dancing, her education, and her assorted eating disorders and physical complaints. They were supportive of her marriage to Jerry, too, but it had always been clear to Jerry that it wasn't the sort of match they'd intended for her.

I'm not sure why, but I had the feeling Janet's mother would have been happier and more comfortable having a son-in-law she found sexually attractive herself and could flirt with, and, perhaps more to the point, a son-in-law who flirted with her, especially an Episcopalian. Whether they approved of Jerry or not, they'd given Janet a significant chunk of money when she married. She and Jerry had used it for the down payment on their rambling farmhouse. Lincoln, the heavily wooded suburb where they lived, was lousy with rambling old farmhouses.

"Horrible winter, isn't it?" Janet said. "Just when I was getting used to global warming, we have a normal New England winter. I had to go out and buy the kids a lot of cold weather clothes. They haven't needed any for years now. Jerry doesn't even have gloves, but I figured he could buy his own."

Janet was beautiful in the self-possessed way of dancers. Having overcome body image and diet pill problems and then borne three children, she'd let herself get softer and more curvy. She carried the weight well, as if it were a hard-earned badge of courage. She had long, beautifully shaped legs that were still muscular. Her hair, which I was used to seeing in a little ballerina bun, was now cut into one of those *über*-practical styles that made her look like she belonged to a women's organic farming collective. She was barefoot. She'd developed a bitter edge over the years related to her disappointment at having given up on her career as a dancer—although dancing is one of those careers designed from day one to be given up on.

Cooking

Jerry was standing at the stove, doing something with a head of lettuce. The kitchen smelled of curry and butter. Jerry was a sloppy, adventurous cook who never used a recipe and always turned out delicious meals that were just a little too rich. He had on a dark shirt and greasy apron, but he kept wiping his hands on his jeans. The house did not feel particularly warm, but the top of his bald head was beaded with perspiration and unless it was my imagination, he looked more pale and exhausted than usual. The middle daughter, Felicity, was sitting on the counter, watching him with bemused adoration. She was too transfixed by the sight of her father even to glance in our direction when we came in.

"Greetings, boys," Jerry said, and gave Conrad a hug. "You smell good."

"That's an awfully intimate comment," Janet said. "I think we need wine. Although it's true, you do smell good, Conrad. Are you wearing something?"

"It feels like we're out in the country here," he said, accepting a glass of red wine. Conrad had an innate understanding of how to take compliments and gestures of generosity, as if he were being handed a well-deserved tip for services rendered, one that didn't need to be commented upon. "Food, children, snow on the ground."

"I take no credit for the snow," Jerry said.

"Oh, go ahead," Janet said. "Take credit for it. No one will hold it against you."

She poured herself a tumbler of wine and peered into the oven with indifference. When they'd bought the house, Janet had spent a small fortune redesigning the kitchen. It was an open space with gleaming oversized appliances that appeared to have been built for a restaurant. For years, Janet had been intensely interested in cookbooks, kitchen gadgetry, and learning how to make complicated French pastries, while subsisting mainly on celery sticks and fiber pills. According to Jerry, her academic interest in cooking had vanished completely as soon as she started eating.

Janet slammed the oven door closed and said, "Don't you even say hello to our guests, Lissy?"

This might have been a lesson in good manners, but it seemed related to the fact that the middle daughter was completely focused on Jerry and had been since birth. The little girl made a muffled grunt of refusal, shut her eyes, and shook her head.

"Well, in that case," Janet said, "go into the other room and play with your sisters."

She plucked Felicity from the counter and plopped her down on the floor. Felicity ran over to Jerry and hugged him, giving her mother a challenging look. There was no mistaking the fact that even at age five or six, Felicity knew that she and her mother were rivals.

"I have officially *had* it," Janet said. She pried Felicity off her husband's leg and carried her, screaming, down a hallway.

"This is all shaping up nicely," I said to Jerry.

"Just another day at the ranch. How did you get roped into this mission, Conrad?"

"Innocent bystander. I'm sorry to hear about the surgery."

"Well, I have a feeling having it done is going to be a lot easier than making the announcement. Which is why you're here. Richard's going to zero in on the right moment and drop the bomb into the conversation, since I don't have the courage to do it myself."

"Do I have a speaking role in this drama?" Conrad asked.

"You can improvise your own lines," I said.

"It's nice to see you're in bad moods, too," Jerry said. "It's best when the guests and the hosts are on the same wavelength."

Slapped in the Face

There were two loveseats in the living room, facing each other in front of a fireplace. Jerry and I sat in one, and Conrad and Janet in the one opposite. From somewhere down the hall, we could hear the giggling and squabbling of the children, but both parents did a good job of ignoring it while making allusive asides to each other.

"Sorry I forgot to light the fireplace before you got here," Jerry said.

"You must have been preoccupied," Janet said.

"There were a lot of preparations for the meal."

"Oh? Is that what it was?"

"If you think it was something else, just tell me."

"How about *you* tell *me*? Am I the only one who wants more wine?"

It was like being at a reading of opaque poetry at which the poet is performing for the listeners even though he knows they won't understand a word of it.

Jerry and Janet had always had a slyly affectionate relationship, which I admired. You'd catch them exchanging glances or reaching their hands across the sofa to establish physical contact. Like a lot of happy couples, they appeared to share a delicious secret.

To be fair, I didn't know many couples who were able to sustain their early affection. I knew of only one pair who maintained their glow, a lesbian couple I occasionally saw at fund-raisers for left-wing causes. They'd been together for twenty years, but seemed still to be connected by a wire of taut erotic dependency that had about it an unmistakable whiff of sadomasochism. They often appeared to be sending coded messages back and forth with the most subtle facial expressions or barely discernible hand gestures. Perhaps love and affection were best sustained when you'd negotiated a safe outlet for the inevitable desire to humiliate and punish the person you love.

After half an hour of desultory conversation, enlivened only by Conrad's description of the precise way the best Panama hats were made in Ecuador—a subject of great interest to Jerry, since he owned more than one—there was an awkward pause. I decided it was time to leap into the void; it seemed unlikely we'd be served dinner before the Big Subject had been broached.

But as I was opening my mouth, Jerry, who'd obviously caught wind of my intentions, interrupted and asked Conrad if he and I were making any plans for a summer vacation.

"Richard hates making plans," he said. "Especially since plane tickets are nonrefundable these days." By now Conrad had had a couple of glasses of wine. He was leaning back on the loveseat in a way that looked provocative and hostile. He was too polite to make scenes in public, but I could hear in his voice a desire to peck at me. "And he doesn't care much for my plans either."

"I haven't ruled out the possibility of visiting friends in Paris," I said.

"Oh really?" Conrad said. He turned toward Janet with inebriated defiance and added, "That's the first I've heard of it."

"Interesting," Janet said, in the least interested voice in the world.

"Janet's parents want us all to rent a place in the south of France this summer," Jerry said. "Big family gathering."

"It sounds wonderful," I said, even though I associate family vacations with sunburn, drunken arguments, and wet towels on the bathroom floor.

"It's out of the question," Janet said. "Since the dollar's worth so much less now, it's too expensive. On top of that, I can't take all the antipathy toward Americans wafting off Europeans these days. I don't want the kids to experience that. It's like getting slapped across the face ten times a day."

"We had no problems the last time we were in Italy," Jerry said.

"Our money was still worth something back then and we weren't total pariahs on the world stage and on top of all that you and I were getting along way back then, so everything bounced off us."

Seeing an opportunity, I said, "You haven't been getting along?"

Janet folded her arms. "Now what would possibly make you think that, Richard? Surely Jerry hasn't said anything to you?"

"We've had some discussions," I said.

"I imagine so," Janet said. She looked at Conrad, her chosen ally, a few inches from her on the loveseat. "I can see them at their gym discussing their adventures."

"I wouldn't call what we've been discussing recently 'adventures,'" I said.

"I'm trying to avoid using the word 'affairs,' which personally I find more threatening than 'adventures.' As for what you call your situation with your married friend, Richard, that's up to you."

I couldn't blame Jerry for having discussed Benjamin with Janet; you can't expect complete discretion when you discuss something with a married person since sooner or later they're bound to tell their spouse your secret in the hope of making themselves look better. I avoided making eye contact with Conrad, which would have been as good as an admission of guilt. A grinding silence went on a moment too long and finally I said:

"Look, we're here to talk about Jerry."

"Oh really? I thought you were here for a long-standing dinner engagement."

"The idea of the dinner is long standing," I said. "But it's true we didn't nail down the exact date until a couple of hours ago. Jerry asked me here because he wanted moral support for something he needs to discuss with you."

"Moral support? I didn't realize the affair was that far along, or that you're now an authority on morality, Richard. Well, if Jerry thinks he's going to leave me, he can think again. I'm not raising three kids on my own."

"Stop it," Jerry said. "You know me better than that."

"Jerry went for a physical recently . . ."

"I know that, Richard. You think I wouldn't?"

". . . and they found some problems they're going to have to address with surgery."

Janet looked at me and then at her husband. She put her glass down on the coffee table in front of her. "What is this, a joke? You went for the physical over a month ago."

"I've been waiting for the right moment to bring it up. It's not a big deal. Just a little heart thing that needs to be taken care of."

"What the *hell* is a 'little heart thing'?" Her face was beginning to get red from anger, and her mouth was slightly contorted.

"Now that we've got this out in the open, how about you and I discuss the details of it later, after dinner?"

"You actually think we're going to have dinner?" she said. "Are you joking? Jesus *Christ*, Jerry. You tell Richard about this and not me?" She started to cry and whatever she was saying became incomprehensible.

"I don't think that's the important point right now," I said.

"Shut up, Richard. It's none of your business."

Conrad put his arm around Janet. She was still crying a minute later when Felicity ran into the living room and leapt on her beloved father's lap.

"Why is she crying?" she asked.

"She's a little upset." Jerry squeezed her against his body and pulled her head to his shoulder, and he began weeping. "But everything is fine. Everything is absolutely fine."

Dinner?

When we left, it was snowing again. There was at least an inch of it piled up on my windshield, and I had to stand in the driveway, sweeping off the windows while Conrad stood by, stomping his feet and clapping his gloved hands. The exhaust pipe was spewing clouds of white into the cold air. Perhaps this was the last gasp of winter, the final storm in what had been a long and wet season.

"It's too bad about the meal," Conrad said.

"I know. It smelled good, didn't it?"

"Yes, it did. Is there anywhere to stop on the way home?"

"I'm sure we could find something. Are you hungry?"

"Yes, as a matter of fact, I'm ravenous." He moved closer to the car and began brushing off the passenger side of the windshield. "At least we won't run out of things to discuss over dinner."

"I don't know a lot of details about Jerry's health problems."

"That's not what I meant."

Poison

"So I have a question for you," I said to Benjamin.

He rolled onto his side and looked at me a little sadly. "Based on your tone, I have a feeling it's going to be embarrassing."

"The question isn't, but the answer might be."

"Well, go ahead and ask." He sat up in bed and pulled a pillow against his chest protectively, blocking from view a smattering of gray hairs that had come in during the few weeks since I'd last seen him. Despite a tendency toward being scatterbrained, I had an exact memory for the small details of his body; freckles, hair, blemishes. In several ways, I knew it better than my own. "I can't guarantee I'll answer," he said, pouting ruefully, like an adolescent.

We were both on extended lunch breaks and had arrived at the Club more than an hour earlier. We'd spent the preceding sixty minutes engaged in the kind of frantic sexual activity that's only possible between two people who see each other infrequently, at least one of whom believes that what he's doing is fundamentally wrong.

However shy, mild-mannered, and conservative Benjamin appeared on the surface, he was completely unhinged in bed. I'd never known anyone who rose to the same level of disinhibition so quickly, possibly because there was so little time for more gradual transitions and withholding. We might arrive at the Club, spend five minutes discussing a problem he was having at his office, and then I'd see a cloud pass over his face; his gaze and his coloring would change and all the controls of his carefully organized life would fall away. In the time it took him to drop to his knees, he became a completely different person—greedy, insatiable, and almost maniacally focused.

I'd come to the conclusion that he believed—each time we fucked—that if he let go completely, held back absolutely nothing, explored every repressed craving, he might finally get it all out of his system and no longer be troubled by the need for me or for men in general. What I saw as an act of erotic and sensual indulgence and an expression of affection he viewed as exorcism. I hoped the gratification I carefully planned and tried to provide for him would, on some level, make me indispensable to him; he hoped it would make me unnecessary.

It was a fairly common attitude among married men and religious fanatics, even if he manifested it in an unusually volatile and schizophrenic way. And yet, the greediness and go-for-broke attitude was irresistible to me. He was a prisoner being served his last meal, and I was the main course. While I had initially viewed this as Benjamin's chief attraction, I had realized during his weeks of withdrawal that the thing that I most looked forward to were the stray moments of tenderness and affectionate companionship that were possible between the two of us only in the spent aftermath of all the loud and rough sex.

"You haven't called me in weeks," I said. "You haven't answered any of my e-mails or messages. So what, all of sudden, made you agree to meet me today?"

He looked at me with sad resignation, his skin winter pale and a little damp with sweat. "I was afraid that's what you were going to ask. I had to come, if you must know."

"I must," I said. "Tell me more."

"As soon as I got your message that Conrad was out of town, I starting thinking about meeting you here. I couldn't turn it off. I wasn't getting anything done at work. I was snapping at clients and even at Giselle and the kids. It was like I had a poison I had to get out of my system."

When Benjamin tried to minimize his desires or rationalize his behavior, I saw him as pathetic and thought of his situation as hopeless. But when he admitted openly to his inability to control himself, I was swamped with fondness and wanted, more than ever, to protect him and help maintain the untenable balance of his life. Looking across the bed, I felt I would have done anything for him, met according to his erratic schedule, helped concoct whatever story he needed to maintain his deceptions. It was a stretch to interpret being associated with a "poison" that had to be purged from his system as a compliment, but since I was a part of the antidote as well, I was happy to take what I could get.

The early afternoon sun was blazing into the sliding doors to the balcony. At this stage of life, direct sunlight wasn't an ally, but there was something exciting about the combination of bare skin and unobstructed winter view—the slate sky, the jumbled angles of deconstructed Tuscany, the indistinct people down below who had more to do or less to do on this late-winter afternoon than Benjamin and me. I pulled him down on top of me and hugged his body to mine tightly. He looked handsome and weary, boyish and aging at the same time, even though, this close up, I couldn't make out his features very well. His waist was thicker than the last time we'd been together.

"I'm glad you didn't implode," I said. "I'd miss you terribly."

"I'd miss you, too," he said. "But let's not get sentimental. It'll make me feel worse."

At some point in my life, it would be nice to once again be in a relationship in which affection is shown openly and joyfully, without first calculating the repercussions; but since I had no immediate plans to acquire a pet, that point was probably far off.

"And you're really fine with Conrad leaving again?"

I had told Ben that Conrad had left for Columbus, but I hadn't dared to mention the circumstances surrounding his departure: the argument over Irrelevant and the way in which Janet's revelation of the existence of my own Insignificant Other had rolled over my objections to Conrad leaving. Conrad had been ready to abandon his trip, but in the face of this new information, he decided the sacrifice wasn't necessary. He had flown off three days earlier with an open ticket, supplied by the well-heeled Clarke. I hoped a good chunk of Clarke's money turned out to have been inherited; there's something infantilizing about trust funds and inherited wealth, no matter how desirable they are. Yes, Conrad admitted, it was a fling, but not necessarily more than that. He had business to do in Columbus, as well. No point in making more of a case out of the whole thing and getting melodramatic.

"Conrad and I are both investing in having a mature and sophisticated relationship," I said. Intellectually, it was true. "We're partners, but there's room to wander, too. Not perfect, but a design for living."

"I can tell that's a reference to something. Give me points for realizing it's supposed to mean something, even if I don't know what."

"Congratulations. It refers to Noel Coward. A British chain-smoker."

"Thank you. I've heard of him. 'Mad About the Girl.'"

"Close enough. Next thing you know, you'll be hanging out in piano bars singing Yip Harburg's greatest hits."

The central tragedy of Benjamin's coming out, if it ever occurred, would be hurting Giselle and the kids. In the wake of all that, there would probably be a bachelor pad and a lot of black towels and leather sectional sofas, and a sudden interest in house music and Ecstasy, things I was even less eager to witness.

I crushed his ribs in a bearish hug.

"Don't forget," I said, "people are more likely to leave a relationship when they feel confined and trapped."

"Oh really? Then why am I still married?"

"I'll tell you why, Ben. You like your life and you adore your kids and you love your wife despite the fact that she doesn't have a penis. The idea of crafting a whole new life is too daunting at this point. I feel the same way. Buying a new coffee maker and a mattress and box spring? Who can face that?" His skin felt warm against the whole length of my body, and I realized how much I'd once enjoyed this kind of intimacy with Conrad, and how much I missed it now. "I'm willing to let you disappear for as long as you like since I know it's the best way to keep you around."

"Probably true," he said. "But I thought we were talking about Conrad."

Disney

His cell phone started to chirp somewhere in the pile of clothes beside the bed. He leaned over and picked through his pockets until he'd located it. I could tell from the way his eyes widened when he saw the number that it was Giselle. He always looked like a chastened boy when his wife called, even when he was fully dressed. As he presented the facts, Giselle was dissatisfied with his level of success, despite the fact that his architectural firm was doing well. A workaholic, she was always encouraging him to be more aggressive in his professional life, and to make more money. Yes, she liked the idea of the income, but more success would give him the leeway to take more risks with his design.

Perhaps it was all her way of trying to help him out, or perhaps she had a frisson of suspicion and was trying to make sure Ben didn't stray. In many marriages I'd observed, there was an attempt by the wife to keep her husband in thrall to their domestic life by making him feel unmotivated and inadequate, the very feelings that make most men roam. It was learned behavior from countless television commercials in which dopey, distracted men are duped about their finances and their breakfast cereal by their wives and six-year-old kids.

He plugged in his headset and made a few adjustments to his hair. "What's up, my love?"

It was when Ben was on the phone with his family that he sounded most convincingly heterosexual. The terms of endearment he used for Giselle, even during periods when he claimed they weren't getting along, the loving tone he took with his cherished daughter, or the stern disciplinary attitude he had toward his son, all reassured me that what he and I did together didn't distract him from his other obligations. The incongruity between what we'd just done and "my love" stung me, though. But then, like any number of other major and minor inconsistencies throughout the day—the diet soda to wash down the chocolate cake, the lie about the report being finished, the long lunch that has nothing to do with lunch— the absurdity and unfairness of it began to fade.

He and Giselle were planning a two-week family trip to visit relatives in Florida and then Disneyworld at the end of the month, overruling Tyler's objections to the plan. I listened to his end of the conversation while they discussed hotels, keeping to my side of the bed and avoiding eye contact as an inadequate nod to discretion.

I had never asked Benjamin about his sex life with Giselle, and he had never volunteered much information. Nothing would have surprised me in the sex department, from active erotic experimentation to the desultory monthly fuck. I'd known bisexual married men who had both types of relationships with their wives, and in Ben's case, it was easiest not to know. I'd once had the audacity to give Benjamin advice on something he might try with Giselle, and later, he'd thanked me with typically guileless enthusiasm.

When he got off the phone, he complained about Tyler's attitude toward the upcoming trip.

"Why doesn't he want to go?" I asked.

"He *does* want to go. He just doesn't want to admit it. He likes to resist every suggestion I make. He thinks we're going because Kerry wants to go. He's somehow got it in his head that I care about Kerry more than him. That I'm more lenient with her, that I give her whatever she wants. I can't stop worrying that he has some intuition about all this." He cast his eyes around the bland studio apartment and the pile of clothes beside the bed.

In the past six months, his reports had made his relationship with Tyler sound increasingly fraught. No matter how much time I spent reassuring him that everything was fine, I'd begun to think that Tyler had in fact picked up on something different about his father, even if he couldn't yet articulate what it was. Perhaps he'd caught a wayward glance Ben had made at another man. Or perhaps, out of panic, Ben was physically retreating from his son as Tyler leaned into adolescence, and Tyler had felt the awkwardness. In a few years, Tyler would probably piece the information together and discuss it with a girlfriend as a way to exorcise his own fears about his father or him and to show how much he trusted her. As personal information goes, his father's bifurcated sexuality would become a marketable commodity, a line on Tyler's résumé that made him marginally more sympathetic and complex. If it made the girlfriend like him a little more, he'd start to appreciate Benjamin more. It would probably bring father and son closer.

"I thought things were better since you took him to the movies."

"That was weeks ago. Our friendship lasted about five days, which, you're right, is better than nothing. Do you have any more suggestions?" He was propped up on his elbow, looking at me sweetly.

"Why don't you give him the option of skipping Florida altogether. Tell him he can stay with your sister or some friend's family, if they'll take him. He'll choose to go, and then it will be his decision and he won't be able to take it out on you."

He touched my face with something like tenderness and paid me what parents seem to think is the highest compliment they can pay someone: "You would have made a good father. You don't ever regret not having kids?"

Undoubtedly, my life had less shape and structure as a result of being childless, but it was a price I was willing to pay. The world of parents was divided between those like Benjamin who, worries about Tyler notwithstanding, had unqualified love for their kids and saw childlessness as a disability, and those like my sister, Beth, who had ambivalent feelings about their offspring and therefore labeled childlessness as unmitigated selfishness. The glorification of reproduction was mainly capitalist propaganda. I could understand applauding procreation if the world had just emerged from a nuclear winter or if you were a member of a religious cult, but given the crowded planet and related environmental disasters, the mania for breeding was wasteful excess, like watering your lawn during a drought.

And yet, there were moments when I heard Benjamin talking to his kids or thought about my odd, endearing nephew that I felt the stirrings of disappointment.

"I told you I don't do regret," I said. "Especially about kids. I'm sure all of you will end up having a great time in Florida, no matter what it takes to get you there."

"It will take about five grand. We probably shouldn't be spending the money. The calls just haven't been coming in in the past few weeks."

"Something's brewing?" I asked.

"Yes," he said, as if he'd never heard the phrase before. "That's it *exactly*."

"Daddy"

He reached for his clothes a little wearily, and I saw on his thighs a web of fine stretch marks, like cracking on aging plaster. I found his lack of vanity around me more erotic than physical perfection. The more casual disregard he had for flaunting his hint of paunchiness, the greater number of stretch marks he fearlessly displayed, the more exciting I found him because of the trust and intimacy it symbolized.

On the whole, I found having sex with seasoned men (those who claimed thirty-five, a number that usually translates into mid-forties) more satisfying than with the enormous twenty-something crowd in student-heavy Boston. In between my abandonment of monogamy and meeting Ben, I'd wasted a considerable amount of time arranging meetings with men when Conrad was out of town. I'd been astonished to discover that it was far easier to attract the attention (for an hour or so; not bad, given the epidemic of ADD) of people half my age than of those who'd been born before the Reagan presidency. The former group seemed to crave aging men they could refer to as "daddy" or the even-less-likely "coach." The Internet had made it possible for them to explore their Oedipal fantasies without the embarrassment of having to be seen in public with an aging troll. I'd had to stop coloring my hair and start wearing boxer shorts and black socks in order to find sex partners. Unfortunately, the twenty-somethings tended to want to be driven places after having sex—being of the generation that had been spoiled by their parents hauling them around to soccer practice and clarinet lessons—or they insisted you meet them at "their place," which usually turned out to be a dormitory.

Again?

As Ben and I were going down in the elevator, I began to emerge from the artificial glow of the Club. The warmth of the overheated studio apartment, wasteful but comforting, was drained off my body by the cold of the afternoon as soon as we stepped outside. At street level, the expensive, surreal building down the street looked odd, but in a more ordinary and tasteless way than it did from the windows on the eighteenth floor. Ben, having had his last meal, had shifted his gaze to some work-related problem or to some self-flagellating regret that needed immediate attention, and I could tell that his mind had drifted far from me. I wanted to grab his arm and drag him back upstairs to bask for a while longer in the make-believe atmosphere of our sublet concrete aerie. The bubblegum smell of his cheap hair pomade had gotten onto my scarf, and for an indeterminate period of time, I'd have to content myself with that.

So I was surprised to get a call from him the next day in the middle of the afternoon. He sounded cheerful and calm, and thanked me for my suggestion about Tyler. He'd given his son the option of staying home instead of going to Florida and Tyler had dragged his feet, and then, as predicted, opted to go with the rest of the family.

"Giselle and I were so relieved, I can't even tell you."

"I hope you got the appropriate credit."

"I got credit, but it certainly wasn't appropriate that I did."

He'd called me on my cell phone, and although I was in my office, I had the door open. Anne was shuffling papers at her desk, no doubt overhearing me. It unnerved me that she seemed to know so much about me without my having told her anything. With her eerie combination of pitch-perfect intuition and detective skills, she probably knew who I was talking to, his address, and Social Security number.

Ben had a meeting late in the afternoon on the following day, he told me, and Giselle was taking the kids out for dinner.

"You're a bachelor," I said.

"Briefly. I thought maybe we could meet."

"Again? Twice in one week? Aren't you afraid that's pushing it?" In all the time I'd known him, I don't think I'd ever once been in his company after 5 P.M. and it was increasingly rare that we saw each other more than a couple of times a month.

"I thought we could do something crazy like go to a movie," he said.

I told him I'd think it over, panicked by the idea of this sudden intimacy, but knowing I wouldn't be able to resist it.

As Anne was leaving the office that afternoon, I asked her if she'd received the money from Sarah.

"Brandon handed me an envelope," she said. Since she hadn't complained about the wedding fund in days, I decided to interpret this as success.

Multiplex

The next day, Ben and I arranged to meet after work outside a movie theater not far from his office. I let him pick the movie and the time, and although it was a moronic-sounding thriller that didn't interest me in the least, I was excited, and I headed over as if we were on a first date. The idea of doing something as ordinary and public as attending a movie seemed more forbidden and kinky than putting him in a dog collar and strapping him to the bed.

The theater had opened within the last year, and was one of those incomprehensibly large downtown multiplexes, the lobby of which made you feel as if you'd stepped into a three-dimensional advertisement for exuberantly fizzing soft drinks or a video game that was impossible to win. We made our way up a network of escalators and finally found the tiny auditorium after first stepping into several other identical ones.

The movie was a sprawling music video kind of production with such short scenes and so many abrupt cuts it was hard to know if it had been filmed or merely spliced together from discarded frames of dozens of other movies. There were no real characters to speak of and a plot that was so complicated I gave up trying to follow it about a quarter of the way through. Every few minutes, a new international location was announced by text streaming across the bottom of the screen, but the locale hardly mattered since every brief scene was of the putative hero running through a similar-looking shadowy alley with an unnamed pursuer (who apparently had the same travel agent and vacation itinerary) chasing him.

I'd been pressing my knee against Ben's since the opening credits, and at one point, I leaned over and asked him if he was following any of it. "No, but the guy's cute," he said. I knew it was a big deal for him to say this openly at six o'clock at night, in an auditorium of people. I put my hand on his thigh, and he wound his fingers through mine, and I watched the rest of the carnage contentedly.

Test Drive

We decided to go for a drink. I suggested the lounge of a nearby hotel. I'm not much of a drinker, but hotel cocktail lounges instantly make me envious of alcoholics. They're always dark and filled with travelers blissed out on expense accounts and liberated from the constraints of their home addresses and mortgages. But halfway to the Copley Plaza, Ben asked me if we could go instead to "someplace gay."

I wasn't sure what was suddenly fueling his eagerness to indulge in another side of his character. Perhaps it was nothing more than a "now or never" sense of urgency and opportunity.

We changed course and made our way to the South End. It was one of the warmer nights of the winter so far, an indication that we were gradually slipping into another season. There was a thin fog that softened the streetlights, and a moist haze infused with the faint smell of melting snow and mud.

I took him to a neighborhood bar where Conrad and his cohorts often ended up on their way to or back from an opening. It was a quiet, unassuming place, and at that hour, there were only a handful of people sitting at the low round tables and sprawled on the leather couches, a mix of men and women, everyone's sexual preference hard to determine and, ultimately, unimportant. A decade earlier, the place would have been crawling with people at this hour, drinking and cruising. But since it was so much easier to lie about your age and physical assets online than in person, hardly anyone went to bars like this anymore.

As I watched Ben glancing around in a restless and anxious way, I had a sudden visceral understanding of how difficult his loneliness must be. There was all that pretending in his daily life, but even here, he couldn't be completely relaxed. It would be nice to think he was honest around me, but I had the sense that the meaning of this evening, the movie, the drink, the gay bar that was a vestige of another time, was that Ben was trying on an identity for a few hours, to see how it felt, the way you might test-drive a Honda. No wonder he had ulcers.

Not that I was in a position to judge, having hidden my relationship with Ben from Conrad all these years—but at least when Conrad found out about it, he hadn't discovered some shocking and hidden side of my identity that he'd never had cause to guess at. I put my arm over Ben's shoulder, as if we were just a couple of good friends, and asked him if it was okay for him, being here.

"Of course," he said, perhaps with too much enthusiasm and cheerfulness. "It's just another place with weak drinks and not enough light." A moment later he said, "You know what worries me the most? Trying to figure out what I'd do or say if Giselle ever asked me."

"We've gone over that," I said. "You might be surprised to know I've even got some suggestions written down. I can e-mail them to you."

"Suggestions. You mean lies."

"They're things you could say to make it possible to continue the life you both want to preserve."

"Lies."

"All right, if you insist."

As we were walking to his car in the fog, I told him, to assuage some of my own feeling of loneliness and imbalance, the rest of what had happened between Conrad and me the night of the dinner at Jerry's—the comment Janet had made, and how hearing it had made it impossible for me to stop him from going to Columbus. Ben listened carefully, looking straight ahead, and then pulled his striped prep school scarf around his neck.

"So what you're telling me," he said, after an unnervingly long pause, "is that Conrad knows about us."

"I wouldn't put it in those terms. As far as specifics go, he doesn't know anything he didn't know before the dinner."

"That's hairsplitting, Richard. He knows. That's the bottom line. I wish you'd told me before now. I never would have suggested we get together like this."

By then, we were standing beside his car in a garage beneath the city. Being in underground garages always makes me feel simultaneously protected and vulnerable, as if I'm in a secure bomb shelter that's about to collapse. I could see a child's knapsack in the rear seat of the car. "Like what?" I asked. "We went to a movie and had a drink."

"You know what I mean. It doesn't feel right to me."

"I had a nice evening, Ben. I thought you did, too."

"I did. But that just makes it worse."

I walked across the top of Beacon Hill and down one of the steep, narrow streets that lead to the flat near the river where I live.

It was dark and murky and it felt even warmer than it had earlier in the evening. Through the fog, I could see into the well-preserved townhouses in this wealthy section of my neighborhood, the rooms tidy and flatteringly lit. Lives often look ordered from a distance, but having consorted with Benjamin for so long, I knew that once you start to peer into the inner rooms, they get cluttered. Ben had test-driven the Honda and didn't much care for the ride. He was re-lieved, I realized, that I'd given him a good excuse for not buying it. Or maybe I'd given him the wrong answer when he asked what he should say to Giselle. Either way, I knew: I wouldn't be hearing from him for a long while.

A Whole Lot More Interesting

There were days when the impracticality of the design of the Connectrix building—the dizzying walkways and the winding staircases, the lack of privacy and the glare of sun through the skylights on summer afternoons—was disastrous, almost to the point of being laughable. But there were certain hours of the day when the big open spaces and the sparkle of lights could be breathtaking. There was something about the excessive beauty of it and the sheer extravagance that gave the enterprise of the company itself shape, importance, and even glamour. It was the exact opposite of the boringly functional buildings Ben's firm special-ized in designing, and overdone though our building was, it sometimes made me sad about the profitable trap Ben had cre-ated for himself.

It must have been in the architect's mind that this design resem-bled a model of the body, through whose transparent plastic skin you could see the blood flowing and the organs pumping. I could always tell the collective mood of the company a few minutes after walking in the door. When things were running smoothly, there was an atmosphere of jovial, almost celebratory conviviality. When a project proposal had been finished or a contract had been secured, word spread quickly and the walkways and staircases were filled with people flowing from one office to the next. The building became a productive hive.

By contrast, when I walked into the building from the gym one rainy afternoon a few days after my date with Ben, there was morose silence that hung in the air of the atrium. The walkways were empty, and there was a gray light filling up the space that seemed to come not from the glass roof and the rainy sky, but from an inner mood.

As I climbed the staircase up to my perch, I began to feel the pervasive gloom seeping into me. I'd been at the gym, and in an attempt to distract myself from the concerns I had about Ben and the fact that I hadn't heard from Conrad in three days, I had insisted that Walmi put me through a rigorous workout. He'd more or less risen to the occasion, but now I could feel the endorphin elation turning to exhaustion.

Anne was diligently tapping on her computer and barely acknowledged me as I walked past her.

"Quiet around here," I said.

"Really? I hadn't noticed." She pushed her big square glasses against her face and went back to whatever she was doing. "Cynthia needs me to finish something before I leave. One of the boys hurt his arm at soccer practice last night, and I have to take him for an X-ray. I'm heading out a little early. You don't mind?"

"Of course not. I hope he's all right." Her big eyes, wobbling and magnified behind her glasses, made me wish I didn't distrust her. The last I'd heard, her husband spent his days prostrate on the sofa, occasionally shuttling the kids to physical therapy or the emergency room. "Is your husband back at work?" I asked.

She scoffed at this without letting up her rapid typing. "The Slob hasn't been 'at work' in eight months. The last time I asked him to deal with something like this, he got lost on the way there."

"It must be tough living with someone you don't trust."

I'd meant it to sound empathic, but Anne's shoulders stiffened visibly.

"We're not 'living together,' Richard. It's a marriage. We're married. And, no, it isn't tough. I believe nothing he says and have to do everything myself. I always know exactly where I stand."

I again had the feeling she was referring to something in my personal life she had no reason to know about. As I turned from her desk, she told me that the complainant's lawyer in the Randy Trask case had called for me.

"Now that they've agreed to start negotiating," I said, "they think I should be on call all day. We'll let them wait until tomorrow."

"He called three times. He said it was urgent. My impression is that the situation is about to get a whole lot more interesting."

What's Going On

"You've heard what's going on, Richard," the lawyer stated, curt and unfriendly in the arrogant way of people who know they've got something on you and are in no mood for social skills or manners.

"I haven't heard anything," I said. "I just got back to the office a few minutes ago."

There was a pause on the other end, long enough to make me start to worry. "My client," he said, "was attacked outside his apartment building early this morning."

This produced what I assume was the desired effect: a shock to my system. I looked out to the atrium and managed a composed, "Attacked?"

"He was beaten up pretty badly."

"Is he all right?"

"He's in the hospital. I'm not sure 'all right' is an option at this point. What we're waiting to find out is how bad it is. He needed stitches on his ear. We're hoping it doesn't get much worse than that, but we don't know yet. They're trying to make sure he doesn't have a concussion."

I'd once had a chair thrown at me by a schizophrenic patient who went off his meds. He'd cracked two of my ribs, and on especially damp days I could still feel a ghostly soreness. But I was lucky in having had no corollary for that kind of behavior in the context of my daily life where anger was usually expressed as depression or passive-aggression. It didn't seem possible to me that a reasonably functional person I worked with would beat someone up that way. I looked through the glass wall of my office to the general vicinity of Randy's department.

"Did they catch the guy who did it?" I said.

"It happened in the alley behind the building, Richard. It was at an hour when most people are at work. It appears to have been planned. His wallet, with cash in it, was untouched, so we've ruled out the possibility of robbery. Hopefully, the security cameras caught something."

"Yes, hopefully. What hospital is he at?"

"I don't see how that's relevant."

"Naturally, we'll want to send flowers."

"At this point, I can't imagine he'd be happy to get flowers or hear from anyone associated in any way with Connectrix."

I was able to take some comfort in knowing that neither one of us was going to mention the obvious, and that the coded language of the business world married to the formal language of law assured discretion of the let's-not-state-the-obvious variety.

"Because of the lawsuit," I said, "I understand there are some bitter feelings. But with something like this, so sudden and random and unrelated, I want him to know we are behind him and rooting for him."

"You can use your own judgment, my friend. He's in the ER at Mass General. I doubt he'll be there overnight."

What's Going On (II)

"You've heard what's going on?" I asked Cynthia, not really doubting that she had.

She was sitting behind her desk, pulling on knee socks in preparation for putting on her high leather boots. It was a slow process she was performing with a degree of sensual intensity I found distracting. At the moment, she appeared to be caressing her small calves.

"I have," she said. "Assuming we're talking about the same thing."

"I assume we are. I can't imagine there's anything more interesting going on around here."

"Let's hope not," she said. She smoothed the sock against her right leg, admired it, and moved on to her left.

"Initial thoughts?" I asked.

"Horrifying. And yet, not surprising."

There was something irritating in the calm, disinterested way she was talking and in the fact that she seemed more concerned about her appearance, as if this matter was mine alone to deal with. "I'm curious about something. How did you hear about this before I did? Did Anne tell you?"

"That's the least of your worries, Richard."

"That's possible," I said, "but at the moment it's at the front of my mind."

"I heard. It might have been simpler just now to pretend I hadn't, but that seemed silly."

"I don't suppose anyone's talked to Randy directly," I said. "Judging from the quiet around here, the whole building has heard, so he probably knows anyway."

"Oh, I'm sure he knows." Her tone suggested she was taking a degree of pleasure in this. "But one thing's certain, he didn't hear about it here. He didn't come in today."

"He called in sick?"

"No. He didn't call in anything. He's been working on a project, and he's several days behind turning in his report, and he simply didn't show up this morning for an important meeting. I suppose he had other things to do. His supervisor called him to see what was up." Cynthia was finally satisfied with her knee socks, so she looked up at me. "Randy told her he has something bronchial."

"There's a lot of that going around," I said. "Half the staff has been coughing since January."

"I hadn't noticed. For everyone's sake, let's hope that's what it is."

I was mystified by Cynthia's attitude toward this and her sudden coldness toward me. Maybe she assumed there was some advantage for her in the whole mess.

"I find it pretty upsetting," I said, "that word of this leaked out to everyone. I've been working on the case, and I come in and find the whole company knows more about it than me. We ought to assume Randy's innocent until there's some evidence against him. How's he supposed to come back to work now?"

"What does any of that have to do with me, Richard? I'm not responsible for the fact that your personal life has you out of the office too much to control what's going on here. At the gym and whatever. And yes, Anne gossips, but you can't blame her for being upset after the way you handled that donation."

"That again? She wanted her twenty-five dollars back, and she got it. I thought I handled it rather well."

"She feels as if you paid her off to keep quiet. Which is basically what you did."

"I'm a little tired of her spreading gossip and rumors," I said. "Since this case involves an ongoing lawsuit, it could be grounds for disciplinary action."

At first, Cynthia appeared not to respond to this comment at all. But then she zipped up her boots, gave her legs one more approving glance, and turned to me with an icy, deliberate stare. "It's upsetting," she said. "Someone we know, or knew, even a little bit, was attacked and is in the hospital, and someone we know a whole lot better could, very possibly, be involved. It's so upsetting, that it's probably easiest to focus on a distraction rather than what was done and what role your inattention might have played in it. But if you're threatening that somehow or other you're going to take out your own anxieties on Anne, or use this as an excuse to punish her, I'm here to tell you you're making a big mistake."

"We'll see about that," I said.

At least I know where she stands. At least the gloves are off. At least I don't have to pretend to be interested in her plants and her feet anymore.

Sick Days

Randy answered his phone after a few rings, and to my surprise and relief, his voice had the phlegmy rumble of someone who's just finished wrestling with a coughing fit.

I told him I'd heard he was out sick and was checking up on him to find out how he was doing. He told me he found this odd, since no one had ever called to check up on him before when he'd been out sick.

"I was looking over your records," I said, "and it doesn't look like you've ever called in sick before."

"The records are wrong," he said. "I had my wisdom teeth pulled the first year I was at the company, and I was out for three days."

"I'll look again. When do you think you might be back?"

"When I'm feeling better? Since I have such an outstanding attendance record, Richard, I wouldn't think missing *one day* would be something HR would get involved in."

"Well, you're right, Randy," I said. "There is something else I wanted to talk with you about."

He snorted as if he was blowing his nose or laughing at me. "In other words," he said, "you're about to get to the real reason you called me."

He reacted to the news about the attack by not reacting at all and then, after a moment of heavy wheezing, said, "So am I supposed to pretend I'm sorry it happened?"

"Given the circumstances and the legal case, it might be better than pretending you're not. And by the way, you don't sound especially surprised."

"Why would I be surprised? The police have been here already. Lucky for me I was at the doctor when it happened."

"I'm sorry you're sick, but I'm glad it's confirmed you were at the doctor."

"Don't worry, they're checking it out. I'm sure the little shit is going to try and frame me, but fuck it."

Bridged

Although the winter had been longer and colder than in recent years, I hadn't heard massive complaints about the temperature and snow, largely, I suspected, because awareness that the planet was overheating and stifling in the waste products of mankind's excesses had spread to the general population. For once, there seemed to be a sigh of relief that there was an element of normalcy in the weather, even if it wasn't always pleasant to deal with. The only person who continued to complain about the snow and cold was my sister, Beth. Living in Buffalo, she had more justification than most, but when I'd called her to describe a new restaurant that had opened up in my neighborhood, she'd gone on at such length, I couldn't help but feel she must have been in the middle of a fight with her husband or a moment of midlife angst. When I told her I thought it was at least a good sign that we'd had a winter at all, given the crisis of the warming planet, she had scolded me for pessimism.

"You're so negative about everything, Richard. I feel bad enough about bringing two children into a dying world, don't try to make me feel worse."

As I was crossing the Longfellow Bridge back to Boston the evening after talking with Randy, I felt a current of mild air blowing in from a southerly direction and looked out along the river to see that all traces of ice had disappeared from the banks. I stopped in the very middle of the bridge and walked out on one of the stone galleries that hang out over the water. The sun in the west was a dark shade of red in the cobalt sky, igniting the low horizon and turning the river into a golden road leading to an undisclosed location. I leaned against the stone railing and looked at the water below, choppy and dark, and thought about all the mistakes I'd made with Randy, whether he truly had an alibi or not. I'd treated him more like a patient than an employee, and I'd failed to make him feel any better about himself.

It was a nicely flowing train of self-indulgent thought that led me back to Conrad and all the mistakes I'd made with my lover over the years. When he'd first moved in with me, reeling from being dumped by Mort, his beloved, aging meal ticket—the breakup being the first cold indication that he was aging out of a certain market—and I was reeling from the death of Sam, we'd often walked across the bridge at twilight in spring and summer and stood at this point catching a breeze and looking out at the setting sun. You could lean against one of the bridge's towers and gaze at the river without being seen by the cars going by on the road or the subway trains or the joggers and pedestrians passing on the sidewalk a few feet away. It had been easy and comfortable then to stand there with him pressed against me and my arms around him, and sometimes we'd talk, in that giddy way that people do when they first get together, about how lucky we'd been to have been on the ferry to Provincetown at the same time, and what a happy stroke of fate it was that he'd decided to leave a day sooner than he'd originally planned.

I turned and saw the building that housed the Club. It had been there rising up out of the buildings in Kendall Square back then as well, but of course it had been nothing to me but another undistinguished column of apartments scarring the landscape.

I'd been living on those feelings for a long time, associating Conrad with the mood of those early days, even though the reality had been different for many years. I'd thrown all my energy in the wrong direction, onto the distractions, like Ben and insignificant others, instead of into the main event in my life. With the warm air blowing in a new weather system, it seemed possible that I could redirect my attention, and start making up for lost time with Conrad. Or at least that I could throw some effort into trying it.

There's a category of powerful, successful middle-aged men who marry and divorce every few years, usually to increasingly younger women. I've always admired their ability to start all over with a new person and a heap of messy legal formalities. But it's probably easier to hurl yourself into a new relationship when you're expected to contribute only cash and can leave the exhausting business of learning your spouse's name to your lawyer. For those of us with less power and money, it's best to try to reinvigorate your old life.

In my turning-over-an-old-leaf mode, I phoned Doreen.

"Every time you call," she complained, "there's wind howling in the background. Do you get bored on your walk home and start dialing?"

"Not bored," I said. "Just curious about how things are working out with Conrad away."

"I have more free time. I'm trying to decide whether that's a good thing or not."

I asked her if she'd like to come to dinner the following Tuesday. "When I put my mind to it," I said, "I can be a good cook. I'm not sure if that matters to you, but it's true."

"It's preferable to being invited to dinner by a bad cook, if that's what you mean."

"I don't picture you being a big eater."

"I suspect we're evenly matched in that area. I'd be happy to come."

We arranged a time, and I mentioned that I hadn't had much communication with Conrad since he left. She offered nothing in return, so I was forced to ask, "Have you?"

"We talk daily about business. Less frequently about other things. But my suggestions in that area don't seem to have had much influence on you anyway."

"I tried to convince him not to go, but I ran into a few roadblocks," I said. "Maybe you and I could revisit the subject."

"I'll bring my appetite. More than that, I can't promise."

Off the Charts

Instead of going home, I went straight to the basement gym. I'd already spent an hour at my other gym earlier in the day, apparently a crucial hour, since that's when news about the attack had started to leak out. My worry about that misstep made me more anxious and therefore more eager to get on an exercise contraption where I could sweat out my anxiety and guilt.

Now that January was a distant memory and almost everyone's

New Year's resolutions had morphed into milkshakes, the dank basement was even emptier than usual. The color scheme of the place was your basic black on black with a bit of thick silver paint covering up the pipes and duct work, undoubtedly to hide the rust. At moments, I appreciated the grim practicality of the decor; the unpleasant appearance seemed to make all the exercise I did there somehow count for more, since fun obviously had nothing to do with it. But that night, I didn't feel much besides revulsion.

A spinning class was going on in the dark, unventilated corner exercise room, and even though it had begun ten minutes earlier, I sneaked into the back and started to pedal, more or less in time to the thumping house music the instructor was playing. The bass was so heavy that one of the tinted Plexiglas walls that separated the room from the rest of the gym appeared to be pulsing with every beat, sending shivers of light up the wall.

The teacher was sitting on her bike at the front of the class-room, her dark hair pulled into a ponytail at the top of her head. As she bounced up and down on her seat and called out supposedly en-couraging announcements ("C'mon you guys, don't pussy out on me!") her ponytail swung back and forth faster and faster. Although she was doing her best to be upbeat in her bubbly cheerleader way, there was an unmistakable undercurrent of despair in her voice. The ropy sinews of her biceps made her look like an underfed stray. Gazing into the mirror at the front of the room, I could see what she was seeing, and from this vantage point—from any vantage point, no doubt—it was discouraging: perhaps twenty-five people sweating and pumping, bobbing up and down, not in unison, not with any particular destination in mind or even a clear purpose. Mouths open, eyes drooping. Despite the loud nightclub-in-Ibiza music and the manic encouragement from the wired instructor, it was one of the most joyless groups of people I'd ever seen.

For some time, I'd thought of this crowd as my tribe. But in the past, if I'd meant it in a generally self-deprecating way, I'd also

seen the upside in it, the commitment to fitness and a concern for
health and all those other familiar euphemisms for an inability to
relax. The Intensifier, the ubiquitous fanatic I saw every time I came
here, was a few bikes down from me, standing and pedaling—
gasping, despite the vast amounts of time he invested in fitness. He
was the least pretty sight in a sea of desperation. But not quite the
least: the moment I stopped looking at him and caught a glimpse of
myself in the mirror was when I got a real shock. For years I had
been thinking of the Intensifier as the image of what Benjamin
might look like if he channeled all his repressed sexuality into exercise instead of me, but I'd missed the most obvious point, which
was, *of course*, that he and I could have been twins, except for the
fact that I was undoubtedly older.

I started up one of my imaginary conversations with him, telling him that for his own good, he really ought to get off the bike. *I
mean look at you. You don't look attractive, and you certainly don't look
healthy. What's the point? Isn't there something better you could be doing
with your time? What possible good is this doing anyone in the world?*

It didn't help a bit. I was gripped by a peculiar feeling of competition, almost as if I had to find out who was going to require
oxygen first, the Intensifier or me. I aimed for some middle
ground—slowing down, let's say—but that didn't blossom into
anything more promising than a desire to go faster.

The worst part of the class by far was the instructor's ritual of
standing at the door and complimenting each of us with a high-five
and a meaningless word of encouragement as we hobbled out. "Too
awesome!" "Looking great!" "Nice effort!" My consolation prize
was "Off the charts!" "What charts?" I wanted to ask her, but I was
too demoralized to bother, and I figured the answer wouldn't be
pleasing in any event.

I went into the locker room and took a shower in one of the
narrow stalls with a cold, tiled floor and moldy shower curtains. An
older man with slack buttocks and freckled arms was masturbating

with minimal success in the stall across from mine. Although the gym didn't have a reputation for attracting gay members, like all gyms, as far as I can tell, it did have a lot of this kind of pointless activity going on in the shower, activity that was sexual in the same way that chewing gum was food—not really. Whenever I saw it going on, I was reminded of a dog scratching its fleas. Two men drying off outside the masturbator's stall were ignoring him as they discussed an all-you-can-eat buffet at a steak house in the suburbs.

I stopped at the front desk on my way out. The clerk appeared to have been fitted into his red T-shirt many years earlier, when his body was a different size. He had muscular upper arms, but the rest of his torso looked as if it had been inflated with a bicycle pump, something I'd once seen Julia Child do to a duck in preparation for a French variation on a Peking recipe. His hair was absurdly dark.

"Something wrong?" he asked.

The main job of the staff at this gym was to field complaints about broken equipment, mildew, and assorted bad odors. They all seemed to have been trained to head off criticism by posing this question in a tone that silently added: "And if there *is* something wrong, it's your problem, not mine."

"I want to freeze my membership," I said.

He frowned. "You can do it tomorrow when the manager's here."

"You can't take care of it for me?" At the moment it seemed like an important step to take, and by tomorrow, I might have lost my resolve.

"I didn't say I can't, I was just giving you another *option*." He had one side of his ass on a stool, and he sighed himself off it. He bumped into his computer screen, and I saw he was looking at the job opportunities on Craigslist.

He found the form, filled in a couple of lines, and looked up at me critically. When you have the misfortune of unexpectedly seeing yourself as you are, you have no choice but to assume that everyone else does, too, and probably has for a long time. "You're freezing for health reasons, I assume."

"What are my other options?"

"Let's just put down health reasons, okay? No one's going to question that."

It was probably the easiest way to fill out the form and his comment had no deeper meaning. But in my current frame of mind, I couldn't help taking it personally.

Fish Stew

A few days later, Conrad called me. I was in our apartment, reclining on a black leather chaise longue Conrad had recently brought into the house. Upon freezing the basement gym membership, I'd started to spend a considerable amount of time in the evening in this piece of furniture after work, and was amazed to discover that something that appeared so austere—all steel and leather—could be so comfortable. I was reading the final pages of Trollope's monstrous *He Knew He Was Right*. One of the central characters is driven insane by jealousy over his wife's friendship with another man, and as I approached the tragic end, I was feeling virtuous about having avoided such a fate myself. I'd always assumed the gym calmed me down, but I was finding the chair and the book equally effective. I'd been falling into a similarly relaxed state more frequently in the past few days, despite the upsets at work and the disappearance of Ben. While I'd initially been horrified by what I feared was age-related slowing down, I had noticed that my whole body was freer than it had been in years of the aches, pulls, and pains I'd grown accustomed to, and had associated with fitness and good health.

"How are things going there?" Conrad asked.

He usually phrased this type of inquiry as "Everything all right there, I assume," as if he didn't want to be troubled by an answer, and so I was surprised by the open-ended nature of the question; it sounded as if he actually wanted to know.

"They're all right," I said. "Although things have taken a messy turn at work."

"Oh really? How so?"

"To have it make sense, I'd probably have to supply more background information than you'd care to hear," I told him.

"I have plenty of time," he said. "I'm cooking. And this recipe requires a ridiculous amount of prep work."

I readjusted the chair so my head was no longer lower than my feet and put the book on the floor. For someone with fluctuating self-esteem, I had never been especially insecure about myself sexually. It would have been nice if this translated into more generalized confidence, but I suppose if I'd had to choose one area of confidence, this would have been it anyway. So I was not especially troubled by the idea of Conrad romping around in someone else's bed. After mulling it over for a while, I decided it helped that the someone else was, apparently, quite rich. Although I didn't have massive experience to back it up, I believed that showy wealth and sexual prowess were incompatible, not counting a few pop singers here and there. I've always found vast bedrooms and fancy hotel suites, infinity swimming pools, and Egyptian cotton sheets to be anti-aphrodisiacal anyway—too obvious and insistently "sexy" to be arousing. And when someone's focus is on impressing you with material goods, how likely is it he'd go to the trouble of being attentive in bed?

Still, it galled me to think of Conrad standing in a gleaming and immaculate kitchen, preparing a meal for Clarke. I wasn't worried about competing with Clarke's dick, but I wasn't so sure about his six-burner range.

"What are we making?" I asked.

"A fish stew. It's not quite a bouillabaisse, but it has some of the same virtues. The problem is that you have to start off with a fairly complicated roux, and I ruined my first attempt."

"A roux? Really, sweetheart? Forgive me for pointing it out, but you haven't been doing a whole lot of cooking around here in the past few years."

"If it comes out well, I'll make it for you when I get back."

"I'll save my appetite. When will that be?"

"Oh, who knows? I just got here." Not quite true, but why quibble? "Tell me about the work crisis."

I filled him in on Randy Trask. He asked reasonable follow-up questions, even while doing what sounded like a lot of whisking and sautéing. The sizzle of food in fry pans and the clatter of the stove created a homey background noise, not unpleasant, even though it was someone else's home.

"I guess," he said, "it will be a simple matter of arresting this Sandy person once they've got the pictures on the tapes."

"Randy," I said. "And I'm afraid it isn't that simple. It turns out there were no security cameras and he supposedly has an alibi, but it's not clear about the exact time the attack took place. Randy's so disorganized and inconsistent, I can't imagine him planning anything like that. There have been a few break-ins in that neighborhood in the past couple weeks. The connection with Randy could be an unfortunate coincidence. He was back at work at the end of the week, and he did look a little sick."

Conrad sighed deeply upon hearing this. "You're so naive," he said. But his tone made it seem as if he found my naïveté more charming than frustrating. Similar to his taste in art, his assumptions about guilt and innocence tended to lean toward the safely obvious—guilty until proven innocent; motivation: insurance money; it's always the husband. "Be careful. You don't want to sacrifice your job to prove a point about a lunatic."

It was pleasantly incongruous that we were having one of the more civil conversations we'd had in a long time and that he was showing concern for me while he stood in a kitchen in Ohio preparing dinner for his rich paramour. But maybe there was something predictable in that; I'd failed at keeping him from his travel plans and he could therefore afford to be more generous.

"I'm having Doreen over for dinner next week," I told him.

"You've been seeing a lot of her, I gather."

"I wouldn't call one dinner a lot."

"Billy told me he bumped into you in the Square a while back and that you'd just come from her apartment. I was in town at the time."

"Ah. You didn't tell me you knew that."

"A lesser offense than not telling me you'd gone. You'd be surprised to learn how many of your supposed secrets I've known about for some time."

"Really?" I said. "You never mentioned anything."

"A snack now and then," he said. "It never spoiled your appetite for me, so why bring it up? Are you growing fond of Doreen?"

Benjamin a snack. That certainly was the way I'd thought about him, at least at the beginning. "I find her coolness sympathetic."

"I thought you might. It makes sense that the two of you connected, and it makes me feel a little easier about leaving town for a while."

Ah, Conrad, I thought. Pimping off his abandoned friends on each other in order to make himself feel less culpable. There was a sudden flurry of indistinct noise and Conrad got off the phone. A culinary crisis or the arrival of Clarke? I decided that it didn't matter.

I reclined my chair again and finished the novel. A few minutes later, I found myself feeling unaccountably full of melancholy and yearning, so I called my sister. Unfortunately, no one was home.

Sliced Open

One of the strange things I noticed about Jerry was that as the date of his surgery drew nearer, he began looking healthier and younger. Once Janet had been told, he started coming to the gym regularly, and was working out in an easy but determined way that I hadn't seen in years. I looked at him out of the corner of my eyes one afternoon as he was changing into his gym clothes. His skin had grown tauter and the curve at his belly had disappeared. Although he was by almost any standards—except his own—a handsome and attractive man, I had never felt a moment of attraction to Jerry. For all his comfort in discussing homosexuality, I don't think he had even a flicker of attraction to other men, and I've never been able to spark a sexual interest in anyone who has absolutely none toward me, straight men especially. Benjamin's public persona as heterosexual was infinitely less appealing to me than his private role of subservient geisha. I told Jerry that he was looking better than he had in years.

"The surgeon told me to lose ten pounds before I get sliced open," he said.

"Did he use the words 'sliced open'?"

"Well, no. But whenever they start flinging around the euphemisms they use for any of this, I hear the whine of a saw in the background."

"Whatever you're doing, you're looking good."

"You like this?" He ran his hand over his chest a few times, and I noticed that it was completely smooth. The balder Jerry got, the hairier the rest of his body became. It was something he frequently complained about. Now that he'd pointed out the smoothness of his chest, I was surprised I hadn't noticed it sooner.

"I thought they did that in the hospital," I said. "Right before they slice you open."

"I'm sure they would have, but Janet did this the other night.

She thought it would be good to get it out of the way. We both got turned on by it. Do you think that's weird?"

"No." But it was the kind of personal information that hovered on the edge of overshare. "It's probably a way of taking control of the situation," I said, trying to neuter the news and prevent further details. "Doing it yourselves instead of passively waiting for it to be done to you."

"I suppose that makes sense. It was fun, which isn't what I was expecting. All of this has brought us together more than I would have guessed."

In the past month or so, the gym had been losing members at a rate that was almost alarming. They hadn't yet started firing staff, but as I looked around, I saw a few attendants wiping down surfaces they'd wiped down five minutes earlier, or refolding one of the dozens of stacks of fluffy white towels, all in an attempt to appear relevant.

"You don't think this place is about to go belly-up, do you?" I asked.

Jerry glanced around. "It's a little last-flight-out, now that you mention it. But the whole country feels like that right now. I'd hate to die while this moron is running the country. That and wasting the last eight months on my gym membership."

Act III

"The funny part," Jerry said to me, "is that the whole experience has made me realize I've been worried about exactly the wrong things all along." We'd moved into the gym and he was standing on one of the elliptical cardio machines, sliding his feet back and forth. "One of the reasons I was afraid to tell Janet is that I thought she'd start seeing me as an old guy."

"And she assured you that isn't true?"

"No. She told me she'd always thought of me as an old guy and that was part of my appeal for her. And I'd rather not hear any analysis of that, if you don't mind. It's a huge weight off my back, a worry I wasn't even aware of having had is gone."

When my beloved Sam was dying, there had been a lot of moping and weeping around his bedside. At one point, he had whispered that as he saw it, he was merely leaving the play before the third act. "And everyone knows the third act is often the weakest part of the show, so I'm not especially sad about missing out on it."

It was typical of his generosity to make a statement like that, denying his own sadness and regrets to cheer up his friends in a small way. But the older I got, the more I appreciated the truth in what he'd said. I had no desire to slip out of the theater yet, but the third act was looking less and less inviting as the second drew to its conclusion. The trick would be to find the beauty in the otherwise unattractive aspects of aging. One of the reasons I would never seriously consider surgical renovations of my face is that I'd never find out what I would have looked like if I'd let nature take its course. Maybe this is just another form of vanity and self-absorption, but *at least it's inexpensive*. The trick was to talk yourself into believing that there was something appealing about the chin situation or the eyelid situation, the irritations of the professional life you'd chosen, and the less-than-ideal home life. Apparently, even the open heart situation had some pluses, and Jerry had managed to find them.

"The other strange thing, which I wouldn't tell anyone, is that even though I'd give one of my testicles to not have to go through this, I'm kind of looking forward to lying in bed for a while and having Janet and the girls take care of me."

"A common male fantasy."

"I'd appreciate it if you'd sit with Janet in the hospital during the surgery, Richard."

"Please, Jerry," I said. "It's not that I object, but Janet and I aren't all that close. We've pretty much established she doesn't like me all that much. Don't you think she'd rather have someone she's closer to?"

"I'm afraid she'll surround herself with her hysterical dancer friends and they'll make her miserable during the waiting. Sometimes when you're with someone you don't like all that much, you put on a good front—she won't let herself get weepy in front of you. That could end up helping her. Besides, since you stepped into the middle of it by telling her about the surgery, you're associated with it somehow. This will just round everything out."

"What can I say? I'd be honored."

Walmi Approves

Walmi had deepened his suntan, possibly to celebrate the approach of spring. Perhaps it was a simple matter of a tanning machine, but his skin was so smooth and firm, and the color of the tan so uniform, it looked as if he'd painted it on in layers. Undoubtedly one of those spraying techniques so much in vogue. As people demand less and less be done to their food chemically, they seem to be insisting that more chemicals be applied directly onto or into their bodies; painted tans, injected lips, pharmaceutically elongated eyelashes. In the sunlight streaming in the wall of windows in the workout room, Walmi appeared to be gleaming. Once I got past the artificiality of the "tan," it looked beautiful, like a fake flower you have to admire for how beautifully fake it is.

To develop my back, he was directing me in an exercise with dumbbells designed to simulate the mechanics of a rowing machine. Perhaps, I suggested, I should just use the rowing machine, which was designed to simulate actual rowing and would thus bring me one step closer to reality. What we were doing, he told me, was better. How so, I asked. The rowing machine, he reminded me, was designed to improve on the real thing by eliminating all unnecessary movements, and this was designed to improve on the machine. One more improvement and we could just do away with everything, I told him.

"This is not the usual speed you do things, Richard," he said. "What is the slowdown today?"

I set the dumbbell on the floor beside the bench. "I'm not sure," I said. "I'm making an effort not to push as hard as usual. I hope you don't mind."

He looked at me in his slow and methodical way with a gaze that was somewhere between suspicion and evaluation. As much as I respected his lackadaisical knowledge of musculature and movement, his sleepy gestures made it hard for me to take his opinions about exercise too seriously. I wasn't sure why, therefore, I had such a strong desire for his approval. Even after listening to the details of his insane relationship with Marco for many months, I wanted him to approve of my life and relationships. In both instances, I suspected that he had a deeper understanding of something than I did—probably spontaneity and passion. If I had his approval, I would be on the right path to attaining his attributes, even if not his physique.

"But this is what I have been trying to teach you all year!" he said. "Slow down. At this stage, what is the point? I'm happy it is sinking in, finally."

"I'm glad you approve," I said. "It means a lot to me."

"I can see it in your face." Having said this, he went to the mirror and studied his own hair, pulling at a few strands to make sure they were falling across his forehead the way he wanted. "You looked fuller. Puffy. Less tired. The wrinkles are filling in with fat."

Apparently, I had been on the wrong track to winning his ap-

proval, trying to prove to him that I was as vigorous as I'd been decades earlier when instead I should have been showing him how
much I'd slowed down.

"How did you get into this business, anyway, Walmi?" I asked. I
put the weights back in their cradles and stood beside him, both of
us gazing into the mirror and both of us, appropriately, admiring
him.

"What else would I be doing when I look like this?" he said. He
turned a little, modeling his appearance, but in a way that was
earned rather than an act of hollow narcissism.

"I see what you mean." His looks had sealed his fate. This job
confirmed his beauty. But it struck me as anomalous that someone
who took such meticulous care of his hair, skin, and musculature
would carry on a relationship with a violent substance abuser whose
actions might destroy the carefully preserved package at any
moment. But that was what great beauties always do, I suppose, so
it was his fate as well.

"You haven't mentioned Marco today," I said. "What's happening there?"

"I'm worried, so I don't want to talk about it. He has been very
sweet to me lately. He drives me to work every day this week. If I
find out he is fucking someone else, I will kill him."

"I'm sure it's not that," I said. "He'd have to be crazy to go
with someone else."

We caught each other's eyes in the mirror, and for the first time
I saw a glimmer of bemused understanding in his face, a small indication that he understood perfectly how silly and contradictory his
relationship seemed. But it lasted only a second, and then he said,
"I am having the baby sent up from Brazil this spring. He needs
me. His mother is drinking. I cannot have that. And I need him. It
will be good for the relationship. Marco will make a wonderful
father number two. He is very loving underneath, and the baby will
make him realize it. I will have a big party for the baby's arrival.

You will get an invitation. You and the friend you live with. You can be good role models for Marco and me."

For the first time, I was not insulted by this kind of comment from him, possibly because it seemed so completely unearned on my part. I couldn't imagine Conrad sitting around a house in Revere playing with Walmi's child, but at the moment, the idea of being there appealed to me a great deal.

"I would love to come," I said. "I've mentioned you and Marco to my partner for months now. He's very eager to meet you."

It was only later that I realized that the only time I'd referred to Walmi with Conrad, Conrad had made a disparaging comment about the whole industry of personal training, and that it was Benjamin who'd expressed an eagerness to meet him.

Lewis Disapproves

Men who are handsome in the virile way that my boss, Lewis, was handsome and who exude his air of friendly congeniality turn incredibly ugly when they suddenly drop the charm and good humor and get down to business. The big white teeth start to look dangerously sharp and the twinkling blue eyes pierce right through you.

"We're taking you off Randy Trask," Lewis said to me. For once, his gaze was directed at me from the outset, no diversionary glances over my shoulder. This, apparently, was the real him, and he had no need to look away for fear of being caught in a moment of bad acting.

The idea that Lewis was in here making out with a mistress or secretly drinking was absurd. The little office sealed off in its windowlessness from the rest of the building was where the true work of the company went on, and it was that that must be done in privacy.

"It's become way too complicated, and we're going to let our lawyer handle everything. In the meantime, you don't need to call his lawyer or ours anymore. And you don't need to talk to Randy, either. It's all being handled."

"For the record," I said, "Randy does appear to have been sick that day."

"I'm not disputing that, but it's being disputed. The immediate problem is that everyone got it in their heads that he was involved and now no one feels 'safe' around him anymore. When did safety become a guarantee, Richard? Isn't it obvious life isn't safe and never has been?"

Dead Zone

The meaningful portion of the conversation having been disposed of, his gaze drifted off to the ever-appealing dead zone over my right shoulder, and he mopped at his face with his hand.

"Richard, dude," he said. He wiped at his face again and then said, "What the hell is going on?"

Inappropriate as it was coming from his mouth, I was relieved to hear him say "dude," a signal that his fangs had temporarily been retracted.

"I'm not sure how you mean that," I said.

"The wide world, amigo. It's never been easy getting accounts. Okay, not true. It once was easy to get accounts. Everyone wanted a U.S. company like this on their side. It gave some crap start-up company somewhere in New Bedford or New Zealand a leg-up, a few bragging points to have us install their communications networks. We have a Cambridge address, so everyone assumes there's a pneumatic tube connecting us to Harvard and MIT. Now it's all a liability. How come? Japan is where it's happening now. My oldest wants to study in Japan so she can get a 'decent education.'"

He snorted loudly through his nose. I'd heard rumors of co-caine use, but he'd once told me he had nasal polyps and was put-ting off surgical removal due to fear of flesh-eating viruses and was thinking about going to Thailand where medical treatment was cheaper and more reliable. I had never discussed politics with him, but I saw encoded in his jovial condescension a libertarian streak.

Personally, I blamed George Bush for everything that had gone wrong in the universe over the past several years. His handling of Katrina, for example, had damaged global views of American know-how, skills, and efficiency, but while on the subject, why not blame him for the ferocity of the hurricane itself? It was his loud denial of climate change coming back to slap him in the face. The empire was collapsing.

"You can't be number one forever," I said.

"True, but some of us can't afford to be philosophical."

"How bad is it?"

He mulled this over in his distant, distracted way, as if he were trying to recall the batting average of a minor ballplayer. "We'll be making cuts. At some point, it's all going to turn around, but I don't see that happening in the immediate future."

"Care to be any more specific about the cuts?"

Lewis worked hard at maintaining the appearance that he didn't work at all. Perhaps the walls in his office were intended to keep his diligence a secret, not his distractions.

"If you're asking about your own position, champ, I wouldn't worry too much. There are a lot of peripheral things that are going to go by the wayside, that's mainly what I'm talking about. The yoga classes, the bicycles, the iPods."

"I see. Even though we know that's a lot of what keeps people on?"

"Two things to say there. One: They have fewer places to go get another job, so they're more likely to stay without the fucking free bike, and two: If they do go, all the better." He glanced around the office impatiently. "Cool shoes, by the way. Where do you buy something like that?"

I could recall at least six times that he'd complimented this very ordinary pair of shoes. "I'm not really sure. Buying them wasn't a memorable experience."

"I want to start getting trendy and metro. It just isn't happening for me."

I interpreted this piece of irrelevant information as a dismissal, and left his office.

Wants

Since I was usually the one avoiding Beth's calls, it was a lesson in humility to have to wait more than a week for her to return one of mine. When she finally did, the excuses she used to explain the delay sounded as if they were ones she'd learned from me: she was busy, work was stressful, there was a lot going on at home.

"I understand," I said. "I was just concerned when you didn't call back."

"Thanks for the concern," she said. "But don't get carried away."

"It's not urgent," I told her. "I was just wondering if you'd decided on the hotel. The sooner I book it, the more choice we'll have."

"What's with you, Richard? You haven't let up on me. I should be flattered, but it makes me nervous. It's so unlike you."

"I just want to get everything nailed down."

"But why? For twenty years you've been sidestepping coming out here or canceling plans at the last minute. And now all of a sudden I have to make hotel reservations months in advance. Is there something you're not telling me? You're not sick, are you?"

I heard several dogs yapping in the background, the high, insistent pleas of displaced vagrants. The racket made it feel as if we were in a busy restaurant and half of what I was saying was getting lost in the aural muck. It made talking easier somehow. I started telling her about my work problems and the potential catastrophes there, and then, without meaning to, I told her that things at home were getting confusing, too. Conrad was seeing someone else, and I had been seeing someone else but now that seemed to be over, and I'd had all these gym memberships, and my friend Jerry, did she remember my friend Jerry? I stopped talking when I realized the dogs had quieted down. On my end, there was one of those strange moments of early evening silence when the persistent din of traffic and the clatter of the city just stopped. I thought I could hear Beth's breathing, but I wasn't sure.

"Are you there?" I asked. "I'm sorry about the rant. I didn't mean to unload all that. Was it too much?"

"Oh, I don't know, Richard. Listening, I realized that I have a lot invested in thinking of you as the irritating brother whose life is all together. It's nice to imagine you as stable, especially when I'm not feeling so pulled together. It's a little like the way I enjoy reading about the weather in Argentina when it's two degrees here. It makes me feel a little shaky to learn you're such a big mess."

"Big mess might be a bit extreme."

"The affairs, the job, even the tone of your voice. To tell you the truth, it's a little overwhelming."

"I didn't mean to overwhelm."

"I think the worst of it is that in all that, the whole confession or whatever it was, you didn't once mention what you *want*. You were like that growing up. It was your way of hovering above everyone else, like you didn't have any real desires. You acted as if you were only concerned with everyone else. But really, I think it's that if you never say what you want, if you never figure out what you want, you never have to worry about being disappointed in not getting it."

She stopped talking and the dogs started barking. I could hear her daughter screaming and giggling in the background. It's such a burden, I realized, to have someone tell you what they really think, especially if it's about you and most especially if it's accurate. Except I wasn't sure she was entirely accurate. I had wanted things, and I'd always known what they were; but from an early age, I'd somehow understood that they were, by the standards of my family and measured against the expectations for boys in general, the wrong things. You start clamping down on a few urges here and there, and before you know it, your life is headed in a very different direction from the one you really want.

"I hope I've at least made it clear that I want you to come visit me."

"You have. But you haven't told me why."

"You're my sister. Do I have to have a reason? Let's say I want to be a more attentive uncle. You said yourself that Nicholas and I are a lot alike."

"If you really mean it and you aren't going to cancel, I'd love to. Nicholas has already picked the hotel he wants. It's the most expensive one."

"I've been making good money for a while now. I insist."

Indoor Golf

On the appointed day, Brandon and I took the subway halfway to his golf school. I convinced him to walk the rest, arguing that it would be a little like golfing, forgetting that no one walked on golf courses anymore. It was one of those days that seemed to shift from unseasonably warm to unseasonably cold at whim. Brandon was in a jersey while I was still bundled up in winter attire, and both of us looked inappropriate. Walking along the streets of downtown Boston, I found it almost impossible not to feel belittled by Brandon. I've always considered myself of moderate height, but due to a disturbing shift in the American diet, an evolutionary trend, or some environmental breakdown involving solar rays and ozone layers, six feet was becoming the norm. Brandon's rangy six foot five was barely sufficient to attract the attention of a basketball coach. I insisted upon striding along at a ridiculously brisk pace to give the impression of vigor and masculine confidence. It pleased me that Brandon had trouble keeping up, despite his enormous legs and his youth. He hadn't brought his own clubs today, preferring to use the golf center's, he reported, to even the playing field with me. Maybe he was, after all, a gentleman.

This particular golf temple was housed in a former movie theater. Like so many things I'd grown up with—landlines, record players, *Playboy* magazine—movie theaters with large auditoriums were beginning to have a feeling of quaint irrelevance, appearing to be a vestige of another time, now that everyone was watching movies on the two-inch screens of their iPods. This place was located on the edge of an old Boston neighborhood with dark, narrow streets that had once been a hub for sailors and streetwalkers, the latter being another cultural artifact. The theater had been built at a particularly gaudy moment in the 1970s and like much of the architecture of that period, it looked as if it had been designed to age quickly and spectacularly. The lobby was a time capsule of scratched and unwashable glass walls, clunky tubular gilt railings, molded plastic seats, and golden frames on the walls that advertised nothing.

"I like it already," I told Brandon. If something's going to look bad, it's best that it look really bad.

"Just wait. I booked us for two hours, but don't feel bad if you get bored before it's up."

In the converted auditorium, netting was draped from on

high, and the gently raked floor was covered in green carpeting that bore a vague resemblance to artificial grass. The place was doing a thriving business with groups of loud co-workers standing at the tees and whacking balls into the netting with an earnest effort I found a little incongruous, given the venue. Since joining the business world, I'd been able to spot co-workers from a mile off. They always treated each other with a combination of intimacy and distrust, a little like the way you treat a seatmate on a long flight.

"Kind of like a driving range," I said to Brandon, proud at having dredged this term out of some locked vault in my brain.

"This is only for starters. The real fun goes on in the back room."

"I've always found that to be so."

"We'll begin here, practice some, and then go back."

If Brandon maintained an air of bewildered engagement at the office, here he appeared to have come into his element. I was touched by his eagerness to set me up with the right clubs, to make sure I was comfortable, and, in general, to show me the ropes. It became clear to me that any antagonism was my own, and that his goal was just to have a good time and share his enthusiasm.

After taking a few humiliatingly misplaced swings, I discovered I could hit the ball effectively if I followed Brandon's instruction, and even more surprisingly, that there was something satisfying in the physical contortion required—a spinal twist, yoga without the spiritual claptrap—and in the sensation and sound of the driver making contact. It was all about letting loose your aggressions in a calculated way and then watching the effects on a helpless little ball, which perhaps explains the popularity of the sport among Republicans.

"I have to be honest," Brandon said. "I expected you to be much worse."

"I'm going to take that as a compliment. You're a born teacher. It's why you've been so successful at Connectrix. And it's one of the reasons you should stay."

"Ah come on," he said. "We're having a nice time. Let's not get into that."

The Back Room

At some point in its life cycle, the theater appeared to have been used for live performances. We made our way through a door and along a narrow passage into the space that had been the back of the stage. The lights were low, and compared with the front of the house, it had a hushed, almost reverential atmosphere. Black curtains had been used to divide the space into a dozen or so little carrels.

"This is for the serious golfers," Brandon explained. "You can play on some of the world's best courses here."

"Really."

There were screens in front of the driving pods, and projected onto these were scenic vistas of famous golf courses from all over the globe. You could change course midstream, an unlimited number of times if the mood struck you. With his hostlike generosity, Brandon let me choose the course. I went for something in Scotland, figuring the virtual climate there would be more to my liking than Palm Springs or some similarly overheated setting.

The whole thing seemed silly to me, especially since Brandon, and everyone else in the place, was taking it all so seriously. Or maybe my notions of the difference between what was real and what was pretend were skewed and out of date; increasingly, this *was* the real world, these images projected onto a screen with a computer in the background somewhere calibrating the ball's speed and progress. While there were a few women scattered around, the crowd was overwhelmingly male. There were sounds of good-natured jocularity in the air, but on the whole, there was something so earnest in the rapt attention of the "golfers" and such a complete lack of irony about the whole venture, I felt it was one of the most utterly hetero-sexual environments I'd been in, in a long time. How different the whole place would have felt, for example, if "the boys" were hacking their way through a golf course in one of the little carrels.

A few minutes after piecing together this observation, I heard a familiar voice, and looked down to the far end of the back room to see Benjamin standing with a group of men, golf club in his hand. He had on a light green jersey and a pair of ridiculous brown and white golf shoes. His demeanor was so different in this setting, among his friends, that I realized I had never seen him in the con-text of his own world before, surrounded by the trappings of the life I'd invested so much time pretending I was helping to preserve. It had been a couple of weeks since we'd gone to the movies to-gether, and I hadn't heard from him since. I felt a sharp stab of desire, an urge to push him behind one of the curtains and make out with him, followed by a fantasy of whacking him with a golf club.

"You've lost your concentration," Brandon said. "You're six above par on this hole already."

I didn't think that Ben had seen me, but I couldn't be sure. He'd obviously had his hair cut, and far from looking out of place in this sunless little world, he looked surprisingly, annoyingly, in his element. He fit in convincingly with his friends as he leaned on his club and joshed with his pals. I flashed on some of the more lurid things I'd done with him at the Club over the years and found myself feeling confused, perhaps in the same way that he was con-fused. Was that the real Benjamin, or was this? In the midst of the confusion, I felt myself growing possessive of him, wanting to rush over to his friends and tell them that however well they thought they knew him, I knew him better.

"Sorry," I said to Brandon. "I got a little distracted. I think I recognized someone I know." I motioned toward Ben's little group. "The guy in the green shirt. Recognize him?"

Brandon studied Ben for a moment and said, "Looks familiar. But corporate guys all look pretty much alike to me. I figure it's one of the reasons I have to get out now, before I look the same as those guys do."

"He's an architect," I said. "Not exactly corporate."

The distinction was insignificant to Brandon, and as the two of us looked over at the group, Ben turned and saw me. I smiled at him, gave a discreet wave. He nodded in my direction, but that was as far as he'd go. In all the years we'd known each other, we'd never discussed how we'd behave if we saw each other in public. Maybe I should have ignored him.

"What's the connection?" Brandon asked.

"Just a friend."

"You're all red."

"It must be the excitement of the golf."

So these were Benjamin's friends. A ragtag collection of uninteresting people. Identical to one another, as Brandon had pointed out. Why did he bother with them? As a cover? The wife and children were not enough? In the time I'd known Ben, he'd been devouring histories and vast biographies of political figures from around the globe. His main interest seemed to be discovering their hidden flaws, and he'd become the world's leading expert on the buried sex lives of virtually every political dynasty in history. Most of them—in his reading, anyway—involved homosexuality. Looked at from Ben's perspective, the history of the civilized world was a record of mistakes leading to downfalls, most related in some way or other to bad decisions made under the influence of lust for a moderately attractive, intellectually inferior other. What did this group of bloated middle-aged men know of Ben's reading or his prurient interests? And why did the half-assed little nod he'd made in my direction make me feel I'd been exiled to a leper colony?

I threw most of my anger and resentment into the golf game, a tactic that proved surprisingly successful at bringing down my score. Brandon was delighted at first, but then discouraged.

"I never much liked this course," he said on the fourth hole. "Mind if we switch? There's a great course in Bermuda I think you'd like."

"Go right ahead," I said. "Is this how you'll be spending your free time once you get to Nevada?"

"Whatever time I spend golfing out there won't be spent in a converted movie theater, I promise you that. And don't try to make me feel bad about the move, Richard. I can tell from the tone in your voice that there's still some resentment there."

"There's no resentment. But aren't you at least a little flattered by the fact that Lewis and everyone else want to keep you on? If it were me, that alone would give me pause about burning bridges."

He looked at me with a knowing, almost surly grin I'd never seen before. "Let's not joke around, all right? We both know why Lewis wants to keep me on. It's the opposite of flattering. You think I don't know why I was hired? Give me a little credit, Richard. My parents will be pissed off for a while, but the way I see it, I'm doing them a big favor. I'm sparing them from one more kiss-ass who's trying to use me to get on their coattails."

The last thing I was expecting was for Brandon to turn self-aware. I started babbling something to try to cover up the role his parents had played in his hiring, but attempting to do so seemed insulting to Brandon, and like all such efforts it was doomed to fail.

I did find the Bermuda golf course appealing. It was less challenging than Scotland, and with the azure ocean in the background, I felt myself unwinding, as if this change from one imaginary place to another mattered. Then again, everything mattered here in unexpected ways. I was playing an imaginary game in an imaginary place while my imaginary paramour was a few bays away playing with his imaginary friends, who imagined him to be someone completely other than who he was.

A few minutes later, Brandon leaned on his club and said, "So tell me something, Richard, that friend in the green shirt—is he a friend with benefits?" He said this with a grin that was self-satisfied, but lacking in malice.

Pretty much my entire relationship with Ben had taken place in the anonymous confines of the Club, and I never expected that anyone in my daily life would have cause to see me with him. I'd invested so many hours in thinking up excuses for Benjamin, should he be asked something, I hadn't had time to think about answering questions that might be asked of me. Jerry was the only person I'd told, but he'd never set eyes on Ben, of course. "Why would you say that?" I asked Brandon.

"People talk about your long lunches. I guess I can tell you that since I'm leaving."

"I spend a lot of time at the gym."

"Whatever you say."

But as soon as he relented, I felt as if I'd lost an opportunity to make my relationship with Benjamin the slightest bit more real. I was committed to protecting Ben, but surely I had some rights to claim something for myself.

"Actually," I said, "he is a friend . . . with benefits."

Brandon glanced back toward Ben and shrugged. "You could probably do better."

Nice Meeting You Here

We both agreed, after the ninth hole, to call it quits, and I excused myself to go to the men's room. I walked past Ben's group, stopped, and stuck out my hand. Ben was forced to shake it. A ridiculously formal and polite gesture.

"Nice seeing you here, Mr. Lamartine," I said, enjoying for a moment that I was making him uncomfortable.

As soon as I got into the bathroom—more lurid 1970s appeal, including enough urinals to satisfy the needs of an entire auditorium of moviegoers—I realized I'd only come in the hope that Ben would follow me. I was washing my hands and giving up on that hope when I looked into the mirror and saw him enter. He cast a furtive glance around the room and gave me one of his broad, cheerful smiles. "The coast is clear," I told him. I saw in his smile the sweetness I'd always admired in him, and in his hesitation some of his awful loneliness. Someone else, I realized, was going to have to be angry at and disapproving of him. I wasn't up to the task.

"What the fuck are *you* doing here?" he asked, amused, despite everything.

"Golfing," I said. "And I'm better than you might think."

"This is the last place I expected I'd ever see you."

"Thought you were safe, eh?"

We were standing at the sinks facing each other, and I suddenly found the ridiculous golf shirt and even the awful shoes boyishly attractive. I also saw in his pretty eyes what I took to be a glimmer of genuine affection for me. Perhaps it was even more than that. Without thinking about it, I grabbed him behind the neck, pulled him to me, and kissed his mouth. His body went slack in the satisfying way it so often did. I could smell his familiar sweat, his bubblegum hair goop, his laundry detergent.

The outer door to the bathroom squeaked and we had just enough time to part before the inner door opened. We were standing at the sinks with the unmistakable look of guilt, our bodies automatically shifting with awkward and unconvincing movements. It was not, apparently, anyone Benjamin knew. I laughed a little and Benjamin gave me a harsh, disapproving look in the mirror and stormed out.

Ugly

As soon as I heard the outer door bang behind him, I followed, and in the dark little hallway outside the bathrooms, I said, "I wish you hadn't walked away from me like that. It's rude."

He glared at me with a toughness I'd never before seen on his face. "You wish I hadn't walked away? Really? Well, I wish you hadn't done that to me. In public. What if that had been someone I know, one of my friends?"

"Is that what you call them? They don't even know you."

"Don't get ugly, Richard."

He started to walk away from me again, as he had minutes before and as he had been doing, in essence, for all the years I'd known him. Infuriated, I grabbed his arm and dragged him toward an emergency exit. If he'd wanted to break free, no doubt he could have easily enough. While much of our sexual relationship had been based on my dominance of him, he was at least my match in strength. Outside, I angrily pinned him against the side of the building, my hands on his shoulders.

"You've been avoiding me for weeks," I said. "You heard Conrad was out of town and so you came over and got off, you made a big show of going to the movies with me, and then you did another of your disappearing acts."

"Stop it. We don't have any obligation to each other, and you know it. That's always been the deal."

"I'm getting sick of the deal. Especially since you don't seem to feel an obligation to simple decency and friendship."

"Don't say that. You're the best friend I've ever had."

"I find that pathetic. What does it mean that you can't even shake your best friend's hand in public without blanching?"

"You weren't shaking my hand in the bathroom."

Since he had on his ridiculous jersey, I could see that he was getting cold, and despite being angry at him, I wished I had a sweater or a muffler I could give him. I wished I had a stronger will and the ability to sustain my anger without these inconvenient interruptions of tenderness.

"You haven't been paying attention to Conrad," he said. "You've been letting him slip away from you, and I don't want to be responsible for that. It's the same as you not wanting to fuck up my marriage. Why do you have such a hard time believing that?"

"Because it's not honest. You're just panicking about your own life again and using Conrad as a convenient excuse. You're so used to hiding things from people, you don't even know what you're feeling yourself."

"As if you're so in touch with yourself," he said. "As if you're so much better than me just because your wife is another man. After all the time we've known each other, I'm happy to finally hear what you think of me. You should have gotten it off your chest sooner. You would have felt better."

I still had him pinned against the wall, and there was an element of seduction in all of this, almost as if we were playing out a variation of our roles at the Club.

"It's been a difficult week," I said. "I'm sorry if I wished I could have seen you for an hour in there somewhere."

"I'm leaving for Florida in ten days. I have to get the kids ready. I have to settle everything at the office before I go. You have no idea what's involved, how complicated it gets. I thought you understood that that has to be my priority."

"Oh, stop it," I said. "Of course I understand. But can't you even send a text message. 'Hello, goodbye.' I'm that insignificant?"

"You're not insignificant to me and you know that. I wish you were; all of this would be so much easier, wouldn't it?"

"I'm sick of everyone putting such a high value on easy. What's so terrible about complicated?"

"I'm freezing," he said. "I'm confused and unhappy and now I'm freezing. I have to go off to Florida and be a good father and a good husband—something I vowed to do a long time ago, by the way. How can I do that when there's this other side of my life here, waiting to explode, mattering too much to me? Please, let's just call it quits, once and for all. Help me with this, Richard. You've always helped me. I tried, okay? We went out. I can't do it. Let's call it all off. Please. Help me with this."

It was strange to hear him pleading with me for the end of our relationship in a tone of voice that was identical to the one he used to beg for sexual favors and erotic requests.

"What's the point, Ben? We both know we'll be right back where we were in a few weeks. You can't just turn it off. It isn't like that. You'll call me or you'll call someone you care less about and he'll make you feel even more rotten."

"Maybe this time I won't. Or maybe if I do call you, you'll do the decent thing and refuse me."

The sun had disappeared, and the gray afternoon felt like winter again, as if it was about to snow. It had been a couple of weeks since I'd seen Ben and in the gray light, his face looked ravaged, his skin mottled in a way I hadn't noticed before, and his eyes weary. He'd been wrestling with himself since we'd last met.

- *At least we're not in love.*

"You're starting to shiver," I said.

- *I might be in love with him, but at least I've never told him how I feel.*

"I suppose it would help," I said, "if I just dropped the lease on the Club."

He looked at me sadly, now that there was apparently nothing more to argue about.

"It would make getting together a lot tougher." He reached into the pocket of his pants and pulled out his set of keys for the Club, attached to an unlabeled plastic tag.

- *At least he carries the keys with him.*

"It's the only set I have."

I took the keys and reached up to cup his face in my hands. One of the keys scratched him and left a faint red line along his cheek.

"If I never told you how I really feel about you," I said, "it's only because I didn't want to hurt your feelings, I didn't want to worry you and upset you. But if we're ending this, it doesn't matter anymore. I might as well get it off my chest, like you said. I think about you all the time. I have since five minutes after we met. You're impossible to deal with, and I've spent as much time being pissed off at you as anything else, and I'm sorry if this is a big betrayal, but I love you. I'll get over it eventually, I promise, but that's how I feel. And please don't say anything right now."

He didn't look at me, a small favor I was happy for.

"Have you finished your game in there?" I asked.

"Oh, shit. No. They probably wonder where I went to."

"Don't worry," I said. "Whatever they think, at least they won't guess this."

I tossed his set of keys into the Dumpster across from us.

- *I told him how I felt about him, but at least we officially ended things.*
- *We officially ended things, but at least I told him how I felt about him.*

A New Attitude

Brandon was waiting for me in the lobby, slumped in a plastic chair with his enormous legs thrust out in front of him. "That was an awfully long trip to the bathroom." He said it without any disapproval, clearly content to sit there forever if that was how long it took for me to return. He was shifting his feet from side to side in front of him, like windshield wipers.

"I was thinking things over," I said. I sat on the arm of his chair and put a hand on his shoulder. "While I was in the men's room, I decided to take a new attitude toward you."

"Oh really? Am I going to like it?"

"I decided you're probably right about leaving. Sometimes, you just have to know when to let go of people, and if you hang on to them too long, things start to get uncomfortable for everyone. So I'm going to stop bugging you about staying, not that it was doing any good anyway."

"I appreciate that," he said.

"I have one last job for you to do."

"I'm still on the payroll," he said.

There was a flurry of snow in the air when we stepped outside the theater. It was undoubtedly the last gasp of winter, and against the bricks of the low townhouses in Bay Village, it looked pretty and harmless.

"I want you to help me figure out a way to get Randy to resign. It's partly my fault, but he's turning out to be a liability. It would be hard to fire him, so it has to be his decision."

Brandon mulled this over for a minute as we walked through the snow to the subway. "I thought my specialty was figuring out how to keep people on."

"This is just the flip side of the same thing. Think about it for a while, and we'll talk. But let's keep it between us."

"Got it," he said. And then added, as if it just occurred to him, "Is it my imagination, or is it snowing?"

You Eat?

Doreen arrived at the apartment exactly on time, carefully dressed, as if for a date. She always dressed like this, in stylish clothes that had an air of formality, as if she were part of a performance. Maybe that was how she viewed her social life. Maybe, in the end, that's what a social life is, a protracted, unpaid performance in front of a small audience. It had been a mild day, and when she entered the apartment, she brought with her a smell of fresh air, combined with the more acrid scent of her perfume, a scent that seemed to have been designed to draw people's attention but then, ultimately, to keep them away.

It was she who commented on scent as I was taking her coat. "It smells wonderful in here," she said. "I rarely cook and few people ever invite me to their houses for meals, so I'm not used to it."

I led her into the kitchen, apologizing for the fact that since it was only the two of us, she'd have to sit and watch me prepare. "I tried to get it ready ahead of time," I said. "It didn't happen. A lot has been going offtrack recently, but I'm trying to put things right. I'm making a chicken—a recipe of Conrad's. In any case, it's something he used to make frequently."

"I'm sure it will be delicious, and not because it's his recipe."

She looked slightly ridiculous, dressed as she was and wearing a pair of one of her art-opening shoes, sitting at the table in the kitchen, amidst the detritus of ordinary life: an empty grocery bag, a bunch of carrots I hadn't put away, a stack of Conrad's unopened mail. I showed her the bottle of wine I'd bought—since I know nothing about wine, I'd just grabbed something expensive—and she approved of the choice with vigor. After a few sips from her glass, she asked if there was anything I needed help with. I looked across the room at her from my station at the counter;

she was sitting upright in her chair, nursing her glass of wine. Although she was overdressed and bizarrely stiff, I was stabbed by a pang of empathy and sadness. Her lovely clothes, her expensive perfume, her careful manner all served mainly to cut her off from people, as if she'd built a low wall around herself. She could say it was what she wanted, but it still made me feel she'd made a mistake somewhere along the line and I longed to invite her in.

"As a matter of fact," I said, "I would appreciate a little help cleaning the lettuce."

She recoiled a bit and drew her chin in as if appalled. It probably hadn't been a sincere offer. I looked through a drawer until I found a long white apron that had been Conrad's back when he was cooking. She gamely slipped it over her head and tied the strings tightly around her waist, cinching in the waistline of her dress. She looked slim and silly, like a socialite serving meals at a homeless shelter. Still, once she set to work tearing up lettuce, rinsing it off, and tossing it into the spinner, she showed a good deal more confidence and adeptness than I'd have guessed.

"You seem at home doing that," I said.

"I prepared meals for my father toward the end of his life. I'd make a week's worth of dinners and lunches and pack them into containers and freeze them. I can't say I enjoyed it, but anything I do, I try to do well. Does that sound conceited?"

"Not at all. Ambitious at worst."

We Both Know

When the food was ready, I served what I hoped were realistically small portions and brought them into the dining room. As Doreen was sitting down, she said, "Would you mind if I kept the apron on? I feel overdressed, and this helps minimize the miscalculation."

"Please, be my guest," I said.

She looked chic in it, with her hair pinned up in a way that made her neck appear even longer than it was. As she was cutting into the chicken with tentative delicacy, she said, without looking up, "Has enough time and small talk passed to bring up the subject we both know I'm here to discuss?"

"Yes," I said. "I think so."

"Good." She sipped from her wine and folded her hands on the table in front of her. "I won't ask for details about why you didn't manage to prevent Conrad from going to Columbus, but I find it disappointing, as you know. I assume it has something to do with your wonderful unspoken agreement. More than that, I don't need to hear." She picked up her knife and fork and began pushing food onto the fork. I loved watching the way she did this; I tend to feel clumsy and hurried and worried that my manners are boorish or betray a lack of good breeding. "However well your agreement has served you in the past, I don't think it's working in your favor now. Just stop me if at any point I'm being too blunt."

"I'm tougher than I look," I said. "I expect you are, too. Go on."

She smiled at this, proudly, it seemed, unless I was misreading. Although I'd often felt, when she and Conrad and I were together, as if I were the third wheel, I'd always been aware of the fact that she was the outsider. After all, Conrad and I lived together. We were lovers. It was me he slept with, no matter how much time he spent with Doreen. But something had clicked into a different position. Conrad had abandoned both of us, an instant realignment.

"I spoke with Conrad yesterday," she said. "This visit seems to be going very well. At least from his point of view. You're not going to blame the messenger, are you?" She asked this question with a degree of sincerity that touched me.

"No," I said. "Of course not."

She sighed and put down her implements. "Conrad told me he and Clarke have found the perfect building for a gallery. Naturally, I didn't take it all that seriously at first, but the more he went on, the clearer it became that he was in earnest. I suppose you have more reason than I do to find it galling, but on the other hand, my relationship with Conrad is important to my career and a good part of my livelihood. I was infuriated by our conversation and the blasé way he expected me to be happy for him."

"I can understand why."

"Well what about you? I'm mystified, to be honest, by your casualness about the whole thing." She looked over at me and the mask of brittle aloofness she always wore dropped from her face. "For Christ's sake, Richard. Do you care or don't you?"

She leaned in a little across the table, and I felt as if I was with a 100 percent flesh-and-blood person for the first time in the years I'd known her.

"I do care," I said. "I always have. But I've cluttered up my life, and that's made it hard for me to realize it."

"And now?"

"I've been editing."

The spicy, carefully prepared chicken dish was congealing on the plates in front of us. "Shall I clear these off?" I asked. "I'm getting the feeling neither one of us wants more."

She waved her hand. "I know you think I have a vile eating problem, and I suppose in the context of the way a lot of people indulge, I do. However, I am, overall, a spectacularly healthy person. As for the chicken, it's not bad. But the flavors are muddy. There's too much of many things and not enough of one thing in particular. You should always strive for one strong note. It's not even all that important what it is, as long as it dominates with the rest of the flavors providing a sort of orchestral background music."

I cleared off the plates and brought out her salad. She'd made a dressing out of a few simple ingredients, and it had a clean, pure flavor that was welcome after the muddy chicken. When we'd finished with that, I suggested to her that we go for a walk. She protested—her shoes—and then gave in. It would probably do her good, she said.

The Whole Truth

We strolled down the uneven sidewalks of Charles Street, past all the shops and mullioned storefront windows that could have been a set from a *David Copperfield* remake. It was the first time I'd been outside with Doreen, and it was clear that this unfiltered air was not her natural habitat. She had her arms folded across her chest even though it wasn't cold. The coat she was wearing was beautifully designed, but so weighted toward style over function, it didn't close effectively. I decided to risk rejection and offered her my arm. To my surprise, she took it, and we walked along in companionable silence for a block. She stumbled a little at the curb and slid against me, and we continued on with her leaning lightly against my shoulder. In the weeks since she'd told me about her husband, I'd found myself wanting to ask her a few direct questions. Despite extensive knowledge of bisexual married men, I had rarely discussed the matter with the woman involved. The out-of-doors might not be where she was most comfortable, but it was increasingly clear that she wasn't the delicate hothouse flower I'd always assumed either.

"Do you mind me asking your husband's name?"

"It seems highly irrelevant," she said, "but no, I don't mind. It was Robin. The boys say I should have realized he was gay as soon as I learned his name. I was young. That's my defense. I suppose that was his as well."

"He eventually told you about himself?"

"Not exactly. He made himself less and less available to me. In small, intangible ways at first, and then more dramatically, canceling plans we'd made, refusing visits with friends. One day I realized he didn't seem to like looking at me very often; and not because he didn't like my face, but because he was ashamed to do so. And he didn't want me looking at him." She stopped and adjusted her shoe and started walking again. "To my astonishment, I asked him, in so many words. I wasn't even aware of having that particular suspicion—it just came out. 'Are you?' Later, it was another item I had to add to the litany of complaints and resentments I had—the fact that I had to be the one to ask, to formulate the words, to define it for him. More work for me."

"Work?"

"Emotional work, psychological work. Nurture, protect. Women's work. And of course I couldn't feel any clean, completely justified anger because I was still in love with him—and by the way, very much enjoyed being touched by him—and felt I had to understand all of his pain and sympathize. Because what would it mean about me if I didn't? Hateful? Reactionary? I ended up feeling responsible for the fact that I wasn't a man and therefore couldn't please him."

As she said all of this, she looked straight ahead, and I didn't dare to look at her. Her voice kept getting softer as she spoke, not as if she wanted to stop, but as if she wanted to draw me closer.

"The only person I could tell was my father and, naturally, that didn't go over. Let's say he was a bully and had never liked Robin. Too quiet, too sensitive, all the safe euphemisms. He dropped that language and used other words to describe Robin once it came out. That only made me feel more protective. If it had been another woman, at least I could have been openly enraged."

"Yes. At least."

Trying to picture this, I could see that Doreen had been a different sort of person than she was now, perhaps very different. In the aftermath of what had been a trauma, she'd turned herself into a Personality, which probably made it easier for her to not feel anything.

"You separated?"

"He moved to San Francisco. He wrote and called from time to time, but I never responded. A few years later, I got a call from a man—possibly his lover, I never found out—who told me that he was sick and that he wanted to see me. I waited too long to visit. Something I regret but would probably do all over again. We never divorced."

"Do you think about him much now?"

"I occasionally think about what it would have been like had I gone out to see him. Silly fantasies, I know, to ward off thinking about what the real end undoubtedly was like." She laughed, a surprisingly deep and earthy laugh that sounded as if it belonged to someone else, perhaps the person she might have been, given other circumstances. "One of the reasons I never talk about this is that it's nearly impossible to do so without coming across as bitter or ridiculous or full of blame. I hate people who are full of blame."

"I guess that means there's something you blame him for."

"I'm not sure. The whole thing made me feel so unsexual in a way, as if there were something wrong with me for having loved him in the first place. For wanting the tenderness he gave me instead of real passion. I'm attracted to fey, effete men. Some women are attracted only to football player types or only Asian men or only rich men or only brooding types with heavy beards. Why not only gay men? I suppose that's why I like being around the boys. If being married to Robin made me feel less desirable, being around the boys—being their mascot, why avoid the word?—makes me feel beautiful and sometimes a little glamorous. I have to put up with a lot of tiresome discussions about the size of everyone's penis, but I get to wear the silly, impractical clothes I want to wear and attend openings and amusing events and have a specific role that's reserved for me, and then I get to go home and have my quiet life, which is not, you'll be happy to hear, lonely."

As It Had Been

We had walked all the way to the Boston Common and were standing in front of the old Ritz hotel, now renamed by the multinational chain that had purchased it. I offered to drive her home, but she insisted on taking a cab. As I was opening the door for her, I asked if she would accompany me to the airport when I went to pick up Conrad.

"You don't think you should do it yourself?" she said.

"I don't think so," I said. "I think he'd be happy to see us both, and maybe it would remind him that he has a whole network of friends and obligations here."

What I wanted to ask her was whether she wished she'd never known about Robin, whether she would have preferred to go on in their marriage as it had been, instead of finding out the truth. But it was an absurd question, especially given Robin's fate, and besides, I'd closed the door to the cab and it had started to pull away.

Good Listener

As soon as I'd stopped trying to convince Brandon to stay, he started buttonholing me throughout the building to confess his concerns about leaving. I met with him to discuss strategies for getting rid of Randy, but we spent most of our time together talking about his future.

"It seems like such a big risk," he said one afternoon. "It's so impractical. Maybe I shouldn't be burning so many bridges. What do you think, Richard? Is the whole plan completely nuts?"

I was sitting behind my desk, and he was stretched out in a chair across from me with his feet up on a hassock. He had his face tilted toward the ceiling and his eyes closed. It was like being back in private practice, except here I could give my own opinions without worrying if I was talking too much or about how many of my own feelings I was projecting onto him.

"That's the brilliance of your plan," I said. "If it were practical, you'd know exactly what you were going to get out of it. This way, it's all up in the air. Playing cards in Las Vegas. It's genius."

"My parents will be completely freaked out by the idea."

"You can't live your whole life for them, Brandon. You put them into the mix, but once you start making decisions because you're worried about their reactions, you've established a pattern. It's now or never to set the right pattern."

"But the truth is, I kind of like the work here. Well, I'm not sure I like the work, but I like that everyone appreciates me and approves of what I do. Believe me, it's not like that in a poker game."

I threw up my hands. "I'm only going to say one more thing, and you can take it or leave it. A long time ago, I made a decision because I thought it was the practical one, and in some way or other, I've felt as if I was on the wrong bus ever since."

I was hoping he'd ask me what decision I was referring to, even if I wouldn't have told him the answer. But I was long past the age at which someone of Brandon's generation would care about my past.

"I've never taken a bus," he said.

"Ah, well." I sighed. I was convinced I hadn't heard the end of this topic, a thought that I found comforting. "What would be helpful," I said, "is if I could have a rational conversation with Randy, like this one. Lay it all out for him in casual terms."

"That isn't going to happen, Richard. He's not rational and he's taken a pretty strong dislike to you. He's going around the office telling anyone who'll listen—a smaller and smaller number, by the way—that you fucked him over."

This upset me as much as anything else I'd heard about Randy's behavior. I'd only tried to help him out. It hadn't turned out well, but my motives had been pure.

"Maybe you should meet with him outside the office," Brandon said. "Take him out for a drink."

"He doesn't drink."

"A meal. It's obvious he eats. Have you seen how much weight he's gained?"

"I can't see that happening either."

"Go to his place and knock on his door. It wouldn't be a business thing, more like a friendly visit. Your advice isn't great, Richard, but you're a pretty good listener."

Salvation Army

Randy lived in a noisy neighborhood in Allston, in a brick building pleading to be rescued from the neglect of its current owners. Allston was one of the few neighborhoods left in Boston where you could find storefronts with junk for sale spilling out onto the sidewalks, pawn shops, the Salvation Army, and peculiar little stores that sold used records and new comic books, two items that were sold together so often, they had to be connected, although in what way I couldn't imagine. Randy's building was wedged between a Vietnamese restaurant and a Thai bakery, whatever that was. I rarely thought about where the employees at Connectrix lived, but I hadn't expected anything quite this atmospheric. It wasn't pretty or pleasant, but it indicated a degree of imagination and character on Randy's part that took me by surprise. I stood outside and rang his bell. When there was no response, I rang two more times, and finally, I heard his voice crackling out of the speaker.

"It's Richard Rossi," I said, answering what had to have been his question.

He buzzed me in. The entry hall was overheated and smelled of frying fish, and the walls were covered in grimy yellow tiles. I went up the staircase to the second floor. Randy was standing in the doorway of his apartment. He still had on his work clothes—a white shirt and dark pants—and if he was surprised to see me, the surprise didn't register on his soft face.

"It's warm in this building," I said.

He pushed the door open and stepped aside to let me enter, almost as if he'd been expecting me.

Despite the heat and the smell of fish from the restaurant below, the apartment was organized and appeared to have been cleaned recently. There were pairs of shoes and winter boots lined up neatly beside the door to the hallway. The living room windows were all open, and the sounds of traffic and pedestrians from the street below were ridiculously loud. The furniture looked brand-new, with the lines and the unmistakable stamp of IKEA. A decade or so ago, someone in Randy's position would have shopped at one of the junk stores in the neighborhood or the Salvation Army, but I suppose IKEA was pretty much the same thing, only less expensive.

I had a fond memory of going to IKEA with Conrad shortly after it opened outside Boston. My reaction to it reminded me of my first visit to a bathhouse in Chicago, decades earlier. I'd approached with enthusiasm and excitement, and had, upon entering, felt overwhelmed by the plethora of possibilities. Fifteen minutes later, though, after adjusting to the light, I'd started to notice the flaws and potential hazards, and I realized there wasn't much I wanted to take home and nothing I'd care to see on a daily basis.

"You've got this place nicely decorated," I said.

"My girlfriend's furniture," he said. He pointed toward a boxy sofa and I sat.

"I'm glad to hear you got back together."

"We didn't. She hates me so much she doesn't want to come by to pick up her shit. I don't even know where she's living."

"At least you got the sofa."

He sat opposite me in a spindly blondwood rocker without commenting. He appeared calm and exerted proprietary control over the room, although I could see that his face had started to flush, not a good sign. His voice was more disturbingly monotone and without affect than usual.

"You're probably wondering why I'm here," I said.

He sat in his chair and rocked. "It's not like it's a big mystery," he finally said. "I wasn't thinking you dropped in for a beer and a joint."

"No. I don't smoke."

"Me neither."

He was obviously enjoying watching me squirm, so I decided I'd better get to the point. "You do know I'm not involved in your case anymore."

"I heard. I guess they figured it was too hot for you to handle, now that everyone thinks I tried to kill that guy."

"Don't talk that way. There's no evidence you're responsible, and until there is, I for one am happy to believe you're not."

"It's more convenient that way, isn't it?" He started rocking faster, pushing his feet against the floor with pent-up frustration.

"The point is," I went on, "that since I'm not handling the case anymore, anything I say to you isn't said to you as management. It's all meant on a more personal level."

"Oh, I see. We're friends now."

"I'd like to think that in some way or other, we always have been."

"Give me a break, Richard."

Although I'd opened my coat and taken off the scarf I'd been wearing, the heat of the apartment had started to get to me. "Could I have a drink of water?"

He got up without saying anything, and I realized that my back was damp with sweat from the heat of the apartment and the climb upstairs. In addition to the loud evening noises from the street below, the room was dark. I reached over to turn on a lamp and saw that he was using one of those environmentally friendly fluorescent bulbs. Perhaps I was grasping at straws, but I found this reassuring. Surely a person who'd attack someone else in an alley and send them to the hospital wouldn't bother with an energy-saving bulb. On the table in front of the sofa there was a bulletin from the Animal Rescue League spread open, as if Randy had just been perusing it. It was addressed to a woman, obviously the ex-girlfriend, but the fact that he'd been looking it over was another point in his favor.

When Randy walked back into the room with a glass, I noticed that, as Brandon had said, he did appear to have gained a lot of weight; his pants were too tight, and his shirt was pulling across his stomach. He handed me the water, sat back in his rocking chair, and stared me down. I took a sip and set the glass on the coffee table.

"You *could* use a coaster, you know," he said. He flipped a circle of cork in my direction. "If my girlfriend ever comes back to get her furniture, I don't want it to be all fucked up."

"Have you tried contacting her and having a serious conversation?"

"Tough to do with a restraining order, wouldn't you say?"

"I don't know from personal experience, but I guess it would be."

Suddenly, the light bulb didn't seem so reassuring. It sounded as if his life was spiraling out of control. It's usually one or two small false steps that lead to a series of irreversible blunders, and his mistakes around the firing of Z had been very small indeed. His obsession about the unfairness of the lawsuit had sped him along this disastrous path, despite all my assurances that it was nothing to worry about.

"Your supervisor tells me you've been a little more behind schedule than usual these days," I said.

"Ah. So now we're getting down to the real substance, aren't we? You're firing me."

"Why would you say that?"

"I know you want me out, and I know the reason you want me out is because I'm fucking up your chances for a promotion. Don't look so shocked, Richard. It's a small company. People talk. Your secretary especially. What I don't understand is why you even want the promotion in the first place."

"I appreciate your interest in my life, Randy, but to be honest, I don't see how that's any of your business."

"I thought you were here as a friend. Now you're pulling rank again."

"I've worked hard, Randy. I wouldn't mind a salary increase, more security, a little advancement."

"You just want to get the promotion so Cynthia doesn't, that's all." He said this in a disgusted tone, as if he took my job aspirations as a personal affront.

"I can't deny that has something to do with it," I said.

"What I think is that you'd be a lot better off if you just figured out how much it really matters to you instead of getting into a wrestling match with Cynthia."

"You sound a lot more insightful when you're talking about me than when you're talking about yourself."

"Yeah, well big surprise. Doesn't everyone?"

In his blond rocker, he looked like an overgrown baby—flushed, fleshy, and pouting—making the fact that he'd thought about my situation at all surprising, especially since his insights were so accurate. Aside from a minor salary increase, my life wouldn't improve in any way by the promotion. For years, I'd been making more than I needed and had been putting a big portion of my income into savings. How much did the extra matter? I'd still feel as if I was on the wrong bus.

"I'm sorry all this happened to you," I said. "I'm sorry about the lawsuit and everything that's come in its wake. Losing your girl-friend . . ."

"A lot of it's been my own fault," he said.

"Maybe. But I'm sure it must have been hurtful to be cited as the person responsible for the lawsuit. I'm sure it must have been embarrassing and worrisome. I know it was a big deal for you."

He got up out of his rocking chair and started to walk toward me slowly. When he was a few inches from the sofa, he sat on the edge of the coffee table, lowered his head into his hands, and started to weep. He began muttering something in a thick voice that was so distorted by his tears, I couldn't tell what he was saying. I could do nothing but listen quietly to whatever he was mumbling. I had an urge to offer some kind of physical comfort, but fortunately, I'd sunk too far into the soft cushions of the sofa to actually reach out to him.

When he had his tears under control and had blown his nose into his sleeve, he looked up at me and said, "Why didn't you just say that to me at the beginning? All I've heard from you is how meaningless this is, how I shouldn't worry about it, how I shouldn't care, how it's *no big deal*. Finally you've got the decency to tell me the truth—of course it matters. How could it not? Maybe if you'd just let me know that right off, everything would be different."

He became quiet again, and the ordinary sounds of laughter and car horns from the street filled up the room. Had he paced up and down in this overheated room, formulating a plan, or had he just run out one morning on an impulse he couldn't control?

"What would have been different?" I asked. "I mean specifi-cally."

"That's not your business anymore, is it? You've been taken off the case."

"I have," I said. "But why don't you go talk to Brandon. You're about the same age and he's probably leaving the company soon, so he's impartial. I'm not sure how good his advice is, but you'd be surprised at what a good listener he is."

Thorns

Like a lot of people who don't much enjoy travel, I'm always thrilled by the idea of picking someone up at the airport. Shortly after Samuel died, I'd taken four months off and bought one of those round-the-world tickets that allow you to stop in ten different countries over the course of a few months. I'd visited dozens of places I'd remember for the rest of my life, and I never regretted the time and money I'd invested in the journey, but what had stayed in my memory the longest and most vividly were the handful of sexual encounters I'd had (most of them with Americans or the ubiquitous, equally unexotic Australians), the fact that almost every major city I visited was home to a Foot Locker shoestore, and the way I'd felt sitting in an assortment of airports waiting for the next announcement of departure. People crow about the benefits of travel and even I can't help but feel some longing when I see a passing airplane, but I've always felt bad for the people I see wandering through airports, dragging their suitcases behind them, caught in this strange nowhere land between home and where they're going. Watching the passing parade intensifies my delight at staying put.

Conrad's flight from Columbus was scheduled to arrive in the early evening, so I drove through the late afternoon traffic in Cambridge to pick up Doreen. It was a windy afternoon, typical of early spring in Boston, and the river looked cold but beautiful. As I drove, I was reminded of the winter evening I'd walked to Doreen's apartment, and how, in the intervening weeks, my feelings toward her had changed along with the weather. I was almost as eager to see her this afternoon as I was to see Conrad.

She was standing in the glass enclosure of her building's lobby, waiting patiently. She had on a long black coat that draped off her slim body beautifully, and even if it was a little too formal for the time of day, it made me happy to see her so done up. There was something beguiling, in an insignificant way, about the fact that someone who lived in such a tiny apartment could have such an extensive wardrobe. I'd once rented a summer house with a group of friends. One man had arrived for a week-long stay with a tiny suitcase. But he kept showing up for dinner in neatly pressed shirts and different pairs of shorts. His ability to continually produce new outfits had been one of the most memorable parts of the vacation, followed closely by the brief affair I'd had with him.

The doorman walked Doreen to my car, and I quickly jumped out and ushered her into the passenger side. She was a woman who elicited a certain kind of chivalry in men. She didn't seem to elicit much else, but now I understood that she didn't want to. As we were crossing the river, I said, "You know, I don't think I've ever smelled that perfume you're wearing on anyone else."

"Is it too strong for you?" she asked. She had pulled down the visor on the passenger side, and was pinning up her hair, a gesture that made me feel, suddenly, as if she and I were an old married couple, going to the airport to pick up our prodigal child. It was clear that she was more eager to see Conrad than she was to see me. "I'm sorry to be doing this thing with my hair," she said. "Generally, I hate women who don't fix themselves up before leaving the house. I ran out of time. I had a productive meeting with a client late in the day. It's been good for me, having Conrad out of town for so long. I always assumed I was the sidekick to the more appealing and capable partner, but I'm beginning to think I might have my own skills. As for the perfume, a friend of mine sends it to me from Antwerp. It's made there by a small perfumer. I find the scent just on the edge of repellent. It has a Flemish name; the translation is 'Thorns.' It fits, doesn't it?"

"A while ago, I would have said you were bluffing, but now I'd say yes, it does fit. In a surprisingly nice way."

She flipped the visor back up and pulled her chin in. "I never should have told you my secrets; I won't be able to get away with anything."

Time for a Drink

The soaring cathedral of the terminal created a false and soothing twilight, a netherworld between day and night, the perfect setting for passengers suspended between one place and another. Conrad's flight had been delayed by an hour. Flights were almost always delayed now. Like most things in the country these days, there was a superficial appearance that everything was running smoothly, but a whispered acknowledgment that below the highly polished surface, all systems were beginning to fray from a lack of attention, time, and money. Doreen and I went into one of the bustling chain restaurants that had sprung up in airports everywhere since airlines had stopped serving meals. The menu was a vast cardboard production, coated in a thick layer of plastic. Unappetizing as it all looked, I found myself craving a snack. Exercising less had made me want to eat more, not excessively, but in a way that made me feel more generally satiated than I was used to feeling. I was even taking pleasure, much to my surprise, in the new age–appropriate layer of flesh that had begun to pad my body.

"Will you have anything?" I asked Doreen.

She pursed her lips and put the menu aside in a definite way. "I distrust restaurants that have photographs of food on their menus. If they doubt the patrons can figure out what a cheeseburger is, they can't expect a group with high standards."

Everything in the glossy photographs looked, like so much in life these days, simultaneously rich and unsatisfying. I ordered a bowl of clam chowder. Perhaps Jerry's pending surgery and his need to change his diet in preparation for it made me feel I had to indulge in some of the things he was now forbidden.

The chowder arrived in a bowl formed out of a round, hollowed-out loaf of bread, an unappetizing touch. In general, I prefer a clear distinction between food and the vessel it's served in. I've never much gone in for edible underwear or flavored condoms, either. The chowder was too salty, too buttery, and too thick; exactly what I wanted, in other words.

Doreen sipped discreetly at her white wine. "I envy you eating that," she said.

"Really? I'd love to order you one, if you'd like. Or at very least, ask for another spoon."

"I think not. Like a lot of life's pleasures, it's one I prefer to enjoy vicariously."

"How's the wine?"

"Not good, but effective." She studied me for a bit longer. "Are you nervous about seeing Conrad?"

"No," I said. "I have a clear goal, and that helps."

The restaurant was open to the immense, twilit concourse, and we were sitting at a table near the front. This was imaginary outdoor dining at a faux sidewalk café. It was at that moment, as I explained my resolve to make sure Conrad stayed on in Boston, that I glanced up and saw a man who looked very much like Benjamin walking through the middle of the silvery light of the artificial evening. In the days since saying goodbye to Ben at the golf center, I'd seen him in a variety of unlikely places—delivering packages to Connectrix in a UPS uniform, cutting meat behind the deli counter of my local grocery store, draped in a towel and emerging from the steam at Fitness Works. It was, therefore, unsurprising to see him here, plodding along in this dreamy light, holding the hand of a little girl.

I went back to my chowder, and then looked up again and realized with a jolt that this time it was not a hallucination I was seeing, but Benjamin himself. I clutched my spoon more tightly. Tonight was, apparently, the night his family was leaving for Florida. He looked slightly confused and especially dashing, strolling along holding the hand of his daughter, Kerry. I felt a rush of affection for the child I'd heard so much about for so many years but had never seen, not even in a photo. She looked remarkably similar to the way I had imagined her—short, somewhat plump with long dark hair and the slight limp that had provoked so many protective impulses and so much consternation. She was wearing glasses, something Benjamin had never mentioned before, and pulling behind her a small pink suitcase with a blue plush teddy bear attached to the top.

They stopped, and Benjamin leaned down and said something to her. She shook her head. He laid his hand on her hair and left it there tenderly. He was dressed for Florida: a short-sleeved sports shirt and light pants—echoes of his outfit at the golf center—and had I not loved him for three years, there was nothing about him that would have made me look twice. I wondered what was going through his head, if he was looking forward to the trip, if he was anxious about missing their flight, or about getting on the plane. He had a brown leather backpack slung over his shoulder, an item so stylish and out of place with the rest of his outfit, I was taken aback by the sight of it.

Later, when I looked back at this moment, I found every detail I could remember poignant: the way he touched his daughter's hair, the short-sleeved shirt he was wearing, his look of anxious distraction. We never worry about the right things, and if he was concerned about the legroom on the plane or their luggage or sunburn or long lines at Disneyworld, he was worrying about the wrong things. In the aftermath of everything that happened, I'd come to think of this moment as the last one in which I saw the person I'd known over the course of so many years. The next time I saw him, and held him while he wept, everything had changed.

A tall, slim woman who was very much as I had pictured Giselle, although maybe even more pretty, stopped beside father and daughter. She had light hair that shone in the way only pampered hair shines. She had shapely, beautiful legs, although there was something in her posture that indicated she didn't know it. Not quite the arrogant, self-confident woman Benjamin had described, or more accurately, imagined her to be. The boy beside her was obviously Tyler. They had the same light coloring and the same angular features. From where I was sitting, it didn't appear there was anything of Ben in him. He was skinny in the way of an adolescent, with long, lank hair, and he was doing something with his cell phone. He leaned over and showed his mother what he'd been looking at, and she grinned and gave him a little nudge with her shoulder. The bonds between father and daughter and mother and son were so obvious, they could have been two couples traveling together, not one united family.

I'd become so fixated on this tableau that I'd forgotten about Doreen, about everything really. I was surprised to hear Doreen say, "Your soup is getting cold."

I looked down and saw that I was still holding the spoon, suspended somewhere above the ridiculous bread bowl.

"I just caught sight of someone I didn't expect to see here."

"So I gather."

She followed my gaze. Benjamin and his family had stepped into the line in front of the ticket counter, and Tyler, prompted by Giselle, was showing his phone to his father.

"You're friends with the whole family?"

"Yes." I paused to let it sink in, but I couldn't leave it there. My friendship with the whole family was imaginary, and that was never more apparent to me than right now. "Not really," I said. "Not at all, in fact. I've known him for a few years, but I've never met the rest of them. She's attractive, don't you think? His wife?"

Doreen studied the little family as they regrouped themselves into their happy twosomes. "Very," Doreen said. "She has lovely legs."

"She's athletic, I believe."

"No doubt. It's easy to imagine her on a horse, or swinging a tennis racket at a country club." She sipped at her wine again and cradled the glass in her hands. Her nails, as always, were shiny, perfectly shaped, and painted a deep shade of red. "Even so, she has the unmistakable look of uncertainty and suspicion. She's angry at her husband and clinging to her son."

"I think you're reading an awful lot into a glimpse," I said. "Especially at this distance."

She smiled and gazed at me in a flirty way that would have been impossible to imagine even a month earlier. "In fact," she said, "I was reading into your reaction on spotting him. I can barely see them. How much does she know?"

Since Doreen seemed to have guessed at everything, I saw no point in trying to pretend she wasn't right. It was my second betrayal of Benjamin's secret life, and it was easier than the first. "Nothing, and if he has his way, she'll never know anything. He's worked hard at keeping his marriage together. He's had to give up some things that meant a lot to him." I looked again at Ben and his family. What I'd said sounded credible and final to me, and there was something appealing about the way it seemed resolved, finished, a task completed. "I've been trying to help him."

Doreen's reaction was so subtle—a blink that might have been dust in her eye—I wasn't sure she'd even heard me, but then she said, "Naturally, it's sad. She'll end up doubting herself, doubting all the years of their marriage, the point of it all, wondering what happened to her youth. But she's attractive. She looks intelligent. She'll get stronger, even if it's not in the most appealing way. As for you, protecting someone from the truth is just a self-serving way of lying to her."

I wished that she had made this comment with some of the icy bitterness she'd shown for most of the time I'd known her. Unfortunately, she'd said it quietly and sadly, and then laid her hand on top of mine briefly, letting the comment sink in.

Quarantine

Increasingly, the people getting on and off airplanes were quarantined in the far reaches of the airport, cut off from the rest of humanity, impossible to reach, unless you had a special pass. You could see them at a distance, going through screeners, removing articles of clothing, tossing their bottles of water and perfume into bins.

I stood with Doreen outside the quarantine area and watched as groups of people reentered the world. There was a reversal going on in travel—madly competing bus lines were offering luxury coaches to New York from Boston with onboard Internet service, movies, immense seats, and lavish meals, while airlines were offering increasingly cramped conditions and fewer amenities. People staggering off planes bragged to their waiting relatives about how horrible the experience had been, how uncomfortable, how delayed, how brutal. It was almost a status symbol to be stranded on a runway for hours or forced to spend an evening on the floor of an airport.

Conrad appeared in the middle of a group of weary travelers and strode forward, grinning but exhausted. He had on jeans and a rumpled white shirt and one of his expensive blue sports jackets. He stood out in the crowd as the most attractive man, the most nicely dressed, almost as if a light were shining on him—but one operated by himself. He reminded me of people I'd seen when I lived in New York, returning home from a nightclub at dawn—pretty and happy, pleased with their hard-earned dark circles, but spent and too apparently in need of coffee and aspirin. I told myself I was excited to see him.

He kissed Doreen on both cheeks. "Unh," he said. "I feel as if I've been gone forever. You look different, sweetheart," he said to me. "Have you been sleeping more? What a hideous flight. Bumpy, late, cramped. And babies. It was like a nursery school on a field trip."

As I hugged him, I noticed a different smell than his usual spicy Italian shower gel. Recycled cabin air and the traces of cheap hand soap from the airplane bathroom. "I missed you," he said in my ear. "I'm so happy to be back."

Looking over his shoulder, I saw his black leather suitcase—usually so slim and tidy—bulging with books and papers, looking almost as weary as Conrad himself. He grabbed the handle and pulled the exhausted thing behind him. Clearly, its traveling days were nearly done.

A More Proper Hello

Later that night, as we lay in bed, Conrad explained himself. It had been a mistake, all of it. The extended trip to Columbus, the very idea that Clarke might have been an appropriate person, even if just for a brief fling. The thought was enough to provoke a hearty laugh from Conrad, a real one, although tinged with an edge of bitterness that made me wonder if he was telling the whole truth. It had been one of those moments of self-doubt, he went on. It had had more to do with his own self-image and probably his age and his fears of economic insecurity—and maybe an inkling that I'd been up to something—than it had had to do with Clarke himself. And certainly, it had had nothing to do with his feelings for me. Really, if I saw Clarke, I probably would laugh. Well, maybe not laugh, but I would wonder what Conrad had been thinking.

I listened in a lazy way, staring up at the ceiling. For days I'd been formulating a plan of how I was going to lure Conrad back to

Boston, reel him in, and now, all of a sudden, the line had gone slack. The work had been done for me. The hurdle had been moved out of the way. The sound of his voice kept growing dimmer, almost as if I was floating up from the bed and out of the room, to some distant and perhaps more interesting place.

I could barely feel the weight and warmth of Conrad's body when he lay down on top of me and began telling me how much he'd been looking forward to seeing me again, running his thumb across my lips, moving his body in a way that let me know he was eager for a proper hello. Then he put his mouth near my ear and said, "I gave up my distraction, Ricky. I want you to give up yours."

I ran my hands up his back and then down the curve of his ass, appreciating his shape in a distant and disinterested way.

"I already have," I whispered. "Given him up. That's over."

Conrad stopped moving. He propped himself up on his hands and looked down at me. "Really?" he said. "Over over?"

I nodded.

He looked confused, as if his plan, too, had been blown off course. He rolled over onto his side of the bed and lay, as I was, with his hands behind his head, staring up at the ceiling. "So that makes everything clear, doesn't it," he said. "With them out of the way."

"I think it does."

He mulled this over. "You don't mind if I read for a few minutes, do you?" he asked.

"No, of course not," I said. "If you're up before me, make sure I'm awake by seven."

As It Turns Out

Brandon was, as it turns out, a good listener, and his advice was solid as well. He convinced Randy to come clean about the attack.

It was a confession that made Randy's departure from Connectrix swift and inevitable. From Lewis's point of view, things could not have worked out better. There was potential to turn the whole event into a story in which Brandon played the role of hero. His parents were certain to be pleased.

"I suppose you've heard about the rest of what's coming for the whole company," Lewis said to me.

Since his most vague comments were almost always preface to bad news he didn't want to deliver, I braced myself. The climate control system in the building was the latest casualty of the wonderful aesthetics, and Lewis's tightly sealed office was stifling after a week of spring warmth.

"You'd be surprised how much I don't hear," I confessed. "Especially when it relates to me."

"I did my best to negotiate for you, but in the end, the decision was made to offer the new HR position to Brandon. I know it'll be a little awkward for you, but I did as much as I could. Management wants a new face, fresh ideas. If I were you, champ, I'd feel proud to be the one who got Brandon this far. I know you'll understand. It's not what you wanted, but I'll make sure his folks know you played a role in this, and all things considered, it could turn out very well for you."

I did understand, and given the recent decisions I'd made about my life, the news about the promotion wasn't upsetting to me or even particularly relevant.

"I think you made a wise decision," I said. "Brandon has a lot more substance than you'd guess at first. Although to be honest, I'm halfway hoping, for his sake, he sticks to his Plan A."

Having delivered what he assumed was the bad news, Lewis returned to his more jovial mode. "He's already accepted. It's a huge relief all around. I suppose Cynthia is going to be unhappy about it, but once we start the big restructuring and downsizing, everyone's going to have to adapt anyway. She's got the nursing thing, too. There's always a need for that."

A Start

When I left the office that afternoon, the sky was still light, and the sunset was turning the buildings on Beacon Hill golden. I kept gazing across the water as I walked toward the Club, wondering what Conrad was doing and what new pieces of art and furniture he'd brought into the apartment. We talked on the phone regularly and had had dinner together several times, but a few days after he'd come back from Columbus, I'd started sleeping at the Club. Now that the Insignificant Others were out of the way, it was easier to see what we actually wanted from each other, or more to the point, what we didn't want. It was shaping into a very nice friendship, surprisingly free of power struggles.

I was happy to have the news of Brandon's promotion, and in the long run, it might turn out for the best that he wasn't going to Las Vegas. He could put away a lot of money now. Then, if he really wanted to change his life around, he could go off to play golf and poker—with some security behind him—at any number of overdeveloped desert oases around the world. I was feeling much more sanguine about the possibility of making fresh starts, no matter how much effort it took. My plan for my own life—graduate studies in literature in my fifties—was even less practical than Brandon's had been, but I had money in the bank and most of the books and the impracticality of it was a good part of its appeal. Conrad thought it was a brilliant idea.

As I stepped into the Club, that delightfully small and blank apartment, I felt my phone vibrate in my pocket. Benjamin had sent me a text message. I suppose I hadn't expected him to stay away forever, but if I'd done my math correctly, he was still in Florida. I lay down on the bed where he and I had spent the majority of our time together, and read his message.

It would be a couple of weeks until I heard the whole story of what had happened. Florida, he'd tell me then, had been baking in an unseasonable hot spell for most of the time his family was there. Nerves had frayed. The visit to his relatives had gone badly. Giselle was accused of being a condescending snob by Ben's sister, and Ben had insisted they leave early and move to a hotel. The little family of four in exile on the Florida coast, driving from one hotel without a vacancy to the next. Tyler in the back seat, surly and overheated, regretting his decision to come, hostile to his relentlessly upbeat sister.

By the time they got to Disneyworld, only Kerry—limping, her glasses fogging from the humidity—was still cheerful. For the rest of them, it was a matter of waiting in the heat to get somewhere they had no interest in going. The make-believe world, the people in costumes, all that American ingenuity poured into the creation of a gaudy, hollow fantasy. Tyler insisted one afternoon on being allowed to go back to the hotel alone, although his sister begged him to remain. Ben took Kerry's side, and Tyler said, zeroing in on a weakness or just using a word that was one more bit of insulting jargon: "Don't be such a *faggot,* Dad."

Ben had never hit him before. How could he have done it then, there in public, slapped his son across the face so hard the boy started to cry? Acting in his own defense, Tyler made things worse. "You're so gay, it's not even funny."

Sometimes, I think he suspects something.

Giselle pulled them apart, but later in the privacy of their chilled hotel room, had wept, and asked him point-blank. He'd stormed out, not enraged, but terrified and confused, and had sent the text message from the giddy, freezing lobby.

Trouble. Help. Please. Tyler knows. Said it. G asked outright. What do I do? Please.

I got up from the bed and walked out on the apartment's narrow, unused balcony. Down below, the surrealist Tuscan village was glowing in its crazy disorder. I had planned for this sort of crisis for most of the years I'd known Ben. I'd feared him calling or writing me for advice on what to say, on how to proceed, and I had that roster of responses stored on my computer, ready to send him—plausible excuses, diversionary tactics that might not be entirely believed but would at least provide a way for everyone to move forward exactly as they had been doing. What were the other options? An expensive, acrimonious divorce, a reevaluation of decades of deceit, a lot of leather sectional sofas? An attempt by me to live with a shattered man and make friends with his children? I wasn't good at making waffles on Sunday mornings and playing computer games. Although it was true that I was willing to learn. I'd have a new set of keys made for the Club, in case he wanted to use them.

Begin with the truth, I wrote back. *Everything else will fall into place.*

It wasn't going to be easy, but at least it was a start.

Acknowledgments

Many thanks to the Ragdale Foundation, the Cambridge Public Library, Holy Cross Monastery, the Chauncy Street Study Hall, and the Frog Lake Family Singers—Katie Dealy, Dan Doyle, Lesli Gordon, Anthony Rocanello, Jenny Ross, and Chris Tanner.

Also to Amanda Murray. Also to Denise Roy and Denise Shannon. Also to Jonathan Strong. Also to Sebastian Stuart and Bob Nicoson. Also, especially, to Anita Diamant and Amy Hoffman.

WATERFORD TOWNSHIP PUBLIC LIBRARY
5168 Civic Center Drive
Waterford, MI 48329